Sam. Can't be. Can't be can't be.

In all the world, he told himself, there had to be more than one female pilot named Sam. Had to be.

A coincidence. A little quirk of fate.

Out on the shimmering runway, the pilot straightened and moved out of the wing's shadow. Her movements were unhurried...lazy, even. She stood waiting for them to approach, hands clasped behind her, one knee slightly bent, one hip slightly canted...chin up, head tilted back.

How well he knew that stance. She'd stood just that way, he remembered, the first time he'd seen her, that day in the White House.

Anger, joy, resentment, regret, pain, lust—all those things and others he couldn't name—lumped deep in his belly and exploded through his brain like mortar rounds, leaving him reeling. Shell-shocked. Numb.

"God," he whispered, not knowing whether or not it was a prayer.

Dear Reader,

Get ready for this month's romantic adrenaline rush from Silhouette Intimate Moments. First up, we have RITA® Award-winning author Kathleen Creighton's next STARRS OF THE WEST book, *Secret Agent Sam* (#1363), a high-speed, action-packed romance with a tough-as-nails heroine you'll never forget. RaeAnne Thayne delivers the next book in her emotional miniseries THE SEARCHERS, *Never Too Late* (#1364), which details a heroine's search for the truth about her mysterious past…and an unexpected detour in love.

As part of Karen Whiddon's intriguing series THE PACK—about humans who shape-shift into wolves—*One Eye Closed* (#1365) tells the story of a wife who is in danger and turns to the only man who can help: her enigmatic husband. Kylie Brant heats up our imagination in *The Business of Strangers* (#1366), where a beautiful amnesiac falls for the last man on earth she should love—a reputed enemy!

Linda Randall Wisdom enthralls us with *After the Midnight Hour* (#1367), a story of a heart-stopping detective's fierce attraction to a tormented woman…who was murdered by her husband a century ago! Can this impossible love overcome the bonds of time? And don't miss Loreth Anne White's *The Sheik Who Loved Me* (#1368), in which a dazzling spy falls for the sexy sheik she's supposed to be investigating. So, what will win out—duty or true love?

Live and love the excitement in Silhouette Intimate Moments, where emotion meets high-stakes romance. And be sure to join us next month for another stellar lineup.

Happy reading!

Patience Smith
Associate Senior Editor

Please address questions and book requests to:
Silhouette Reader Service
U.S.: 3010 Walden Ave., P.O. Box 1325, Buffalo, NY 14269
Canadian: P.O. Box 609, Fort Erie, Ont. L2A 5X3

Secret Agent Sam
KATHLEEN CREIGHTON

Silhouette®

INTIMATE MOMENTS™

Published by Silhouette Books

America's Publisher of Contemporary Romance

SILHOUETTE BOOKS

ISBN 0-373-27433-5

SECRET AGENT SAM

Copyright © 2005 by Kathleen Creighton-Fuchs

This edition published by arrangement with Harlequin Books S.A.

Visit Silhouette Books at www.eHarlequin.com

Printed in U.S.A.

Books by Kathleen Creighton

Silhouette Intimate Moments

Demon Lover #84
Double Dealings #157
Gypsy Dancer #196
In Defense of Love #216
Rogue's Valley #240
Tiger Dawn #289
Love and Other Surprises #322
Wolf and the Angel #417
*A Wanted Man #547
Eyewitness #616
*One Good Man #639
*Man of Steel #677
Never Trust a Lady #800
†One Christmas Knight #825
One More Knight #890
†One Summer's Knight #944
†Eve's Wedding Knight #963
*The Cowboy's Hidden Agenda #1004
*The Awakening of Dr. Brown #1057
*The Seduction of Goody Two Shoes #1089
Virgin Seduction #1148
*The Black Sheep's Baby #1161
††Shooting Starr #1232
††The Top Gun's Return #1262
††An Order of Protection #1292
††Undercover Mistress #1340
††Secret Agent Sam #1363

Silhouette Desire

The Heart Mender #584
In from the Cold #654

Silhouette Books

Silhouette Christmas Stories 1990
"The Mysterious Gift"

*Into the Heartland
†The Sisters Waskowitz
††Starrs of the West

KATHLEEN CREIGHTON

has roots deep in the California soil but has relocated to South Carolina. As a child, she enjoyed listening to old-timers' tales, and her fascination with the past only deepened as she grew older. Today she says she is interested in everything—art, music, gardening, zoology, anthropology and history, but people are at the top of her list. She also has a lifelong passion for writing, and now combines her two loves in romance novels.

Prologue

He saw Samantha for the first time in the White House rose garden.

"How many people can say *that?*" Cory Pearson said aloud to the computer screen as he slid the cursor to the Save icon and thumped the mouse.

The words he'd written, black letters stark on a vast white field, seemed to shimmer in anticipation. He stared back at them, wrists propped on their ergonomic supports, fingers poised...

Nothing. *Hell.*

It wasn't that he didn't have the words. Problem was, he had too many. Memories, impressions, images, emotions—everything translated automatically into words in his mind, always had, as far back as he could remember. He hadn't understood then, not until much, much later, that not everyone's mind behaved like this. And the fact that his did was something he'd been both gifted and cursed with at birth. And that this was what made him, whether he liked it or not, a writer.

By the time he'd come to that understanding, thanks to the combining of this gift—or curse—with a curious and adventuresome nature, he was already well on his way to becoming one of the most respected war correspondents-slash-journalists of his time.

It was shortly thereafter that those same attributes got him thrown into an Iraqi prison. Which, in turn, had set in motion the chain of events that had resulted in his presence in the White House rose garden on that particular day in May. And was also how he'd come to know, only a few months before that, of the existence of a girl named Sammi June Bauer.

Oh, he had plenty of words. Words swirled in his mind now like leaves in a whirlwind. Experience told him that attempting to force them into a semblance of order and paragraph form would be like trying to catch those windblown leaves in his hands. But he knew, if he was patient, eventually they would begin to settle and arrange themselves into patterns of their own making….

He watched her from a distance as she wandered among the rose beds, noticing how she seemed separate from all the other guests, isolated even in a crowd. It struck him that this apartness must be natural to her.

And, in retrospect, perhaps it was something he should have paid more attention to, perhaps…

What if I had? Cory asked himself as he stared at the blinking cursor. Would it have made a difference?

Probably not. He let out a breath and went back to typing.

The humid heat of a May afternoon, thick with the scent of crushed grass, rose around him as he moved closer to her, stalking her the way a nature photographer stalks a leopard. Through the heat shimmer he saw her throw a furtive look over one shoulder before she bent toward a half-open rose blossom, rather as if she meant to steal the flower itself rather than merely a sample of its fragrance. After a moment she looked up and cocked her head. Her lips formed a pout of disappointment.

"Try this one. It seems to have some smell to it," he said, and felt a surge of strange delight when she gave a start, then turned with the slow dignity of an offended duchess.

As she studied him, hands clasped behind her back, head tilted back and chin out-thrust, he couldn't help but smile. Not much about her resembled the pictures her father had painted for him during those weeks in Iraq, but remnants of the scruffy, combative ten-year-old soccer-playing tomboy she'd been could still be found in that chin and jaw. And that attitude. Oh, yeah.

But for the rest…

For starters, she was a whole lot taller than he'd pictured her—nearly equal to his own six feet in the high-heeled boots she was wearing—and a good part of that seemed to consist of legs. Slim, tanned, well-muscled legs, judging from the portion visible between the tops of her boots and the bottom edge of her dark pinstriped skirt, which was, in fact, a considerable amount. The rest of her was slim, too, but strongly built and athletic, like her father. Her hair—thick and shaggy, a rich blond shot through with gold—was a gift from her mother, but the eyes were Tristan's. Dark and mysterious as moonlit waters. A man could drown in those eyes…!

"I'm Cory Pearson," he said as he ambled toward her, wearing a disarming smile and trying to make it seem as if he'd just happened to be wandering by that way. "I was—"

"I know who you are. I've seen you on television." She gave her shoulder-length hair a toss and her chin jerked a notch higher, if that was possible. "You're the reporter who was with my dad in Iraq."

"Yes. And you're Sam—"

"Samantha," she said in a breathless rush.

Not Sammi June. Not anymore. Of course not. The little-girl name had gone the way of the freckles and pony-tails. She was a grown-up woman now.

He accepted it with a solemn nod, and a peculiar quivering pressure behind his breastbone. "Samantha…"

Cory sat back, his hands grown sweaty on the keyboard. The same pressure was there in his chest now, and letting out a long, slow breath didn't ease it much.

There'd been more to that day, of course. A lot more. He remembered every moment of it, every word, every look, every gesture.

She'd confided in him, for some reason, although his intuition told him she was a private person by nature. She'd told him about ordinary stuff—her life, about soccer and school, and her newly born dream of becoming a pilot, like her dad. And some not-so-ordinary stuff—what it had been like to lose her father as a little girl and get him back again as a grown woman. Amazingly, in the midst of her own emotional turmoil she'd asked about Cory, too, how it had been for *him*.

He hadn't been able to hide his pain from her that day, not completely, though God knows he'd tried. Just the first of many times in his relationship with Samantha Bauer when his will had failed him….

He'd listened to her speak of adult loss with a child's simplicity, and of a child's heartbreak with an adult's passion.

And he'd fallen in love with her. Right there, that day, in the White House rose garden.

He let out another breath as he once more hit the Save icon, then darkened the monitor. He'd had enough. Couldn't do any more, not now.

Nor, he imagined, would he make another attempt any time soon. He should have known it was too soon. That it would still hurt too damn much.

Writing had always been his lifeline in difficult times. His medicine, his therapy, his healing balm, his anesthetic, better than a bottle of Scotch. He'd thought, he'd hoped...it would help get him through this. But it seemed there was no medicine on earth powerful enough to dull the pain of losing Samantha.

Chapter 1

The tiny airstrip simmered in the afternoon heat, denied out of functional necessity even the small solace of trees. To Cory Pearson's eyes the ragged cluster of clapboard buildings with rusting tin roofs that apparently served as hangar and maintenance sheds as well as terminal and business offices seemed to have hunkered down beneath the pounding sun with the silent endurance of penned livestock.

The taxi driver who had brought them from Davao City cut off the elderly car's engine—to keep it from overheating, Cory imagined—which of course rendered the air inside the cab unbreatheable within roughly three seconds. Feeling his breath catch in an instinctive effort to keep that awful heat out of his lungs, Cory hurriedly thrust a handful of bills at the driver across the back of the seat and opened his door. On the other side of the car, his best friend and favorite photographer, Tony Whitehall, hefted the cases containing his cameras onto his knees and did the same. Hot air rushed inside the car like the breath of a ravenous beast.

"God," Tony said, the profanity halfhearted and forlorn.

"Beats a monsoon, or so I'm told," Cory said cheerfully as he hooked the strap of his laptop carrier over his shoulder and climbed out of the car. "Hard to see how, but if we're still here in a few weeks, I guess we'll find out."

Tony just grunted.

The two men waited in stoic silence while the driver—spare, wiry and apparently eternally cheerful—retrieved their bags from the trunk of the cab. Returning their nods and muttered thanks with more nodding and smiling—Cory's tip had been generous—the driver climbed back behind the wheel and started up the engine with a rackety explosion of noise and exhaust. He drove off with a full-armed wave of farewell from his open window.

"You couldn't have picked a hotter month to do this?" Tony inquired as they stood motionless and watched the taxi undulate and seem to hover above the ground in the distant shimmer of heat waves. Moving from the spot seemed almost too great a task; the heat sat on their shoulders like a burden.

"Believe me, it was a whole lot cooler when I started negotiations last November." Cory bent and picked up his bag and Tony did the same, and the two men began walking slowly toward the uninviting-looking cluster of buildings. "When Fahad al-Rami finally gave me the go-ahead to do the interview, I didn't argue. I said, 'Tell me the time and place, and I'm there.'"

Tony paused and set his bag down long enough to fish an already damp handkerchief out of the pocket of his jeans. "Yeah, well, I just hope we get something out of this—besides one hell of an interview, I mean."

Cory glanced at him. "The hostages, you mean." Tony, in the process of tying the handkerchief pirate-style around his shiny mahogany-colored head to protect it from the blazing sun, didn't reply. Cory faced forward again, squinting even though the photosensitive lenses of his glasses had already adjusted to the glare. "Goes without saying. Not that I'm holding out much hope."

Tony's sunglasses flashed toward him briefly as he picked up his bag. "Why not? They've released other hostages."

"For money. The Lundquists are missionaries—in most cases like this the churches back home are too poor to pay the ransom."

"Then why the hell'd they take 'em?"

"Probably didn't know who they were getting. Just scooped up a bunch of tourists from a seaside resort. The way I understand it, the Lundquists just happened to be vacationing there at the time."

"Poor devils," Tony said. Then, in a blunt tone and with a thrust of chin that might have been taken for callous if Cory hadn't known him so well, he asked, "So, why keep them? They've had 'em for what, going on a year, now? Why not cut their losses? Turn 'em loose or kill 'em. One or the other."

"I expect they're hoping to get something for their trouble—leverage of one kind or another." Cory pulled open a door marked Office and held it for Tony to squeeze through with his assortment of bags and cases. "Which is why I don't hold out much hope for us securing the release of any hostages through this interview. It's not like I have anything they want."

Tony grunted as he nudged past him, then paused to let his eyes adjust to the dimness. "Other than the interview, you mean," he said as he began lowering bags to the dusty linoleum floor.

"Hell," Cory said with a grin as he let the door close behind him, "they had that for the asking."

Tony took off his sunglasses and tucked them into his shirt pocket, then threw him a grin back. "A *favorable* interview. Maybe they're figuring on holding the hostages over your head so you'll make sure and show them and their cause to the world in a sympathetic light."

It was a possibility that had already occurred to Cory, and another reason he didn't entertain high hopes of bringing those hostages back with him. Not through negotiations, at any rate. As far as other means…he had some ideas on that score.

Which he was keeping to himself, for the moment. What Tony didn't know couldn't hurt him. And it could probably save a whole lot of arguing.

He dropped his overnighter on the floor and eased his laptop down beside it as he surveyed the room. Except for the two of them it seemed to be empty of people, the atmosphere rendered only slightly more tolerable than the outdoors due to the valiant efforts of a rackety fan sitting on a wooden countertop. The counter divided the room roughly in half. Furnishings in the half Cory and Tony occupied consisted of a wooden bench to the left of the entrance and a soft-drink vending machine on the right. Beyond the bench was a door marked with the universal male and female symbols indicating toilets. On the wall next to the door was a cork bulletin board sporting faded pictures of tropical resorts and sunset beaches, and above that, black letters individually pinned in an arch spelling out, WELCOME TO SEA CHARTERS.

On the countertop, a stack of brochures fluttered intermittently in the breeze from the oscillating fan. Behind the counter, a computer monitor sat atop a gunmetal-gray desk, its screen turned discreetly away from public view in the manner of airline ticket counters everywhere. Beyond that, through a bank of windows partly obscured by bamboo blinds, Cory could see an expanse of sunbaked earth interrupted by splashes of yellow-and-brown grass. Beyond the grass, before a backdrop of distant palm trees, a large twin-engine plane sat waiting on a hard-packed dirt runway.

In the shade of one low-slung wing, a slim figure wearing a dark blue baseball cap and khaki cargo pants belted over a white T-shirt lounged against the slanting fuselage. Nearby, moveable steps waited below an open doorway located in the rear of the plane, between the wing and the tail.

"Holy Mary, Mother of God," said Tony—who hadn't been a practicing Catholic in years—as he came to stare past Cory's shoulder. "S'pose that's ours?"

"Pretty much has to be, since it appears to be the only thing out there with wings," Cory said absently, his attention distracted, for the moment, by that distant figure under the aircraft's wing. Something about her...

"That's a damn *Gooneybird*," Tony said as if Cory hadn't spoken, his voice hushed. "I didn't think those tail-draggers were still flying."

"Gooneybird?" Cory glanced over at him, laughing a little. "Come on. That would be Second World War, right?"

Tony was staring reverently out the windows. "Yup. Douglas DC-3. They were *the* workhorse aircraft during World War Two. Commercial airlines flew 'em after the war—hell, they pretty much *started* commercial passenger service. That's a damned *antique* out there."

"Didn't know you were an airplane buff."

"Not me—my dad. *His* dad—my granddad, never knew him myself, he was in the Navy, in the Pacific. The Cee Bees—you know, the construction battalions? Anyway, before he got killed—Guadalcanal, I think it was—he helped build quite a few landing strips for those things. They used 'em for troop transport back then. Dad used to build models of all those World War Two planes—tried to interest me in doing it when I was a kid, but I was more into Nintendo." He threw Cory a look, grinning. "Guess more of that stuff soaked in than I thought."

He looked back at the plane, then did a double take. "Damn. I think that's a *woman*." He launched into a string of his favorite cheerful profanities before adding in an exaggeratedly ominous tone, "That wouldn't be our pilot, would it?"

"Sexist pig," Cory said with a lopsided grin. Coincidence, he thought. An odd little twist of fate. "Women have been known to fly airplanes. Does the name Amelia Earhart ring any bells?"

What surprised him—shocked him, actually—was the twisting he still felt in his guts when her name...her image...flashed through his mind. Not Amelia's, of course.

Samantha.

Before Tony could reply, the door to the left of the windows opened and a man bustled in, showing tobacco-stained teeth in a wide, welcoming smile shaped like a lying-down half moon. He was of indeterminate age and ethnicity, with long salt-and-pepper hair pulled loosely back in a clubbed ponytail that left a halo of loose frizz around his broad, swarthy face. He wore rumpled light tan slacks and a Hawaiian-print shirt that hung unbuttoned over a dirty vest-type undershirt and a solid-looking mound of belly.

"Welcome to SEA Charters," he said, slightly out of breath, in an accent that sounded vaguely Australian, adding, "Sounds like a boat business, dun'it? Stands for South East Asia. We pretty much cover the islands from here to New Zealand…Indonesia…anywhere you want to go. That's our motto. Anywhere you want to go, we can get you there. I'm Will, by the way." In what appeared to be a habitual gesture, and probably explained most of the dirt on the undershirt, he brushed his hand across his belly before thrusting it over the counter to shake first Cory's hand, then Tony's.

"I'm guessing you're the reporters, right? Going to…" Still bustling, muttering under his breath, he dodged back behind the computer monitor, tapped some keys and bent over to peer at the screen. "Let's see…" He glanced up, shaking his head as he whistled softly. "Not too many people going in there these days. Government warnings, you know. That province is in rebel hands. Well—off and on, anyways. Been a lot of government activity goin' on up in those hills lately. 'Government activity'— that's a euphemism for fightin', you know. They been warnin' foreigners to stay away."

"I was told you could fly us in." Cory was fishing in his shirt pocket for the folded paper that contained his e-mail confirmation.

The other man waved it away with a fatalistic shrug. "Oh,

yeah, we can get you there, that's no problem." His lips quirked and his eyes gleamed. "Getting you back could be, though." Then the smile broadened into the half moon again, and his eyes narrowed into cheery little upside-down half moons to match. "Just kidding. Government always tends to exaggerate these things—you know how it goes." He tilted his head toward the windows. "That's your ride, right there, all gassed up and ready to go. So…lemme see…that was Visa, right? I'm just gonna need your card for a minute…."

While Cory was hauling out his wallet and extracting the plastic, Will pushed a sheet of paper across the counter toward him. "And if the two of you'll just sign this waiver…" The half moons came out again. "Just a formality—since there is a government caution in effect. Nothin' to it, really."

Nothing to it, Cory thought as he scrawled his signature on the appropriate line at the bottom of the paper, except several hundred terrorists, a few-dozen tourist kidnappings, an occasional car bombing and a couple of missionaries held hostage for over a year.

He shoved the paper and pen toward Tony, who poked at them and tried not to look nervous.

"So, that's our pilot?" Tony asked with a casual nod toward the windows as he pretended to study the paper. Cory cleared his throat and nudged him with his elbow.

Will looked up from making an old-fashioned slide impression of Cory's credit card to beam at him. "Yep—she's one of our best."

"Wow, a woman, huh?" Tony was still fingering the pen.

Cory elbowed him in the ribs again and muttered, "Sign the damn thing, already. What's the matter with you?"

"Like I said, one of our best." Will brought the credit card slip to the counter and waited for Cory to sign it, after which he tore off and handed him his copy and tossed the other onto the cluttered desk.

"Okay, if you'll come right this way, please." He unhooked and folded up a section of countertop to let them through.

Cory tucked the credit card slip into his pocket and went to collect his bags. Tony, after hastily scrawling his signature on the waiver, did the same.

As they sidled through the door Will was holding for them— and tried not to gag as the heat assaulted them with renewed force—Will said in a chummy, confidential aside, "Hey, man, don't you worry about Sam, there. The woman could probably put that bird down on a tennis court, providing you get the net out of her way." He showed them his teeth and his half-moon eyes briefly as he pulled a cigarette pack from his shirt pocket, then turned away to light one.

For which courtesy Cory was intensely grateful. How would he have explained the look of blank shock that must have come over his face just then?

As it was, his step stumbled as if he'd taken a blow, and to cover it he paused briefly to shift his laptop carrier strap on his shoulder. When he continued on, there was a ringing sound in his ears.

Sam? Can't be. Can'tbecan'tbe. In all this world, he told himself, there had to be more than one female pilot named Sam. Had to be.

A coincidence. A little quirk of fate.

Out on the shimmering runway, the pilot straightened and moved out of the wing's shadow. Her movements were unhurried…lazy, even. She stood waiting for them to approach, attitude relaxed, even arrogant…hands clasped behind her, one knee slightly bent, one hip slightly canted…chin up, head tilted back.

How well he knew that stance. She'd stood just that way, he remembered, the first time he'd seen her, that day in the White House rose garden.

Her eyes, in the shadows beneath the bill of her cap, would be half-closed, he knew, measuring their approach with the cool appraisal of a well-trained sniper.

"*God,*" he whispered, not knowing whether or not it was a prayer.

Anger, joy, resentment, regret, pain, lust—all those things and others he couldn't name—thumped deep in his belly and exploded through his brain like mortar rounds, leaving him reeling. Shell-shocked. Numb.

For which small favor he was fervently thankful. Because the numbness was the only thing that made it possible for him to continue to function. To walk up to her with a steady step, to nod and calmly say, with the coolest of smiles, "Hello, Sam. Small world."

Oh, boy, thought Sammi June, *I'll bet he's mad.*

At least she told herself—half-hopefully—that he must be, and that, as determined as he might be to hide it from her, there would be telltale signs. A steely glint in his normally compassionate eyes, perhaps…those dark blue eyes, set deep behind the wire-rimmed glasses he almost always wore, eyes she'd always felt could see inside her soul…except, okay, right now his eyes were barely visible behind darkened lenses, but there was the tiny muscle flexing in the hinge of his jaw, the set of his mouth, the almost imperceptible hardening…

His mouth…normally so sensitive. So incredibly skilled. She remembered the way it felt like warm silk on her skin…sometimes. And at other times like liquid fire. And it tasted like…

No. I can't. I can't.

A thrill of excitement, of—God help her—anticipation shivered through her, astringent and heady as chilled wine.

"Helluva small world," she replied easily, nodding at him. "Hello, Pearse."

She thought it best not to offer him a hand to shake, since hers were cold as ice. Hoping he wouldn't notice, she tucked them casually in her back pockets to warm them.

And saw the quick flicker of his eyes. Of course he'd notice.

He was a reporter. He noticed everything. Especially if it had to do with her. He always had.

"Been a long time."

"Yes, it sure has." *And what a scintillating bit of repartee this is,* she thought. *How many more of these can we come up with? Long time, no see.... Fancy meeting you here.*

"You two know each other?" The guy with Cory—he'd be the photographer—was looking back and forth between the two of them, a puzzled and suspicious frown apparent, even though sunglasses hid his eyes.

Tony Whitehall didn't look like a man she'd want to mess with if she could possibly avoid it, being half a head shorter than Cory and probably outweighing him by fifty pounds, none of it fat. His head resembled an egg, both in shape and hairlessness, but from roughly his earlobes down he looked to be one hundred percent solid unbreakable muscle. His skin was a warm, glossy mahogany, although his features, including wide cheekbones and a jutting hawk's beak of a nose, hinted at a heritage more Native American than African.

Taken feature for feature he was almost marvelously ugly, but at the same time, in an indefinable, ruggedly offbeat way, she thought, rather attractive.

"Samantha Bauer," she said, smiling at him. And since the circulation seemed to have returned to her hands, she pulled one out of her pocket and offered it to him. "Cory and I go way back."

He smiled as he took her hand. "He and I go back a ways, too, but I swear he's never mentioned you."

As she felt her hand being swallowed by one the approximate size and texture of a baseball mitt, she could feel Cory's eyes on her, intent and unwavering. Broadening her smile to a grin, she said, "Doesn't surprise me. He's just—" she let her gaze slide casually across Cory's "—an old family friend." She was gratified by his barely audible snort.

"Hey, if you were a friend of *my* family's, you can bet I'd mention you." Now there was an unmistakable lilt in his voice. Obviously, the flirting lamp had been lit.

Cory gave another snort, a louder one this time, and said dryly, "Tony's got a thing for your airplane."

Sam retrieved her hand but kept her smile where it was. "Yeah? You familiar with the DC-3?"

"Familiar?" Tony's voice climbed the scale to a squeak that was almost comically unsuited to a man of his size and shape. "Oh, yeah, sure…like at the Smithsonian."

Sam laughed, then wished she hadn't. The laughter served to ease some of the tension that had tied her belly in knots, but without that tension holding her together, she suddenly felt loose and shaky inside. Fighting to keep the shaking out of her voice, or at least camouflage it, she waved Tony toward the steps and turned to walk beside him. "The DC-3 is probably the most reliable aircraft ever built. This one's been restored, of course. She'll probably outlast both of us."

As she followed the photographer up the steps, she felt Cory fall in behind her. Felt his eyes on her. Of course she did; she was conscious of every movement he made—always had been. And the worst part of it was knowing he'd know that. He'd know exactly how aware of him she was, no matter how earnestly she chatted with Tony about the history and merits of the DC-3 aircraft. *He'll know, no matter how I try to hide it. He always knows what I'm feeling. Damn him.*

How, exactly, *was* she feeling?

I can't think about that right now. I can't think now.

I thought I was ready for this. Dammit.

At the top of the steps she moved aside and gestured for Tony and Cory to pass her. "Go ahead and get settled in. I just have a couple of flight details to go over with Will. Shouldn't take but a minute. We'll be underway shortly."

To be truthful, she was feeling on the verge of suffocation as she stepped back through the doorway. At the top of the steps she paused and lifted closed eyes to the merciless sun and hauled in a great gulp of the syrupy air as if it were pure oxygen. After a moment, when her head seemed to have stopped swimming, she clattered down the steps and headed for the shimmering terminal buildings. Halfway there, in spite of the heat, she broke into a jog.

Inside the stuffy cabin, Cory was putting himself through the necessary mental fortifications to deal with the awful heat. It was an exercise he'd learned long ago, and one that had gotten him through far worse circumstances than these. Mind over matter, that's all it was. Mind over matter. The air was only unbreatheable if he thought it was.

Seeing Samantha again was only unendurable if he let it be.

Originally designed to carry around thirty passengers, the restored cabin had been reconfigured to hold maybe half that many. The furnishings were spartan, but the seats were wide enough to accommodate even Tony's massive shoulders, and set far enough apart to afford a lanky six-footer like Cory adequate leg room. By mutual and unspoken agreement, he and Tony selected seats across the aisle from each other about halfway up the sloping cabin and set about stowing their bags in heroic silence.

Having secured his precious cameras to his satisfaction, Tony again took off his sunglasses and hooked the earpiece in the neck band of his shirt. He took off the bandana, wiped his face and neck with it, then sank into his seat with a heavy sigh.

After a moment he sat up again restlessly and looked over at the man in the seat across the aisle from him, the man who was most likely the best friend he had in the world, and who he admired and respected probably more than any other living human being. Nevertheless, and in spite of the fact that the man had a good five years on him, Tony more often than not felt a big-brotherly need to look out for and protect this man. And, at the moment, he felt a strong urge to throttle him.

When looking over a couple more times failed to get his attention, Tony tried shifting around and clearing his throat—not too subtle and a little bit childish, sure, but in Cory's case, it usually worked.

This time, however, Cory went on staring straight ahead at nothing, absolutely still but in no way relaxed, neck and shoulders rigid with tension.

Tony leveled a black scowl at him. He considered himself to be normally a good-natured soul, but his aggravation levels were rising rapidly. They were rising because he was trying to work himself up to doing something completely alien to his masculinity and that he was resisting with every macho bone in his body. And he was becoming royally ticked at his buddy for making all that necessary.

He was about to do something guys, in his experience, simply don't do, which was ask a guy friend a personal question.

"So," he said, after clearing his throat a couple more times and finally hitching himself around in his seat in the heavy, flopping manner of a landed marlin. "What's with you and Amelia Earhart?"

Cory jumped as if he'd been a million miles away—which he probably had been, mentally—and threw him a frowning look. "Who? Oh—you mean—"

"You know damn well who I mean." Tony jerked his head toward the tumble of buildings beyond the wavy window glass. "What's the story?"

Cory took off his glasses and went to polishing them on the tail of his shirt, an activity Tony recognized for the delaying tactic it was. "You heard her. I'm just a friend of her family. Her father's…actually." He put the glasses back on and pushed them up on the bridge of his nose. Since his nose was slippery with sweat, they slid right down again.

"Friend of the family, my *foot*," Tony said, and was rewarded with a sideways look and a lopsided grin.

"Your *foot?*"

Tony shrugged and grinned back. "I don't know, my mom used to say that. I guess it was the best she could do, since Gramma wouldn't let her swear. Anyway, you get my drift. You and I go back quite a ways, too, buddy. I was best man at your wedding, in case you've forgotten. What's maybe more germane to this discussion, I was there during your divorce. I stood by you—"

"Not too much standing involved, as I recall, unless you consider perching on a bar stool—"

"Hey, I was there, that's what counts. Ready and willing to lend you a shoulder if you needed one."

"The way I remember it, you were the one needing a shoulder—not to mention a ride home, and on one memorable occasion, at least, bail."

Tony gave an affronted snort. "Don't try to sidetrack me, Mr. Wordman. Whatever was between you and Amelia Earhart had to be something major. Hell, you know me—when it comes to understanding women, I'm no Dr. Phil, and even I felt it. Out there. Just now. The way the sparks were flying back and forth, it's a wonder you two didn't set the damn plane on fire."

Cory didn't reply, just gave him a hard, steely stare, a look that normally would have had Tony backing off. This time it didn't work, and after a moment Cory put his head back against the seat and closed his eyes.

It took a long, slow ten-count before Tony succeeded in throttling back enough to press on in a calmer, quieter voice. "Look, man, you know me, I don't butt in where it's not my business. But this isn't exactly a picnic in the park we're going on. I mean, here we are, heading into a place that's supposedly so dangerous no commercial airline or boat or bus service is even willing to take us there, supposedly to interview a major terrorist who, if he had his druthers, would probably just as soon kill us as look at us. If you've got history with the woman we're trusting to get us in and out of there alive, I think I ought to know about it."

There was a long, suspenseful silence, during which Tony watched, with a sinking feeling in his gut, the little muscles working in the side of Cory's jaw, and wondered if he was going to have to start looking for a new best friend.

Then, to his great relief, Cory straightened abruptly and said, "You're right, you do." Tony let out a silent, careful breath.

He waited, heart thumping, while Cory glanced over his shoulder toward the terminal buildings, again took off his glasses, rubbed his eyes. Put the glasses back on. Leaned toward him across the aisle and spoke in a soft, conspiratorial way, although there was no one else around to hear.

"You know I was a prisoner in Iraq, right?"

"Yeah, sure—about ten years ago, wasn't it? Special Forces went in and got you out in the middle of the Second Iraq War. Didn't you win the Pulitzer with some of the articles you wrote about it afterward?"

Cory nodded in a dismissive way. "So you probably also remember there was another guy rescued same time I was. Tomcat pilot—he'd been shot down over the no-fly zone between the two Gulf wars. Given up for dead. They'd had him for eight years, and nobody knew."

"Holy jumpin' jeezits," Tony exclaimed, whacking the armrest with an open palm, "I remember that! I was working in Richmond at the time—I think it was maybe my second or third big assignment—they sent me to Andrews to cover his return. Had all us media people corralled away from the action behind a chain-link fence so we wouldn't interfere with the big family reunion. Never got one decent shot. Let's see…I seem to remember he had a wife…a daughter…"

Cory nodded, took a breath and let it out. "He did. And that pilot out there, Samantha Bauer—" he dipped his head toward the windows "—Amelia Earhart, as you call her…"

"Don't tell me," Tony said, in the same reverent tone with which he'd first spoken of the airplane they were sitting in.

"Yep," said Cory, in a voice like the echoes of doom. "She's the Top Gun's daughter."

Chapter 2

"I met her in the White House rose garden," Cory said, following a gleefully profane exclamation from Tony.

He could still smile, remembering that day, but carefully, tentatively, with great care not to jostle the memories too hard. The turbulence of seeing her again had shifted and tumbled them—and the feelings that went with them—inside the compartment he'd stuffed them into years ago, and right now he feared if he opened that door too wide and too suddenly they might tumble out and bury him.

He spoke rapidly to get past the danger.

"There was a reception for us—for him, really—Lieutenant Bauer—I was more or less an afterthought. The guy was a genuine hero, and you know what the media does with heroes."

"Aren't *you* the media?"

"That's why I get to bad-mouth—it's like family. Anyway, you're not the media when you're part of the story."

"But you wrote those stories."

"Yeah, mainly to get through it. Get past it. I wonder, sometimes, how it would've been if I hadn't had that outlet. I know Tristan had a tough time of it—of course he'd been gone a lot longer than I was. They only had me a few months. Him they'd had for eight years."

"Hard to imagine. Impossible, maybe."

Cory nodded, the knots in his belly relaxing a little. He was always more comfortable concentrating on someone else's story. "It was tough on his family. They'd assumed all along he was dead. Jessie—his wife—hadn't remarried, though, which was one good thing. What a mess *that* would've been. Still, it was hard—they had a lot of readjusting to do. But it was hardest, I think, on Sammi—on Samantha. She was just a kid, a ten-year-old tomboy when she lost her dad. That's how he remembered her—how he described her to me, when we were together in that Iraqi prison. He talked about her all the time. A tomboy with ponytails. With bandages on her knees from playing soccer." A smile fluttered like a leaf on the gust of his exhalation. "Let me tell you, that's not what he came back to."

Not even close.

Oblivious to nuances, Tony whistled. "I guess not. She'd have been what, then—eighteen?"

"Yeah. In college. A grown-up woman, the way she saw it."

"Still just a kid, though," Tony said in a musing tone, then threw Cory a quick frown as it finally hit him. "What, you're telling me you had something going with her? I never figured you for a cradle robber, man. You must have, what, ten or twelve years on her?"

"It wasn't my intention," Cory said, putting his head back with a sigh. "Believe me. Well—" the smile this time was brief and wry "—not at first, anyway. Not that I didn't fall for her. *That* happened probably the first minute I laid eyes on her." He threw Tony a look and shifted uncomfortably. "Well, you've seen her." He glanced toward the window and his heart gave a jolt as he saw the tall wavery figure in khakis and a baseball cap striding toward them across the scorched grass.

Alerted by what he saw in Cory's face, Tony, too, turned to look out the window. After a long moment he said in a reverent tone, "I can see how she'd get your attention, yeah. Even dressed like that I can see it."

"It wasn't about her looks, though." Cory waggled his shoulders, uncomfortable even with the thought. Blond hair, brown eyes, long legs...*great* legs...okay, sure, she'd had all that. So had any number of other women he'd met in his lifetime and over the course of his career, in one variation or another. But Sammi June—Samantha—there'd just been something about her. So much...*more.*

"So, you had it bad for the college kid," Tony said. "So, what happened?"

"About what you'd expect, I guess. Didn't work out." Cory lifted one shoulder and closed his eyes, hoping maybe Tony would take the hint and let it drop.

Naturally, he didn't. "Didn't work out? That's all you have to say?" His voice rose in pitch as it lowered in volume. "Look, man, I know you. You'll make a story out of a trip to the 7-Eleven." With his eyes shut Cory felt the voice come nearer, and drop to a conspirator's mutter. "Hey—I saw your face when you recognized that woman out there a while ago. Like you'd been whacked upside the head with a plank." There was another pause while Tony settled back in his seat again.

After a moment he exhaled in an exasperated way. "Look. Three years ago I stood by your side and handed you the ring while you got married to a woman who just *happens* to bear an uncanny resemblance to this pilot of ours—don't think I didn't notice that—*and* I gave up my couch when you divorced that same woman barely a year later—*not* that I minded. I never liked her that much, anyway. Now, I may be crazy, but I'm getting the idea there's a connection there somewhere. So trust me, 'didn't work out' ain't gonna cut it."

"What do you want me to do? I can't very well get into it *now*," Cory threw back at him in an exasperated whisper. "She's gonna be back in here in a minute."

"Yeah, well…don't think I'm letting you off the hook on this one, pal. First thing when we get to Zamboanga—okay the second, but once we've got a couple of cold brewskies in front of us, I want the whole story. I'm not kiddin', man."

Cory let out his breath in a gusty sigh.

Of all things to happen, he thought. On *this,* of all assignments. It had to be the mother of all coincidences.

Or maybe just fate, catching up with him.

Outside on the steps, Sam paused with one hand braced on each side of the door as if she were preparing to withstand a gale-force wind. Which she supposed she was in a way, or at least the emotional equivalent. And so far she wasn't pleased with the way she'd held up in the face of it. No excuses, she'd had plenty of time to prepare. She should have had her emotions battened down a whole lot better than this.

One thing, one small triumph she could cling to: the look on Cory's face when he'd realized who his pilot was. Hah—complete and total shock. His face had gone ash-white. *You might be able to control your expressions and voice, Pearse, but there's not much you can do about your blood vessels.*

He'd had absolutely no clue, she was sure of it. And his re-action to seeing her again told her one thing: The man still had *some* feelings for her.

Okay, so she was probably never going to know exactly what those feelings were, but at least she knew he wasn't indifferent.

A little buzz of *something*—excitement? Triumph?—zinged through her and a smile curved her lips. Indifferent? *Not by a long shot.*

The smile stayed put while she got the steps pulled up and stowed away and the door secured. The smile was still in place, feeling as if it had been molded out of clay and drying fast, as she started up the aisle, nodding at Tony Whitehall, who had turned to look at her with an expression of unabashed curiosity, and a glint in his exotic golden eyes.

She wondered what Cory'd been telling him; she knew Tony *had* to have asked about her the minute she was out of earshot. And what an internal battle *that* must have been, she thought, between Cory's two selves: On the one hand, the reporter, who'd made a life and a career out of finding out secrets, getting to the bottom of things, solving mysteries, telling the story. On the other, the intensely private man who'd mastered the art of protecting his own secrets.

He, naturally, seemed completely unperturbed by her presence, or anything else, for that matter, sitting square in his seat, face forward, head back against the headrest. He looked as if he might even be enjoying a little nap.

But she knew better.

Or did she? Had she ever been sure what was going on behind those deep, all-seeing eyes?

"Air controllers at Davao City airport have cleared us for takeoff. If you-all wanna fasten your seat belts, we'll be getting underway in a few minutes," she announced in her this-is-your-captain-speaking voice, pausing to check that the two men's bags had been properly stowed in their compartments. "We should be in Zamboanga in about an hour and fifteen minutes." She threw Tony Whitehall a smile and a wink.

She didn't look at Cory, but to her great annoyance, felt a distinct prickling sensation between her shoulder blades as she continued up the sloping aisle to the cockpit, an awareness of eyes watching her with unfathomable intensity....

From his seat Cory could see clearly through the open cockpit door. He watched as she ran through her preflight checklist, and try as he would to deny it, felt a little burr of admiration, even pride, begin to hum beneath his breastbone. He'd never flown with Sam at the controls before.

The baseball cap had been replaced by a bulky set of white headphones that left her sun-streaked hair in the kind of sweaty disarray he'd always found particularly sexy. Sexy even now, cut short like this, shorter than he'd ever seen her wear it. Her strong hands and long-boned fingers moved nimbly over the complicated array of dials and switches in a way that brought back vividly the no-nonsense, straight-ahead way she'd always had about her, even when they'd made love. The way she'd had of touching him that was uniquely hers, without shyness or hesitation, with a certain bold edge and a hint...just a hint of wickedness.

And it was that more than anything, he thought, that had ignited the fires in his blood back then. Maybe that part of her had connected with the secret danger-lover and thrill-seeker within him, like two live wires touching....

Come off it, Pearse. It's over. It was over long ago.

One after the other, the twin engines fired with a deep-pitched growling sound that hummed in his bones and put him in mind of old black-and-white war movies, or something he'd watch on the History Channel. The plane sat vibrating in place while the engine rpm's climbed and the growling changed in pitch and intensity. Then it slowly began to move forward.

Cory felt his own pulse pick up speed as he watched the hands that had once stroked him to feverish arousal skillfully manipulate the throttles while she steered the plane in a tight right turn onto the runway, then tight left to straighten out. He saw her reach down with one hand to lock the tail wheel in place. The growling sound continued to grow in volume and intensity and he could feel the vibrating now in his belly as the plane began to accelerate down the runway.

Tearing his eyes away from the open cockpit door, he glanced over at Tony, who looked back at him and hummed the first few bars of "Off We Go, into the Wild Blue Yonder," grinning like a madman. He felt his stomach drop and his body press heavy into his seat, and he jerked his gaze to the window in time to watch the scorched grass and palm trees and tin-roofed buildings drop away under him.

"Hot damn," said Tony with a gleeful chortle.

Cory didn't reply. He leaned forward to stare through the window as Davao City came into view, slowly spreading out below him, with the glittering blue of the water beyond. His stomach dropped and the earth tilted as the plane banked sharply, and when it slowly rotated back into position, he could see Mount Apo draped in haze on the horizon.

And still the plane climbed steadily, the deep growling of its powerful twin engines creeping into his bones and invading his brain until he almost felt as if he were a part of the plane himself, as if he were the one laboring skyward with the sun in his face and the wind solid beneath his wings. He felt a soaring, lifting inside himself, too, to think of the woman he'd held soft and naked and trembling in his arms, in control of such awesome power.

He found the notion damned exciting…a pure turn-on, in fact. Which surprised and unnerved him more than a little.

When he felt the plane level out and the engine growl ease off to a steady purr, Cory unbuckled his seat belt. He got a look from Tony when he got up and stepped into the aisle, but something Tony saw in Cory's face must have warned him, because whatever it was he'd been about to say never got said.

Sam glanced back at him as he stepped through the radio operator's compartment, lips curving in a smug little Sammi June smile he remembered well. He couldn't see her eyes because of her sunglasses. He wished he could have seen them, though he wasn't sure why. Was he remembering the way they'd once lit up at the sight of him, wondering if the glasses were hiding that same glow now?

Wishful thinking, he told himself.

She tilted her head toward the right-hand seat. "Hey, Pearse— have a seat."

He eased past the controls and settled himself gingerly, his fascinated gaze sliding over the bewildering array of gauges and levers and dials to the view through the wide rectangular windshield. "Wow," he said.

Sam said lightly, "I guess this is a first." She threw him a smile. "You've never flown with me before."

"With you at the controls, you mean. No," he said, gazing once more at the hazy horizon, remembering other times when she'd seemed unknowingly to echo his thoughts. "I guess not."

There was a pause before she asked, with a slight edge of impatience, "Well, what do you think?"

He hedged, naturally, since there wasn't any way he could have told her the truth. Which was that he'd lost the ability to think the moment he'd set eyes on her, standing there beside the old World War Two airplane, wearing the arrogance that had always captivated him so, that was like her very own signature perfume.

In that first moment, the years since he'd last seen her had evaporated and it was as if she'd never been gone from his life or his mind, not for an instant. It was all there, in total recall—her face, her body, her voice, her laugh…the way her skin felt, its texture and heat…its softness and its tiny imperfections…the freckles, the way she smelled, the way her hands felt touching him…the way she tasted.

"Of the airplane," he dryly asked, "or you?"

She laughed, that husky chortle he'd always liked. "The plane, of course." Once again her smile quirked sideways. "Me being a pilot isn't exactly news."

"I never had a problem with you being a pilot. You know that."

"Yeah, *right.*"

He shifted in his seat and changed the timbre of his voice, the way driving a car he might have shifted gears to gain traction through a muddy patch. "Somehow I never would have pictured you flying World War Two prop planes for a dumpy little backwater charter outfit in the Philippines, though. The last I heard, you were crewing on passenger jets to China. How in the hell did you wind up here?" He let go of an incredulous huff of laughter. "I'm still trying to get my mind around the coincidence of that."

She shrugged and said lightly, "Long story," as she reached to tap some dials and gauges, an activity that, as far as Cory could tell, produced no changes whatsoever in the plane's behavior.

"We've got time."

Sam felt herself tensing up; she couldn't help it. It was the calm, almost gentle way he said it that got to her—hadn't it always?

As the old resentment flared, she fought the urge to glare at him, kept her eyes fixed on the horizon and said sweetly, "I don't know, I guess it must have been my 'childish lust for adventure.' Isn't that what you called it?"

And she couldn't help the little glow of satisfaction she got from the silence that followed, even though voices were hissing and moaning in dismay in the back of her mind. *Ooh, what did you wanna go and say that for, Samantha June? You don't wanna dredge up all that old stuff again. That's water under the bridge, honey-child…you should just leave it be.*

She could feel his eyes on her again, that quiet, steady gaze that made her squirm because it seemed it must see right inside her.

"You could have warned me," he said mildly.

Now she looked at him, her lips curving in an evil grin. "Deprive myself of the look on your face when you saw who your pilot was? No way."

He chuckled and shook his head, and his eyes found hers even through the shielding lenses of her sunglasses. "Same old Sammi June. Always got to be on top."

Something thumped hard in her belly. She kept the smile, but it no longer felt like part of her face. More like the clay mask again. "You used to like that about me."

He held her eyes for a long, intense, *awful* moment, then eased his shoulders back in the copilot's seat and exhaled, sounding weary. "I used to like a lot of things about you, Sam."

Damn you, Pearse. Damn Will, too, for requesting me for this assignment. And damn me for being stupid—no, arrogant—enough to think I could handle it. What was I thinking?

What were *you thinking, Sam? How about that you're a highly trained professional, with the skills and guts it takes to do this job?*

So, do it already. Focus, Sam. Do your job. So you had an affair with the man once upon a time. Forget it.

An affair. She cringed at the word. It made the whole thing with Cory sound…frivolous. Fleeting. Bittersweet and nostalgic—rather old-fashioned, really. Like something you'd read about in an old diary.

But it wasn't just an "affair," dammit. I loved you, Cory Pearson. You were the love of my life. And you broke my heart. No—you tore out my heart, tore it into itty-bitty pieces and stomped them in the dirt! God, how I hate you for that.

She did—oh, she did. But most of all she hated that she'd never known if she'd succeeded in hurting him back. She'd tried—you'd better believe she'd tried—but if she had managed to hurt him, he'd never let her see it. Not once.

And for that, more than anything, I swear I am never gonna forgive you.

She cleared her throat, took a deep breath. "Look, Pearse…I know this is probably awkward for you—"

"Awkward?" She heard the smile in his voice, and irony that was gentle, not bitter. "Like…*hell* is awkward, you mean?"

So, he thinks seeing me again after two solid years is hell? Well, good. I'm glad.

She *was* glad. So why did she feel a need to grit her teeth and swallow hard before she could answer him?

"Yeah, well…I'm gonna need to know if you're okay with it.

If you're not, just say the word. When we get to Zamboanga—"

"Of course I can handle it," he said softly.

Of course he can handle it, she thought, sarcastically. He'd
handle it the way he handled everything. Like a journalist, clear-
eyed and objective, but careful to keep himself one step removed
from the messy stuff. Stuff like…emotional turmoil. And pain.
It was the way he'd handled Iraq and its aftermath, wasn't it? And
probably all sorts of stuff that had happened to him in his distant
past he'd never been willing to talk about to anyone, not even her.

Seconds ticked by in silence, while the farmlands and forests
of Mindanao unfolded slowly below them.

"So, tell me," Sam said in a falsely bright, conversational
voice, shaking off the strangling sense of futility that had coiled
around her, "how's Karen these days?"

She heard his sharp hiss of exasperation and felt her cheeks
heat with a weird mixture of triumph and shame. What was it
that made her want to needle him? The forlorn hope he might
lose his cool? That was never going to happen. And even if it
did, what would that accomplish?

*At least I'd know he cared. That I'd hurt him, maybe a frac-
tion as badly as he hurt me.*

Okay, the devil made me do it….

"For God's sake, Samantha," he said in a weary voice.

"What?" She threw him a wounded look. "She was your wife
for…what was it, a whole year? Knowing you, I'm sure the divorce was amicable. You probably keep in touch, exchange
Christmas cards…all that stuff, right?" She lifted a shoulder and
turned her eyes back to the horizon. "I was just wondering how
she was doing. She looked like a nice person. I wish her well."

Sure you do. You wish her in hell, is what you mean.

"How do you know what she looks like?" Cory's voice
sounded idly curious, remote and far away.

"I saw the wedding pictures you guys sent Mom and Dad. She

looked…happy. So did you." She looked over at him, chin lifted in defense against the suffocating pain in her throat and chest. "So, what happened, anyway?"

He was maneuvering himself carefully around the controls and out of the copilot's seat and didn't reply.

"Hey," she said in mock dismay, "we're still a half hour out. You don't have to go back to your seat yet."

"Yeah, I do," he said flatly. "If you think I'm going to discuss my failed marriage with you, you're crazy." With one hand on the back of the right-hand seat, the other on hers, he paused as if listening to a replay of what he'd said inside his own head. Then he added in a softer tone, "Not now, anyway. I guess we are going to have to talk, but this isn't the time *or* the place."

It wasn't until he'd left the cockpit and was on his way back to his seat that Sam realized her heart was pounding. And that she felt shivery inside—a purely feminine kind of weakness she hadn't felt in…oh, years and years. Well, two, to be exact. Which happened to be the last time she'd spoken face-to-face with Cory Pearson.

Feminine weaknesses—or any other kind, for that matter— she surely did *not* need. Lord help her, especially not *now*.

Well, hellfire and damnation—as Great-Grannie Calhoun might have said—what was she supposed to do? She hadn't expected to feel so much, not after all this time.

Tony's stare followed Cory down the aisle and into his seat.

"Don't even *think* about asking," Cory warned in a hard, flat voice that carried over the loud click of his seat belt.

Tony promptly closed his mouth. A moment later, though, he opened it again to say, jabbing a finger at Cory for emphasis, "Okay, but just so you know, the minute we get to Zamboanga, it's the brews first, then the buzz. I mean it, man. The whole story. Or you can find yourself another cameraman. Swear to God."

Cory put his head back against the seat and closed his eyes.

He wasn't worried about losing his photographer. In addition to being a close personal friend, Tony'd have to be comatose *and* chained to a bunker before he'd miss this assignment. But he was right—the three of them were going to be depending on each other for a lot during the next week or so, including, possibly, their lives. They were a team, for better or worse. Tony deserved to know about his history with the third member of the team—some of it, anyway.

Definitely not everything.

God, how it all came back to him, the way things had been with Sam and him. Every laugh, every tear, every heart-thumping, gut-twisting, sweaty detail. The chemistry—the fireworks—had been there from the first moment for both of them, although he'd done a pretty good job—heroic, he thought, considering what he was up against—of holding it at bay for as long as he had.

There'd been the age thing, of course, but Sam hadn't wanted to hear about that. Far as she was concerned she was a grown-up woman of legal consenting age, and that was that. Didn't help matters, either, that her mother had been the same age when she'd met and fallen in love with her dad.

Then there'd been Cory's friendship with Tristan, forged during those hellish days spent together in an Iraqi prison. Tris hadn't been happy when his baby girl, the daughter he still remembered as a ponytailed tomboy, had declared her intention of dating a thirty-two-year-old friend of her father's. Cory had been fighting a strong sense of guilt about that the weekend he'd gone to visit Tris, Jessie and Sam at the lake house. Memorial Day weekend, it had been. Lord, how well he remembered that terrible day….

It's been a beautiful day. Last night's thunderstorms have moved on, and the skies have cleared to a typically hot, hazy, sunshiny summer afternoon. The lake is crowded with boats of all kinds, shapes and sizes: pontoons loaded with partying lake-

dwellers waving to neighbors on their docks, flat-bottomed bass boats with solitary fishermen stoically riding out the chop in quiet coves, lots of other ski-boats, and of course the Wave Runners and Jet Skis, zipping illegally in and out amongst them all.

In the midst of all the chaos, Sam is determined to teach me to water-ski. I've never considered myself particularly talented when it comes to sports, but she's patient—or stubborn—and it seems as if I might be getting the hang of it, finally. I've gotten up—again—and this time it feels like I might stay here awhile. Tris is driving the boat, while Jess sits watching me from the spotter's seat in the rear, and Sam rides beside me on her knee board. Above the hiss of the water's spray I can hear her shouting encouragement and praise.

He remembered the feel of the goofy grin on his face, the breathless exhilaration when he successfully jumped the wake.

He remembered the two kids on the Jet Ski, a boy and a girl riding tandem, cutting in close…too close.

I hit the water with that stinging thump that's become all too familiar to me this day, and I hear Sam's yell and Jessie's whoop, and the sound of the boat's motor throttling down, then circling slowly back to me. Jess leans over the back of the boat, calling to me, asking if I'm ready to call it quits.

That's when it happens.

I don't see the accident, none of us do, except maybe Tristan. But we all hear it—that terrible grinding crunch. I hear Tris shout as he guns the boat, and then he's heading away from me toward the mouth of a nearby cove. Far off across the roiling surface of the water I can see the teenagers' Jet Ski floating at a crazy angle next to a capsized bass boat.

Then I'm swimming, swimming toward the wreck, swimming as hard as I've ever swum in my life before, and my heart feels like it's on fire in my chest.

I hear Jessie screaming at Tris, and the sound of a splash as Tris hits the water. And after what seems an eternity, I see Tris's

*head reappear, and next to it that of the unconscious fisherman.
I feel an awful jolt of adrenaline shoot through me a moment
later when I see both Tris and the fisherman slowly sink back beneath the surface of that muddy water.*

*A thought flashes through my mind: No! No way he survived
eight years in an Iraqi prison to die in this godforsaken pond.
No way!*

That's when I haul in air and dive.

Things become confused…I'm operating on instinct.

*I'm underwater, I feel something…I grab hold of it. It's Tris,
and I grab hold of him and try to fight my way back to the surface. And I realize I'm fighting a losing battle because Tris still
has a death grip on the bass fisherman and isn't about to let go.*

I think, God help us, we're all going to drown.

*And then…my head's above water, and I see Sam, plowing
toward us through the water on her knee board, digging hard
with both arms and yelling and cussing like a maniac, and she's
shoving life preservers at me, and her strong hands are everywhere, helping me, lifting Tris, pulling them both up out of the
water.*

*There's a lot of yelling and thrashing around, and everything
is gasping, coughing, choking, sobbing pandemonium….*

In spite of the confusion, some images stayed clear in his
mind: Sam treading water while breathing into the fisherman's
mouth. Jess doing the same for the teenaged boy in the bottom
of the boat while she sobbed and swore furiously at Tris between
breaths. Tris clinging to the side of the boat, gasping for breath
and glancing over at Cory with haunted eyes.

Later that evening, after paramedics had flown the three accident victims off to the hospital in a medevac chopper, after Tris
and Jess, Sam and Cory had all showered and eaten and calm
had been restored, Sam and Cory took the boat and went out
again onto the now-serene and all but deserted lake. To watch
the sunset, Sam said, but Cory had known her real reason for

wanting to get out of the house was to give her mom and dad some privacy. They'd been having a rough time of it since Tris's return from the dead, Cory knew. It was Jess's concern about her husband that had led her to call Cory, to ask for help from the one person she felt might understand what Tris was going through.

How well he remembered that night, too, and what a strange contradiction there seemed to be between the peace and quiet of tranquil water reflecting sunset clouds…the first and brightest star of evening…and the sense inside himself that something profound had happened to him this day. That being here with this woman, a milestone had been passed in his life, one equal in import and magnitude to his parents' death and his sojourn in Iraq, one that would change the direction of his life irrevocably.

"Look," Sam says, "there's the Wishing Star."

She tells me, then, how she wished on that star when she was a little girl, and she tells me the poem and we recite it together: "Starlight, star bright, first star I've seen tonight…"

"What did you wish for?" I ask her, smiling, thinking how very young she is.

"Uh-uh. You're not supposed to tell. Otherwise, it won't come true." And she smiles and tilts her face up to mine.

It was then, in that moment, that he'd forgotten any thoughts he'd ever had about how young she was. He'd remembered instead her strength and her courage. He'd remembered her intelligence and sensitivity, her stubbornness and arrogance and husky, sexy laughter. And he'd lowered his head and kissed her.

Oh, how he remembered that kiss.

What do I expect—something sweet and innocent and virginal, maybe? Instead…I find myself lost. Lost in a sensual jungle…lush, humid, beautiful, exhilarating…terrifying. I'm afraid I may never escape; I don't want to, really. But at the same time I'm afraid, as inside me I feel battlements I've spent a lifetime erecting begin to shiver and quake.

It takes all my wits and will, but I fight my way free, and I'm thinking, How am I ever going to hold out against this?

And I think, Tristan, my friend, I'm sorry—forgive me—but I'm afraid I've fallen in love with your daughter....

He had held out for a lot longer than he'd believed possible, though he hadn't been able to make Sam understand why, even with her long, silky body warm and soft against his, her strong fingers tracing paths on his skin for her eager mouth to follow, when all her woman's instincts and the evidence of her senses told her how much he wanted her, he could still refuse to take her to bed.

Sam hadn't understood, that night on the lake...a night and a kiss so beautiful, so full of sweetness and hope and promise it had made his soul ache. It was only the first of God-knew-how-many times he'd disappointed her.

Chapter 3

"Okay, I just wanna know one thing." Tony wiped beer from his lips with the back of his hand and leaned back in his chair. "If you still had a thing for this Sam chick, why in the *hell* did you marry Karen?"

Cory watched the waiter in his white tunic and black slacks weave his way between tables on his way back to the bar. "Boy, you don't mess around, do you?" he said mildly. "Straight for the throat."

"Whatever works," Tony said, burping agreeably.

Cory picked up his beer glass and sipped, then reconsidered and took a couple of hefty gulps. Talking about personal stuff—*his* personal stuff—never had come easy for him; he figured priming the pump a little couldn't hurt.

He coughed, frowned and said, "It's not that simple."

"Never is." Tony nodded at him in a so-go-on kind of way. "Quit stalling."

Instead of replying, Cory shifted around in his chair, ran a hand through his hair and swore under his breath.

"Okay," Tony said, sitting forward and planting his forearms on the table, "I'll get you started. You met this…"

"Samantha."

"Yeah. You met Samantha right after you came back from Iraq, right? And it was love at first sight. Dyn-o-mite. So that'd make it…" he counted on his fingers "…six—no, seven—years later you married Karen. I have to assume you dated the lady *some* before you popped the question. So, what were you doing during the previous six years? Were you and Samantha together all that time?"

"We dated," Cory hedged, scrubbing a hand over his eyes. "Off and on…"

"Dated…as in, dinner and a movie? Or dated…as in, you give her a drawer in your apartment and she keeps your aftershave on her sink?" Cory glared at him. "Hey, you *were* sleeping with her, right?" Tony waggled a finger back and forth like a tiny windshield wiper. "Look, man, the kind of sexual tension I been pickin' up here, that doesn't come from nothin'. So gimme a break, okay?"

There was a pause while Cory drank more beer, then pursed his lips, steeling himself. "There were long periods when we didn't see each other," he said at last, in a voice Tony had to lean closer to hear. "She was in school in Georgia, I was working out of New York, on assignment a lot of the time. When we did manage to get together, it was like we'd never been apart. Couldn't keep our hands off each other. It was…" he waved a helpless hand "…like touching a match to fireworks. Like dropping a torch in dry tinder. Like that. We couldn't seem to help ourselves."

Tony stared at him for a moment—probably in shock, Cory thought, to hear him give up so much personal stuff at once, and so easily. Then belatedly he nodded, as if in sympathy. Cory glanced at him, shifted in his seat and forced himself to go on.

"Then, the time together would end, she'd go back to Georgia, I'd go back to New York, we'd resume our lives. She had hers, I had mine. Not," he said wryly, "that I didn't spend a lot of my time thinking about her when I wasn't with her. I'd like to think she spent some time thinking about me." He paused for an absentminded sip of beer. "I never asked her whether or not she dated anyone else when we were apart. I have to assume she did."

"Tough way to run a relationship," Tony offered, shaking his head in sympathy.

Cory nodded, then shrugged. "We both had other things on our minds, I guess. For me, I think it was a case of…I was just biding my time, keeping busy, traveling a lot, waiting for her to finish school. In the back of my mind was always the thought that once she graduated, we'd find a way to work things so we could have a more…I don't know, *steady* relationship." Once again the wry grin stretched the unwilling muscles in his face. "As it turned out, she had other ideas."

Tony was nodding, hunched over his beer, apparently staring at the front of Cory's shirt. "Things to see…places to go…people to…uh."

"Something like that." Cory lifted his beer glass, discovered it was empty and signaled the waiter with it instead. "Her big thing was, she had her heart set on being a pilot, like her dad. Her mom wasn't going to hear of her joining the military, so off she went to flight school. Didn't take her long to get her private pilot's license, and again I thought…okay, maybe *now*. But after that…" He frowned, distracted by the waiter's approach. When their order for two more of the same had been taken and the waiter had gone away again, he resumed. "After flight school, she pretty much disappeared for a while."

"Wait a minute. Disappeared? As in…went missing? That's kind of freaky."

"As in, dropped out of sight. Out of my life. Oh, I'd get phone calls from her. Sometimes she'd e-mail me. Always full of how much she…how much she missed me. But also how much she loved what she was doing, how exciting it all was, and that it was what she'd always wanted to do. And if I happened to have some free time, let's say, and suggested we get together, she was always off somewhere 'training.' Well, *hell*," he added bitterly as the waiter arrived with two fresh glasses of beer, "a man can only take so much."

"You got that right," said Tony stoutly, lifting his new glass in a salute.

When the waiter had been disposed of, Cory claimed his glass and leaned in, in a companionable sort of way. He'd been right about the beer; telling his story was definitely getting easier. "I mean, I'd been waiting for the woman for five years. Then, too, I wasn't getting any younger. You know, I was in my late thirties, approaching middle age, and I'm feeling like there's something missing in my life. I'm thinking maybe it's time to be settling down, cut down on the travel, have some kids before I'm too old to enjoy 'em. You know?"

Tony was nodding again, like one of those little dogs people put in the back windows of their cars. "You got the ol' nesting urge. Happens. Hasn't happened to me, yet, but I've heard about it."

"So, right about then's when I met Karen."

Tony went on nodding. "She caught you at a weak moment."

"Yeah," said Cory gloomily, "I guess." But he felt guilty even saying it. It had been a whole lot more complicated than that, but he didn't feel much like getting into it with Tony. Not now. Not with Sam back in his life and "What was I thinking?" the phrase uppermost in his mind.

After a moment he straightened himself up and said, "Hey, I'm not proud of it, okay? She was there and Sam wasn't, and after a while I convinced myself what I felt for Karen was love, and that made it all right, somehow. It was a case of somebody being in the right place at the right time." He tilted his head, considering that. "Or, from her point of view, maybe the wrong place at the right time…. Anyway. So—" he shrugged, drank beer, burped gently and waved his glass in a *c'est la vie* gesture "—I got married. End of story. Or anyway, you know the rest."

"Uh-uh." Tony's head movements had changed direction. "Not so fast. What about Samantha? How'd she take it, you going and getting married on her like that?"

Cory gave him a sideways look. He was feeling defensive again. "Come on. It wasn't like that. Not like I sent her a Dear John—or Jane—letter, if that's what you're thinking. We'd already agreed it was time to cut each other loose…go our separate ways. I sure as hell didn't need her…her *permission*."

Tony said, "Humph," in a thoughtful way, then narrowed his eyes. "Who called it off? You break up with her, or she break up with you?"

"What difference does it make?" Cory said, squirming a little.

"Helluva difference. The dumpee always carries a bigger grudge than the dumper. It's kind of a natural law."

"Look, it wasn't like that, okay? Anyway, I don't know if I even remember."

Oh, but he did, though. He probably remembered every moment of that last night together, every word spoken. The things he'd said to her—gently, he'd thought at the time. Calmly. Rationally. Explaining to her that he wasn't getting any younger, and…oh, all the other things he'd just told Tony, and how patient he'd been, waiting for her all through college and flight school, and as much as he loved her and always would, how long did she expect him to wait for her to grow up?

Oh, boy. He'd realized the moment those words were out of his mouth they might not have been the best choice. Plus, no matter how gently he'd phrased it, what he'd done was force her to make a choice between him and the career she loved, and Sam

never had taken well to ultimatums. He remembered, could feel
it still, the sick, sinking feeling in his stomach when he saw her
eyes harden to cold, dark fury. He felt chilled even now, remembering the implacability in her voice as she'd replied.

"Then don't," she says. "Don't wait for me anymore."

Just that; Sam never has been a great one for words.

*As I watch her walk away from me down a rain-slicked
Georgetown street, part of me—a long-buried, almost-forgotten
part—is howling in pain and anguish like an abandoned child,
all set to hurl myself after her and beg her to forgive me, forget
everything I've said, that I will wait for her forever if that's what
it takes to keep her in my life.*

*But another part of me, the adult part that has governed
me since I was nine years old, is already deadened to the
pain...growing numb with acceptance that this is for the best.
And already growing used to the idea that the woman I've considered the love of my life for so long, I must henceforth remember as the one who got away....*

"Uh-oh," Tony said. "Speak of the devil. Uh...not that I think
she's...well, you know what I mean. Look who just walked in."
He hauled his beer close and subsided, looking vaguely ashamed,
while Cory shot a quick guilty look toward the bar's entrance.

In keeping with the hotel's "tropical hideaway" theme—
which meant many of the guest rooms, including his, were on
stilts, right at the water's edge—the bar's ambiance was lush and
exotic. Reminded Cory of the old Tiki Room at Disneyland,
which he recalled visiting once during his college days. Here,
though, the plants and flowers were real, and the sounds of trick-
ling water came from miniature waterfalls that cascaded invisi-
bly through the greenery. Instead of the clacking of animated
birds, the background music emanating from hidden speakers
was muted, exotic and unfamiliar.

The entrance was a small elevated landing flanked by stands
of bamboo that leaned inward toward each other to form a door-

way arch, illuminated by a soft mellow spotlight. It was like a small stage, and dead in the middle of it stood Sam, looking as though she belonged there, her head held high in that almost arrogant way she had, her short blond hair shining like sunshine, spiked and curling slightly with the damp.

His heart slammed against his ribs, but all he said was, "I see her."

No cargo pants and baseball cap tonight. She wore a wrap skirt in tropical splashes of orange and peach and red that hit her a couple of inches above the knee and set off the soft golden tones of her skin, and a yellow knit tank top that clung to her small firm breasts and slender waist like the hide of an exotic animal. She looked confident and at ease, there in the light, her long, naturally lean body relaxed, but seeming to vibrate with strength and energy held in reserve.

"So does every male in the room—every one that's got a pulse," Tony muttered out of the side of his mouth. "Man, I only wanna know one thing. How in the hell'd you ever let a woman like that get away?"

Cory winced. The question was too close to what he'd been thinking to himself a moment ago. He said in a voice gone unexpectedly guttural, "Like I said, I tried my best. She had other ideas." He took a swallow of beer that seared his throat.

"Think she's looking for us? Hey—she's looking this way."

"No—don't—" But it was too late. Tony had already lifted his beer glass and was gesturing with it in a welcoming way.

"Hey—Captain—over here."

With his pulse a hollow tom-tom beat in his belly, Cory watched Sam give Tony a little smile and a nod, pause briefly to speak to the white-jacketed host who had rushed over to greet her, then make her way unhurriedly through the maze of rattan tables.

As she walked among the tables, it occurred to Sam that her legs felt rather odd. Not weak—she'd *never* say weak—but…as though they weren't all that well strung together, put it that way.

Oh, Lord, it's still there. All these years later, and it's as bad as ever. Like one of those tropical diseases, she thought, that pop out every now and then even when you think you're over it. Like malaria.

She tried hard to keep her eyes on the bald guy, the photographer—*Tony, that's it.* She kept her eyes and her smile focused on him and tried not to look at Cory, but how could she help but see him sitting there? Sort of leaning back in his chair, relaxed as always, wearing a loose-fitting long-sleeved shirt in some kind of coarse, rugged material softened and faded by long wear and many washings.

He'd be watching her, she knew, with his lips slightly curved, eyes dark and intent behind the rimless glasses he always wore. It was the attitude that made him such a successful reporter, that way he had of making a person feel they were the most fascinating and important person in the world, that nothing mattered more than what they had to tell him.

It would only occur to them a long time afterward that they'd spilled their guts to him, told him their deepest, darkest secrets…and that they knew absolutely nothing about him.

"Hey," she said by way of a greeting, in the manner of the deep South in which she'd been born and mostly raised. She slid into the chair Tony had gallantly shoved out for her with his foot.

After risking a glance at Cory, who raised his beer glass a fraction of an inch, tilted it toward her and gave her his enigmatic little half smile, she turned the brightest one she could come up with on Tony.

And found he was already signaling a waiter. "Hey—can we get another one of these over here?"

She started to shake her head, but before she could get a word out herself, she heard, "Sam doesn't like beer," in the quiet, deep voice that always made something thrum beneath her breastbone, like bass synthesizers thumping in the distance. "She's got a sweet tooth. Rum and Coke's her drink.

Right, Sam?" She swiveled her head toward him, braced for that first contact with his penetrating blue gaze. "At least, it used to be."

"Still is," she said lightly, and although it nearly killed her to do it while her teeth were clenched, nodded and smiled at the hovering waiter. *We have too much to deal with tonight,* she told herself. Silly to start with a fight over something so trivial.

"Hey, Captain, you're looking mighty fine tonight." Tony was smiling at her in a way that, though blatantly flirting, still managed to be unexpectedly charming.

The man definitely has charisma, Sam thought with regret. What a pity it was wasted on her. What a relief it would be to enjoy something so simple, so painless, as pure, uncomplicated sexual attraction.

"Thanks," she said, smiling at him as she shook herself back in her chair. "I do like to change out of my khakis now and then. Shower…you know—get rid of the hat-hair."

"You used to wear it longer."

The casual words stung her nerves like wasps. She looked at Cory and—no great surprise—found him staring at her, although something in his eyes…

"Don't like to drink and run…" Tony abruptly shoved back his chair, making her jump. For those few seconds she'd forgotten his existence.

"Don't rush off." She said it automatically, in the time-honored Southern way, and Cory echoed, "Don't you want to eat something?"

Already in the process of taking his wallet from a back pocket, Tony took out some bills and put them on the table, saying as he did so, "Naw, I'll just order something from room service. I've got things to see to—want to sort out my equipment, make sure I've got everything I'm gonna need—you know." His settling-up completed, he flicked her a smile. "What time we figuring on taking off in the morning, Cap'n?"

Sam dipped a nod at Cory. "That's up to you guys. You're the paying customers."

Cory coughed and shifted forward in his chair. "My instructions are to go to the rendezvous point and wait to be contacted." His lips tilted without smiling. "I'm not sure what that means, but I'm envisioning unknown numbers of heavily armed men wearing black hoods emerging from the bushes. So I doubt the timing is all that critical. That said, I'd like to get to the spot with as much daylight ahead of us as possible."

Sam dipped her head again. "No problem. We take off at daybreak, then." She looked at Cory. "You got maps, I assume?"

"In my room."

"I'll need to see those. I'll be filing my flight plan before we leave in the morning."

Cory nodded. "Of course."

"Okay, I'll be sayin' good night, then." Tony winked at Sam, gave Cory a little one-finger salute and left, dodging around the waiter who was just arriving with Sam's drink.

"You having another?" she asked Cory. He glanced up at the hovering waiter, shook his head and politely lifted a declining hand.

The waiter went away. Sam took a sip of her rum and Coke. Through a strange buzzing in her ears she heard Cory's quiet voice say, "What about you? Want something to eat?"

Are you kidding? The way my stomach feels, if I ate anything it'd probably erupt like Mount Vesuvius. That's what she wanted to say. What she did say was, "No, thanks. I'm not all that hungry."

She took another sip of her drink. Not looking at him. Not wanting to look at him. Knowing she had to. Not to look at him was stupid. *Childish.* Sooner or later, with Cory it always seemed to come down to that, didn't it?

So, she shook back her hair and lifted her head and looked straight at him. And found him looking back at her—of course

he was, what had she expected? They looked at each other, neither saying anything, and Sam felt her face grow achy and stiff,
and a horrible and unexpected desire to cry begin to gather behind her eyes.

To head it off, she gave up a bubble of husky laughter. "Okay,
this *is* awkward."

Without smiling, Cory said mildly, "Did you think it wouldn't
be? You saw my name on the charter, you knew who the cus-
tomer was. You had to know this moment was coming. You must
have had…I don't know, *days* to think of something bright and
clever to say."

Cruel, she thought. *That isn't like you.*

But then, what did she know? *Really?*

"Well, I'd have thought *you'd* have more to say," she shot back
at him. "I've never known you to be so stingy with words."

He sat back in his chair. "What is there to say? You told me
never to call you or speak to you again."

"*Jeez!* You got *married!*" *There. Yes!* Anger felt so much better.

"And divorced."

She stared at him through a shimmering haze. "And that was
supposed to make it all okay? We could…what, pretend it never
happened?"

His jaw looked tense; she could see the small muscles working. "We can't talk about this here," he said stiffly. "I need to give
you those maps, anyway. Let's take this back to my room." He
sat forward in his chair.

She leaned back in hers, cringing away from him. "Uh-uh—
no way."

He paused then, and a smile broke wryly across his face.
"Don't tell me you're chicken? Afraid to be alone with me?
Doesn't sound like the Sam I knew."

She bristled, then, as he'd known she would. The one sure
way he knew to get to Sam was to question her courage.

"I'm no chicken, which you know damn well." Though she glared at him still, he could see a faint blush creep beneath her tan. Her lips twitched, and she pressed them together to stop them from softening into a smile. She drew a quick, faint breath. "But if you think I'm going anywhere near a hotel room with you…"

He gazed at her, letting his compassion for her warm his eyes and his smile. His wanting, his hunger for *her,* he kept hidden, a secret thumping heat in his groin, a bitter ache in his heart. "Still there, isn't it?" he said softly, for the sheer pleasure of seeing her eyes flare hot.

She opened her mouth to deny it, and he watched the struggle play itself out in the changing expressions on her face. It was a familiar battle, one he'd seen waged there many times before. Pride versus honesty. With Sam, though, the victor was never in doubt. After a long, anguished moment, she closed her mouth and, chin elevated, turned her head away.

Cory said gently, "If I promise not to touch you, will you let me explain?"

What could she do? True, his gentleness had driven her mad sometimes, possibly because it was impossible to resist. She could feel herself growing shaky inside; the protective walls she'd thrown up so hurriedly were beginning to crumble already. How much longer would they hold? What would happen to her when they fell?

In a desperate effort to shore them up, she stiffened her back and said tartly, "What is there to explain? I came back from training and they told me you were married. I had to hear it from Mom and Dad." And her whole body vibrated with the tension, the sheer willpower it took to keep him from seeing how much that had hurt.

"Sam," Cory said, gentle still, "we'd cut each other loose. We'd agreed…"

Yes, but I never thought…I didn't believe…I didn't know you meant it! I thought…I thought you'd always be there. I thought you'd always love me, and wait for me….

Childish of me, probably, to think so.

"Yeah, right," she said abruptly, then caught a breath. "I know. It was…just a shock, I guess." She gave her head a toss and pasted on a smile. "You should have told me. I'da sent you guys a toaster, or something."

"Sam…" He shook his head, and she caught a glimpse of sadness in his eyes before he veiled them from her with a downward sweep of his lashes and rose to his feet. "Come on—let's get out of here."

Hollow and shaken, Sam didn't wait for him to settle with the waiter. She made her way to the lobby, where she fidgeted restlessly, surreptitiously checking herself out in the mirror above the check-in desk. Satisfied with what she saw, reassured that none of her inner turmoil showed on the outside, she was able to flash Cory a confident smile when he joined her there a few minutes later.

He gave her a nod and they walked outside together. Together, but not touching. As they strolled unhurried along the bamboo breezeway that led to their rooms she thought how odd it was to be doing that, while a memory tumbled out of the past and threatened to inundate her with sadness…a memory of walking like this, the two of them side by side but not touching, down the lane at Grandma's house in Georgia, she with her insides all aquiver with the strange joyous awareness that she was falling in love. How scary that had been, and how beautiful and sweet at the same time. Remembering made her ache with yearning, and she wasn't even sure what for.

It's the air, she thought. *That's what brings it all back. Reminds me of those early-summer Georgia evenings—soft and humid, still warm even this late at night. Except here, instead of cicadas and frogs backing up a giddy whippoorwill, I hear surf sounds and the chirp of night birds I don't recognize making a different kind of harmony with the music from the bar.*

They walked in silence until Sam, feeling easier, maybe, with the cloak of semidarkness around her—not having to see his face—spoke softly...carefully.

"Look—I'm sorry, okay? Divorce is sad and awful. I have friends who've gone through it. So I'm sorry you had to." She paused, waiting for his reply. When none came she ventured on, still focusing on the path ahead. "So...what happened? I mean, it only...you were married for such a short time. Did something..." Her voice trailed miserably off.

Please, she thought, say the words. *Say it, even if it doesn't fix anything: My marriage failed because...she wasn't you.*

After a long suspenseful moment he said in the same slow and careful way, "I think...let's just say we both had expectations the other wasn't able to meet. Leave it at that."

Leave it at that? Why did I dare to hope for more?

"At least," she said lightly, with a soft breath to hide how disappointed she was, "you didn't have kids. That's a good thing. I guess."

"Yes."

She waited, but again there was nothing more. Never known for her patience at the best of times, she felt her frustration level rising with every pulse beat. Inevitably, in spite of every promise she'd made to herself, it boiled over.

"Is that all you have to say? That's what drives me crazy about you. You know what, Pearse? You never let anybody know what's going on inside you. What you're feeling. I know you've got feelings. Nobody could write the way you do and not have feelings. Huge, deep feelings. But you never let anybody see them, me included. In all the years we were together—"

"Don't try to tell me I never told you how I felt about you," Cory said on a surprising note of anger. "Because I did. You know I did. You *knew* how I felt about you."

She considered that, head tilted to one side, ignoring the little thrill she felt at his unexpected display of emotion, however brief. "Did I? See, the thing is, I *thought* I knew, but then it turned out I was wrong. So either you didn't tell me, or I missed something, or maybe you lied—"

"Come on, Samantha. I've never lied to you and you know it."

"No—that's right. You don't lie. You just leave blank spaces."

"Blank spaces? What are you talking about?"

"You, dammit. You're one big blank space."

"Sam, you're being ridiculous."

"Don't you dare go all tight and reasonable on me," she fumed. "Do you realize I don't know anything about your past? Your childhood? How long were we together, and yet, I don't know what kind of child you were—what kind of books you read, what games you played, what songs you sang. Nothing. I've told you every little thing about mine—I even taught you the Wishing Star poem, remember? Almost the first time I met you. But you've never told me…*anything.*"

"You're talking about facts, not feelings. I told you I grew up in foster care," he said quietly. "Okay, you want feelings? It wasn't fun. What else is there to say?"

"You see?" She gazed at him for a long moment, then shook her head and said in a voice tight with frustration, "Maybe it's because I don't know the right questions to ask. That's your talent, not mine. You have that gift, you know? You can get inside people's heads. Before they even know it, they're telling you their life history. I wish I could do that, but I don't know how. Which probably explains why, even after all the years we were together, I don't really know you at all, Pearse. What does that tell you?"

He'd never seen her look at him that way before. The bewildered anger in her face tugged at his heart, but it was the bleakness he saw there that shocked him. She looked…defeated. Sammi June, his Sam, who he'd never known to be any way but upbeat, determined, confident…who went gung ho after what she wanted with chin held high and never even considered the possibility of failure. How he'd loved her arrogance, her self-confidence, and at times, drawn strength himself from her courage. Now, the sadness and defeat in her eyes was more than he could bear. He reached for her, then remembered his promise….

But almost at the same moment, she jerked away from him with a small cry that pierced him like a dart. "No. I'm not going through this again, Pearse. I'm not."

He snatched his hands back, held them up and away from her, then folded his arms across his chest and leaned against the breezeway's rattan railing. The door to his room was only a few feet away, with Tony's next to it and Sam's a little farther on. He glanced at his door, then away, while words, thoughts and emotions pounded like thunder in his head. Knowing any attempt to voice them would be futile, he simply shook his head.

"Why did you do it? Why did you call me…after the divorce?" Her voice sounded so small, but still it managed to hold all the anger and bewilderment, the sadness and defeat he'd just seen in her face. She didn't wait for him to answer, but plunged on in the tiny, wounded voice that was so *not* Sam. "I mean, what did you think was going to happen? What did you expect me to do? Or say?" He looked at her then, opened his mouth to reply, but again she rushed on.

"Like—you getting divorced just…*erased* everything? Hey—maybe getting a divorce erased your marriage, but it didn't erase anything else, you understand?"

She was gazing fiercely at him but tapping her own chest with an angry finger; that, and the stark anguish in her eyes told him what he knew she'd never say: *You hurt me, Pearce. Nothing can fix that or take it away.*

"No, you're right," he said stiffly. He wanted to swallow, to cough, do something to relieve the tight, raw feeling in his throat. "That was a mistake. I shouldn't have done it. What you said to me—I deserved that."

She didn't answer. He heard a faint creak as she, too, leaned her hip against the railing. Beyond it—and utterly wasted on the two of them, Cory thought—the sea shimmered in the light of an almost-full moon like a tropical hideaway ad in a honeymoon brochure.

After what seemed like a very long time, he heard her say in a soft, bleak voice, "Anyway, it wouldn't have worked, because nothing had changed. That was the thing, you know. It still hasn't. I still am a…pilot. I have a career that…well, you know. And you want…"

"Yeah," he said, straightening abruptly. What in the hell *did* he want? He wasn't sure he knew himself, anymore. He'd once thought he did, and look how wrong he'd been.

Right now, all he knew was what he *didn't* want, which was to stand here talking about it with the one thing he wanted and couldn't have—a woman he'd been craving like an addict and hadn't even known it…a woman he wasn't allowed to touch. His whole body, every muscle and nerve and sinew in it, quivered with the strain of denial.

He turned and lurched for his door, at the same time plunging a hand into his pocket and pulling out his room key. It was the old-fashioned kind, the metal fit-into-a-lock-and-turn kind, and while he was struggling with it, he felt Sam come up beside him. Felt her warmth like a tropical breeze on his skin…her womanly scent like an intoxicating drug. His head swam.

The key turned and he shoved the door inward. It was all he could do to say thickly, "Look, I'll see you in the morning, okay? Shall we say…whoever gets up first, rouses the others?"

"Fine with me."

He stepped into the room and turned toward her. Instead of backing away, saying good-night, she followed him in.

Hell. He'd forgotten the maps.

His overnighter was on the floor beside the door. He unzipped the outside pocket, took out the folded maps and handed them over without looking at her. "I've marked the rendezvous point and the location of the airstrip." His breath felt meager, his chest tight.

She nodded—he could see that much as he flattened his back against the open door, making room for her to slip past him. Then she moved, and he had time for one surprised breath before she stepped close, slipped her arms around his neck, lifted herself and pressed her mouth against his.

Oh, no, she's still the same. Still Sam. The confidence, the certainty, the sheer possession in the way she kisses me.

She knew him so well…knew just how and where to touch him…how to slide her body against his…melt her mouth into his. Fire squirted through all his veins; his thoughts turned to vapor, his bones to water.

Oh, God, she's still the same.

"Sam," he said feebly when at last she pulled away, "I promised I wouldn't—"

"You promised," she said in her old, familiar, arrogant way. "I didn't."

She patted his chest once with the folded maps, then went away and left him standing there.

Chapter 4

As the plane droned steadily eastward, the sun rose like an angry red sentinel and rushed to meet it. Sam blinked as its heat struck her face and its light assaulted her eyes even through the dark lenses of her sunglasses, and she drew a long exhilarated breath. It seemed like a personal challenge to her, that sun, a gauntlet thrown down in her path. Confidence swelled inside her, warm and red as the sun.

Yes! Whatever this day brings, I can handle it.

She glanced over when Cory eased into the copilot's seat beside her. Something fluttered in her stomach, up high near her heart, then eased, leaving only the quickened tap-tap-tap of her pulse.

"Hey," she greeted him, not trusting herself with more, for fear the gladness, the exhilaration inside her should leak into her voice. She hadn't expected it, waking up this morning with this happiness, this almost giddy sense of triumph and well-being.

Last night had been a test of her strength and will, and she'd passed it with flying colors. Yeah, sure, the hunger, the lust, the craving for him were still there, and as powerful as ever. But it wasn't an addiction. *I can control this. I can handle it. I won't let myself be hurt again.*

"Hey, yourself," he answered in his neutral way, and she could feel him studying her with his probing, inquisitive reporter's eyes.

"Sleep well?" he inquired.

What with the hurry and hustle of getting everyone up, breakfasting, gathering belongings and equipment, getting to the airport, filing flight plans, prepping the plane and getting underway, it was the first moment they'd had alone together since she'd left him the night before.

"Yes, I did." She didn't try to keep the satisfaction—maybe even smugness—out of her voice. "How 'bout yourself?"

He made a soft dry sound, then muttered something under his breath. Something along the lines of, "Same old Sam…"

The urge to grin made the muscles in her face cramp, and she bit down hard on her lower lip to quell it.

Cory clasped his hands together, then leaned forward to gaze through the windshield at the low, cloud-shrouded smudge on the horizon. Fidgeting. The thought flashed into her mind: *That's not like him.*

She said, "That's the island you're looking at out there. We'll be landing in about…forty-five minutes." He nodded but didn't reply.

After listening to the droning of the aircraft's engines for several minutes, she said, "Mind if I ask you something?" The look he threw her was both surprised and wary—she didn't usually ask permission. "I'm curious—Will and I both were, actually. Why charter a plane for this? Why didn't you just hire a boat? Woulda been a lot simpler—cheaper, too."

He gave her a look and said mildly, "I'm going into a terrorist's hideout to interview one of the most wanted and dangerous men in the world. When I'm done with that, I'd rather not have to get through forty miles of jungle before I'm home free."

"Okay, I can see that. Then wouldn't a helicopter be more practical?"

The look he gave her this time was wry. "I was specifically warned *not* to use a helicopter. Apparently, both Philippine government forces and U.S. Special Ops are active in that area. When al-Rami's troops see a chopper they do their best to shoot it down."

"Ah," said Sam, keeping her voice neutral. "So..." she persisted after a moment, "why did you ask for such a big plane? There's just the two of you. Why not a Cessna? It'd be a whole lot easier to land and take off on those remote airstrips."

He shifted again as if something was irritating him, but replied in a calm, almost conversational way. "That's not a problem. Apparently, there's a landing strip near the rendezvous point that was built by the Americans during World War Two, and the villagers have kept it up—they get most of their supplies that way. The roads in and out of the region aren't reliable at the best of times, and during the monsoon season they're sometimes impassable." He threw her a grin. "You shouldn't have any trouble. In fact, this old bird ought to feel right at home."

Sam frowned at the cloudy horizon. "That still doesn't explain—" Then she broke off as it hit her. "Oh, good God. They have hostages. You're going to try to get them out." He didn't answer. She looked over at him. "Aren't you? That's what this is all about—the interview—" Her hands tightened on the wheel. "That's how you were able to get approval from State, isn't it? I should have known."

Dammit, I should have known. Why weren't we told about this? Same old story...left hand doesn't have a clue what the right hand's doing....

Cory's quiet, reasonable voice broke in on her silent fuming. "I intend to try to negotiate for their release during the course of the interview, sure. How can I *not* try? What else would you expect me to do?"

She let out a short, sharp breath. "Nothing—absolutely nothing. It's exactly what you would do. Like I said—I should have known." She threw him a distracted glance, not even registering the puzzled look on his face or the probing intensity of his eyes as she switched to her captain's voice.

"Uh…look, we're coming into Isabella airspace…I'm gonna need to be talking to their tower…if you wouldn't mind taking your seat…"

"Oh—sure, no problem."

Sam was already fiddling with the radio and hardly noticed when Cory eased out of his seat in the overly careful, oh-Lord-don't-let-me-touch-anything way he had and made his way slowly back through the radioman's compartment. She did glance up, though, to make sure his back was still turned while she tuned her radio to a frequency not monitored by any airport control tower anywhere in the world. Only when she was certain he was out of earshot did she begin to speak into her mouthpiece, in a monotone designed to carry no farther than the confines of the cockpit.

"Uncle Willie, this is Junebug calling. Come in…."

She waited, counting off the seconds, then repeated it. "Uncle Willie, this is June—"

"Hey, Junie-baby, this is your old Uncle Willie. How're ya doin', sweetcakes?"

One side of Sam's mouth quirked upward. "Oh, fair…just fair. Got a few clouds on the horizon…"

"Yeah? How bad? Look like it might spoil our party?"

"Don't know yet. Seems our guest of honor has some plans of his own. Might be a conflict, can't say for sure. Does complicate things, though."

There was a brief and thoughtful silence. Then: "Okay, stay on top of it. I trust you can handle our guest if he gets…uh, difficult?"

"He's not exactly the 'handling' type."

"Be a shame," the voice said smoothly, "if the party had to be cancelled. The other guests would *not* be happy."

"Right." She let out a gust of breath. "I know. I'll take care of it. Oh—Uncle Willie—one more thing." She lifted a hand to her right headphone, then lightly touched the tender spot just beneath a small fresh surgical scar hidden in the thick hair behind her ear. "How're those pictures I've been sending you? Still getting to you okay?"

There was a fat-sounding chuckle. "Gettin' some as we speak, sweetcakes. Nice of you to share. Almost like bein' right there with you."

"Glad you're enjoying 'em," Sam said, grinning. "I'll be in touch."

"You do that, Junebug-baby. Take care now."

"Will do, Uncle Willie. Out."

No longer wearing any suggestion of a smile, Sam returned the DC-3's radio to its regular frequency.

As Cory settled into his seat, Tony looked up from the paper-back novel he was reading to give him what could best be described as a leer. "So, how'd it go last night? You and Captain Earhart patch up your differences?"

Cory responded with a dismissive snort. "Sam's and my differences are pretty much irreconcilable."

"Huh. That your opinion or hers?" When he didn't get an answer, Tony dog-eared the page—making Cory wince—and closed the book. Tucking it between his leg and the armrest, he shifted in his seat in a settling-in kind of way and said in an undertone, "Okay. When last we left the romantic misadventures of Cory Pearson, you were telling me how you'd just, in effect, told the lady you love to grow up. After which, when she took offense—quite understandably, in my opinion—you went off and married somebody else. That doesn't sound like 'differences' to me, man. Sounds to me more like you owe the lady one hell of an apology. Not to mention roses. And diamonds."

"Yeah, well…as it happens, I tried that—the apology, anyway. After the divorce was final. I…I actually called her."

"Yeah? And?"

Cory's smile flickered dimly, like a dying lightbulb. "About what you'd expect. She told me to get lost. Leave her alone. Never speak to her again."

Tony reared back in mock astonishment. "No kidding? What a shock, man. And I suppose you did just what she told you to."

"As a matter of fact I did, yeah." Cory was beginning to find the whole conversation annoying. "What was I supposed to do? Stalk her?"

"*Woo* her, man. That's what she wanted, I guarantee it. Hey— after what you did, a phone call and a simple 'I'm sorry' ain't gonna cut it. You gotta go back to square one, make her remember why she fell for you in the first place. You dig?"

"Easy for you to say," Cory said dryly. It was, too; he'd seen Tony in action. For reasons he'd never been able to figure out, in spite of his strong resemblance to a bald-headed pit bull terrier, the man seemed to possess some kind of magic attraction irresistible to any human female between the ages of six and a hundred.

Tony made a "Tsk"-ing sound and hitched himself closer. "Look, man. Any fool can see she's still got a thing for you. And if the feelings are there, there's no such thing as 'irreconcilable differences.' Know what I mean?"

Would that that were true, Cory thought. He felt heavy and sad, thinking about it, remembering his conversation with Sam last night…remembering the way she'd kissed him. He wished Tony would leave it alone, just…shut up about it. But unfortunately, Tony's looks weren't the only thing about him that resembled a pit bull.

He drew a resolute breath. "It's not about feelings. In this case

I'm not sure they even matter. What it is, is that both of us want something the other doesn't have to give. If that doesn't make it irreconcilable—"

"Ah, come on, that's just bull—"

The cough of the intercom interrupted. To Cory, thoroughly sick of the conversation, Sam's tinny voice came like the answer to a prayer.

"Okay, we're over the island...I'm gonna drop down under this cloud cover and see if I can find us a place to land. Fasten your seat belts, boys and girls...might get a little bumpy."

"That wasn't so bad." Tony was grinning, his jaws working like pistons on the wad of gum he'd been chewing to relieve eardrum pressure during the corkscrew descent.

Cory gave him a look, then went back to scanning the jungle growth that crowded close to the plowed fields surrounding the grassy airstrip. Beyond the jungle, green mountain slopes, terraced for farming on the lower flanks, rose into a feathery gray mist of cloud cover. The air was still and heavy with humidity.

He half turned as Sam came from locking down the plane to stand beside him. "I'd have expected more of a welcoming committee," he said, frowning.

They'd passed low over a village on the way in, but so far the only signs of life they'd seen had been the young boy of maybe nine or ten, wearing only a tattered pair of camouflage shorts, who'd risen from the grass at the edge of a rice paddy as the plane had braked to a halt, then scampered for the trees like a flushed rabbit.

"Most people will be in hiding if al-Rami's men are in the area," Sam said, pausing to wipe sweat from her forehead with her shirtsleeve before putting on her baseball cap. "The villagers around here are scared to death of them. I doubt we'll have long to wait, though...." Her eyes smiled briefly at him before disappearing behind her sunglasses. "That was their lookout you saw running for the jungle as we landed. I imagine he's reporting the news of our arrival as we speak."

"You seem to know these people pretty well," Cory remarked.

She shrugged. "Al-Rami's methods are well-known in these islands. Believe me. Anyway, they'll probably wait until nightfall to contact us, just to make sure we didn't come with an escort. In the meantime we can hang out here with the plane, if you want to, or we can check out the village. Maybe find somebody willing to sell us some food." She hefted the knapsack at her feet. "That way, we can save the provisions we brought for later— you never know when it might come in handy, since we don't know how long we'll be trekking through that jungle."

"By all means," Cory said, then raised his voice to reach Tony, who had wandered off into the rice paddies to take pictures. "What about it—want to see what the village has to offer?"

"Yeah, cool." Tony's teeth flashed white as he grinned. His broad face wore a sheen of sweat that glistened like polish on old mahogany. "Oh, *man,* feel that humidity," he said as he rejoined them, pausing to tie a bandana around his head.

"Building toward rainy season," Cory said. "Feels like it's going to break any minute now."

"I just hope we're out of here when it does." Sam jerked her head toward the plane, parked at its characteristic slant on the elevated strip of grassy ground they'd been calling the "runway."

She didn't have to say more. Cory didn't know what the composition of the soil was underneath that grass, but he'd spent enough time in the tropics to know what a monsoon rain could do to previously firm ground. He didn't care to think about what it might be like, trying to take off in a hurry on a sloppy runway with a planeload of hostages on board.

He slung the strap of his laptop carrier over one shoulder and picked up his tote bag. Sam hitched herself into the backpack— Tony already had cameras and equipment bags hanging from every available part of his body—and they set out along the grass-and-dirt track toward the village.

Although they'd flown over the cluster of buildings nestled at the foot of the mountains on the way to the landing strip, and knew approximately where it was and that it was nearby, the heat and humidity they carried like an added burden made it seem much farther than it actually was. They were grateful for the spotty shade of banana and bamboo groves along the road and between patches where the jungle growth had been cleared for farming.

Houses made of bamboo roofed with scraps of wood and tin sat on the borders between plots of unknown vegetables, or clung precariously to tree-covered slopes farther up the hillsides. Gradually the houses came closer together, until the vegetable plots disappeared and there was only the dusty track where chickens pecked and wandered, oblivious to human fears, threats or omens. Nothing else moved. Except for their footsteps and the contented chuckling of the chickens, there were no sounds…no signs of life.

"Creepy," said Tony.

A cold trickle of sweat chose that moment to meander down Cory's spine.

Sam paused to take off her cap and wipe her face with her T-shirt sleeve as she looked around. "I saw a bigger building when we were coming in. I think it was over that way—at the far end of town. My guess is, if anybody's around, that's where they'll be."

"A church?"

Sam shook her head. "These people practice a local religion—a form of animism—you know, where everything, even rocks and trees, has its own spirit? It might be a community meeting place, though. Or a marketplace."

It turned out to be both those things—and more.

They came upon it a little farther on around a gentle bend,

where the dusty track widened out before a large lanai covered over with bamboo. In the shade of the bamboo roof were stalls, bins, tables and mats where, in less troubled times, homegrown vegetables, fruits, poultry, eggs and perhaps some wild game would be displayed and bartered. Now, flies floated and hummed above empty tables as they passed, birds screeched and twittered in the bamboo roof above their heads, and here and there they caught the flash of a lizard scurrying for cover.

Behind the lanai was the large building they'd seen from the air. It was rather more sturdily built than most of the houses, Cory noted, of boards rather than bamboo. Separating it from the lanai was a screened porch, or cabana, and as they approached it, a narrow screen door creaked open. A man stood in the doorway, holding it wide for them to enter. He appeared to be somewhere around middle-aged, and wore the loose cotton pants and shirt and flip-flops nearly all rural Filipinos wear. His expression, Cory noted, seemed neither hostile nor welcoming, but merely resigned.

While Tony lingered in the lanai, still snapping pictures, Sam spoke to the man in a language Cory didn't know. He replied with a fatalistic shrug and a nod and gestured for them to follow him inside.

"Since when do you speak Tagalog?" Cory asked Sam in a mild undertone as they trooped through the cabana.

"Helps to know the language of the people you work among," she replied with a cryptic half smile.

Just then another of those sweat runnels trickled down his back. He didn't know why, in spite of the heat, it should make him feel cold.

The smell of disinfectant hit him as soon as the door opened, so it came as no surprise when Sam, who'd gone in first and was still talking to their escort, turned as he entered to explain that the building housed a small regional hospital.

"More of an infirmary, or clinic, I suppose. Anyway, they're very proud of it—it even has screens on all the windows, see? A doctor comes every couple of weeks by plane. This man is one of the caretakers—caregivers?—sort of a combination nurse-custodian. I'm guessing he drew the short straw today—he gets to stay behind to look after the patients. And us. He says we must wait here. We are to stay inside, out of sight."

Tony, as he joined them, quipped dryly, "They gonna supply us with bedpans, too?"

"He's afraid," Sam said in an undertone. "Can't blame him. If he doesn't do exactly as he's been told, he and his family may be killed."

Cory swore softly.

"Or worse," she continued as if he hadn't spoken, "he's afraid if government forces find out al-Rami's men are in the area, they may attack and destroy the village in order to kill the rebels." A sardonic smile flickered. "What they call collateral damage."

Tony shifted the strap of his camera bag and swiped at the sweat on his face with a forearm. "So, what do we do now, man?"

"What the man said," Cory replied on an exhalation as he lowered his laptop to the floor. "We stay inside, out of sight. And we wait."

Sam was uneasy, though she felt confident no one would have guessed that to look at her. She lay on her back on a wooden bench in what would be, if the clinic were open for business and the doctor in residence, a preliminary-exam—or triage—room. Her knees were drawn up and her arms folded to make a pillow for her head. To a casual observer she'd appear to be napping, but nothing could have been farther from the truth. In fact, her eyes were not quite closed; every nerve and sense was on full alert, her ears were straining to hear the slightest stirring in the vegetation outside…her skin prickled with awareness. Beneath lowered lashes, her gaze was fixed on the main source of her unease, the man sitting on an exam table on the other side of the room.

He was only a shape—though an achingly familiar one—dimly lit by the lantern hanging from a rafter overhead. Night had fallen at last. Out in the cabana, which would serve as a waiting room during infirmary hours, Tony lay stretched out on another wooden bench. Not much doubt about whether *he* was asleep; she could hear his raspy snores from in here. From other rooms in the hospital came the quiet sounds of restless people…sick people: coughing…a baby fussing…someone calling out in his sleep. Outside, beyond the screens, the night was full of insect noise, but nothing more.

Cory wasn't even pretending to sleep. He sat upright, facing her, with his hands braced on the edge of the table, rocking himself slightly and glancing at her from time to time, evidently deep in thought.

Sam didn't know what to make of his attitude since they'd arrived at the village. Something had changed. He seemed… watchful. Thoughtful. Nothing new there; Cory was always watching…thinking…observing and evaluating. But tonight there was *something*—a new element. He seemed…not exactly *suspicious,* but…well, maybe. She didn't know what name to call it; she only knew it made her uneasy as hell.

Same old story, she thought, with a flare of unprofessional resentment. *Can't ever tell what he's thinking…don't have a clue what makes him tick. No wonder it didn't work out between us.*

She tensed as the object of her frustration slid off the exam table and began quietly to pace. She watched him for a few minutes, annoyed to find her heartbeat quickening, then called softly to him.

"Hey, Pearse, pacing won't make them come any quicker. Maybe you should try and get some sleep."

His reply was a grunt. "Yeah, right."

"Your friend doesn't seem to be having any problems."

This time the grunt was more of a chuckle. "Tony's a battle-field photographer. He can sleep through artillery fire."

She tilted her head back in order to follow him with her eyes. "Why not you? You've seen your share of battlefields."

He paused in his pacing to turn his head toward her, and though she couldn't see it in the shadows, she could hear the smile...the wryness in it. "This is hardly the same."

"No? Why not?" And her breath caught as he prowled slowly toward her.

"For starters, you're here."

An oddly enjoyable tension gripped her chest. "Ah," she said softly, "do I disturb you that much?"

He was standing over her now, looking down at her. "You worry me," he said thoughtfully.

A little thrill of warning shook her—*not,* she told herself, of fear. She sat up and swung her feet to the floor. "*I* worry you? Why?"

Taking her move as an invitation, he sat on the bench beside her. Instead of answering directly, he gazed at her for a moment, then said quietly, "This is a dangerous mission we're on, Sam."

His voice was stern, almost parental. She felt a chilly wash of disappointment. *Same old, same old...*

She said stiffly, "You don't have to worry, Pearse. I *can* take care of myself, you know."

He turned his face toward her and after a long pause replied, "Maybe that's what worries me."

She gave an involuntary hoot of laughter. "What's that sup-posed to mean?" And heard the sigh of his exhalation as he looked away.

"I don't know what I mean." He hitched in a breath, then con-tradicted himself. "This is a dangerous mission, and yet you don't seem to be concerned. Not even a little bit...you know, keyed up. Apprehensive. Nervous. Any of the things any sane, intelligent person should be in this situation. Since I know you to be both sane and intelligent, I can't figure out whether you're simply clueless, don't fully understand the situation…"

"Well, that's flattering," Sam said dryly. "I'm hoping there's an *or* coming."

"*Or,* you know a whole lot more about what's going on than you're letting on—maybe more than I do."

She hitched herself around to face him. It was a defensive move; he'd managed to jolt her in spite of all her preparation, all her training. She fought to keep the anger out of her voice. "Did it occur to you maybe I'm not worried because I have confidence in myself, that I understand worrying isn't going to help anything, and I have the self-discipline to keep myself calm—in short, that I'm a mature adult, capable of reason and self-control?"

"Jeez, Sam." He drew a hand over his face and shook his head in a weary, long-suffering way that only stoked her anger. "You don't ever forget or forgive, do you?"

"Maybe," she snapped back at him, "I'd be more willing to forgive if I could see some evidence you've changed. As far as I can see, *nothing's* changed between us."

"You're right. Nothing has." His voice, as he gazed at her, suddenly had a different quality. A huskiness that should have warned her, but didn't. Before she had any idea he was going to, he caught her by the arms and at the same time rose to his feet, taking her with him.

Once again her breath caught, this time with an audible gasp. *"You promised—"*

"Are you kidding me?" His voice seemed to grind through his chest. "After what you put me through last night, all bets are off."

She felt the rush and heat of his body coming against hers, and his head coming down for the taking. The breath left her lungs and her chest filled instead with the fierce ache of joy. *Yes,* her heart cried, *Oh, yes. Finally.*

His mouth claimed hers with the passion, the roughness she

remembered he could reveal, at times, that had been so much the more thrilling to her for being unexpected, so at odds with the gentle and compassionate man he was. And she thought, *This is why.* Not just the sex, not only that. For the fire and passion she knew were inside him and that he worked so hard to hide—from her, from the world, from everyone.

From the world, she could understand. *But why does he keep this from me? Except at times like this...times when he lets himself go, and it's so good...could have been...*

But sex isn't enough. It could never have worked between us. I know it...have to accept it.

The desire welling up inside her shattered suddenly, like a glass bubble bursting. She felt the loss like pain, and pulled away from him with a sharp and bitter cry.

But his hands still held her head prisoner, gentle again now, fingers splayed wide, burrowing through her hair in a way she remembered with a sweet and terrible ache.

"*Sam,*" he said—just that, in a voice too raw for more.

"Don't," she whispered, trying to swallow. Hurting too much to swallow or speak.

His fingertips scraped over her scalp, touching her nerves with his particular brand of electricity. And found the tender spot beneath its freshly healed scar.

She winced; she couldn't help it. She heard the sharp hiss of his breath and jerked free of his grasp, a reply to the question she could see forming in his eyes and on his lips already balanced on the tip of her tongue.

But the sound that came next was neither his voice nor hers. It was a cough, a polite, almost comical little "Ahem," followed, as they both whirled toward the sound, by a gruff but somewhat feeble, "Uh...guys?"

Tony stood in the doorway to the cabana with his hands behind his head. As he stepped into the room, several dark shapes separated themselves from the shadows and followed him. In the

dim lantern light the shadows became men dressed in camouflage clothing. They weren't wearing masks or hoods, and their
expressions were stoic, their eyes dark and hard. They all carried automatic weapons.

Chapter 5

Still reeling, his senses glutted with the taste, the smell, the feel of Samantha, Cory watched the men slip into the room, seeming to fill it with their silent menace and the threat of violence in their weapons and their hard, cold eyes. His eyes leaped from one impassive face to the next, looking for the one he'd come so far to meet. He wasn't there, of course. These were the messengers, he realized; the retrieval squad, nothing more.

One of them, the designated "spokesman," apparently, motioned with his weapon. *Come.*

Cory nodded. *So far, so good,* he thought as he picked up his laptop and tote bag.

But as he stepped toward the waiting cadre of armed men, the leader again motioned with his weapon, this time holding it up to bar his way, and his hard black stare had gone shooting past Cory to something behind him. Turning, Cory saw Sam, waiting to follow him, her face calm, body relaxed, one hip canted and the straps of the backpack slung over one shoulder.

The terrorists' leader spoke, his voice sharp and unexpected in the stillness. "Who is this?" The rifle in his hands jerked toward Sam.

"She's the pilot," Cory explained, and it took all the self-control he had to say it calmly with every nerve twanging and his heart thumping. When the man's face remained blank, he hooked his thumbs together and made flapping motions with his hands, and for good measure added, "She flies the airplane."

The man jerked half around, and several of his companions leaned closer to confer with him in unintelligible mutters while Cory waited in silent agony, cursing the fates that had conspired to bring Sam into harm's way. This harm *he'd* created. *If anything happens to her,* he thought...

The spokesman turned back, and with yet more jerking motions of his rifle to emphasize his words, said sharply, "*She* stay here. I am told to bring only *you*—" the gun barrel pointed toward Cory "—and *you*—" now toward Tony. "Come, now."

Fear flooded Cory's body and prickled his skin like frost. His heartbeat was a distant booming in his ears. Horrifying images, reports of extraneous captives being beheaded flashed through his mind. He could feel himself screaming, "No!" inside his head in the silent, chest-burning, throat-tearing way of nightmares, and again it was a shock to hear his own voice, sounding calm and in command. "No. She's needed. She's also my interpreter. She comes with us."

The gunman thrust his chin upward in a manner that was both arrogant and dismissive. "*I* speak English. No need for interpreter."

"She goes," Cory said flatly, "or I don't." To demonstrate the conviction of his declaration he lowered his laptop and tote bag to the floor and folded his arms on his chest. "Tell your leader there will be no interview."

The silence that followed shrieked in his ears. The ultimatum was, he knew, a ridiculous, utterly meaningless display of bravado; he had only as much bargaining leverage as these gunmen…terrorists, rebels, insurgents—whatever they might choose to call themselves tonight—decided to give him. And *that,* he was sure, depended solely on how much their infamous leader desired this interview. Or, putting it another way, how compelling was his need to get his message out to the world.

The spokesman's face darkened as he turned once more to consult with his companions in clipped and rapid phrases. Cory couldn't look at Tony or Sam. *Literally* could not; tension had him paralyzed. He felt as if his neck would crack if he tried to move his head. I've put us all in jeopardy, he thought. *My best friend…the woman I love. They may kill us all right now. Or take Tony and me hostage and kill Sam…*

What else could he have done? The only thing he had to balance against the terrible weight of responsibility for the lives of two people he cared about was the utter certainty that if he left Sam behind in this place he'd never see her alive again.

The suspense became unbearable. He began to wonder if he would ever dare to breathe again.

The spokesman turned back suddenly and rapped out a sharp and grudging, "Okay." Then, with a series of gestures—more pointing with the rifle barrel—and barked commands, ordered them to leave everything they'd brought with them behind.

"Hey, man, not my cameras!" Tony took a step backward, clutching his bags to his chest like a mother protecting her young.

Cory thought, *Oh, Lord, here we go again…* as he remarked in a languid drawl, "Hey, look, I was instructed to bring a cameraman. Not much point if he doesn't have a camera." Fading adrenaline had left him drained…he felt loose and weak and much too warm, as if he'd just emerged from a long hot bath.

The spokesman looked at him with hatred, and his words came grudgingly. "Okay. Cameras can go. Everything else—stay here."

"What about my computer? I can't very well—"

"*No.* No computer. We have tape recorder. No need for computer. Leave everything here. *Come. Now.*"

"They think we might be carrying tracking devices," Sam muttered in an undertone from behind him. "Better do as he says."

Cory nodded in grim acceptance. Hell with it—he'd won the important battle. And he'd done interviews before laptops were invented; he could do without one now. It definitely wasn't worth getting killed over. Getting Sam killed over.

With yet more poking and waving of rifle barrels, the three of them were herded outside, through the lanai and into the deserted village, which seemed frozen in silence under the silvery light of the almost-full moon. Nothing stirred as they made their way along the pale ribbon of road, heading in the opposite direction from which they'd come. The only sound was the muffled scuffing of their footsteps in the dusty dirt.

Just outside the main cluster of buildings where more planted fields began, the terrorist leader turned sharply away from the road. The rest of the band followed, then Tony, Sam and Cory behind them, picking their way single-file along the banks that bordered the rice paddies, with two more of the armed escort bringing up the rear. The air was warm and heavy; rain seemed to hover a breath of wind away, like a secret bursting to be told.

Cory felt a familiar exaltation rise inside him, one he could neither explain nor deny. He wondered if it was the sort of thing a hunter feels as he closes in on his quarry, or a scientist as he nears the discovery of a lifetime, a mountain climber approaching the summit. He only knew it was what had him returning again and again to the world's most perilous places in spite of the various dangers and discomforts involved, in search of answers…the truth…a story. He couldn't imagine himself ever doing anything else. Like the explorer seeking one more horizon or the prospector the elusive gold nugget, he knew there would always be new questions to ask, new truths to be revealed, more stories to be told.

Ahead, the jungle loomed like a dark maw, and even as it swallowed him, Cory felt his heart lift and excitement shiver along his spine.

Sam had been in jungles before. The nighttime sounds and smells were familiar to her, and in spite of uneasy thoughts of the kinds of creatures that might be making those sounds, she welcomed the darkness for the chance it gave her to pull herself together, shielded from Cory's all-too-perceptive eyes.

She needed time to process what had just happened to her—and she didn't mean being taken into custody by armed terrorists. Cory's kiss, his touch, and the way she'd responded—not just her body's responses, she could have dealt with those—but, dammit, with her *heart.* Yes—her wretched, pathetic, *stupid* heart, which apparently had no memory of being broken into tiny pieces by that very same man. She needed to face up to that, push against it, *hard,* the way she'd test a twisted ankle to see if she could stand the pain.

He's just like a patch of quicksand, she thought with a shudder. *I knew it was there...let myself wander a little too close...just one tiny slip, and already I can feel myself sinking....*

After a time, they emerged from the darkness of the jungle onto a moonlit grass-and-dirt road that wound like a silver ribbon into the mountains. Cory moved up to walk beside her, and she felt his presence there with every nerve ending in her body. The familiar shape and smell of him overwhelmed her senses.

Memories inundated her....

Lying naked in a patch of sunshine on rumpled sheets, propped on one elbow while my fingers lightly trace the long, elegant lines of his back.... I watch him sleep...the fine, sensitive mouth relaxed, silky dark hair falling across his forehead, and his face stark with the loneliness I can only see when those beautiful eyes are closed and their compassion and curiosity hidden behind shadowed lids and lashes.

*I watch him sleep and wonder what lonely place he's gone to
that he never lets me share, and I ache with wanting something
that always seems to be just beyond my reach.*

In an effort to shake herself loose from the memories, she
leaned closer to Cory, bumped him in the ribs with her elbow
and said in a gravelly whisper, "What were you trying to do back
there, Pearse, get us all killed?"

He grunted but didn't reply. The urge to needle him passed as
quickly as it had come, and after a moment she added a gruff,
"Well...anyway, thanks." And found herself, without meaning to,
reaching for his hand. It, too, felt familiar...big and long-boned...so
warm and good... She squeezed it once, then quickly let it go.

"You're welcome," he said.

She tensed when she felt that same big warm hand lift to the
back of her neck. She held her breath when he began to rub it,
the way he'd done so many times before, finding, as he always
knew how to do, the trouble spots at the base of her skull.

Coming too close to the tender place behind her ear.

"Cut it out, Pearse," she croaked as she shook herself free.

"Sorry," he murmured, not sounding sorry at all. "Force of
habit."

Tears sprang behind her eyes. She swallowed hard—twice—
and stared at the dark shape of mountains against the silver sky.
After a long moment, feeling an obscure need to make amends,
she said gruffly, "Sorry about your computer."

He was so close she felt him shrug. *Too close.* All her nerve
endings were twanging, but she didn't move away.

"I'll get along. I'm surprised they didn't search us, though."

"Oh, they will," she said with a careless shake of her head.
"They'll probably take our clothes away somewhere and go over
everything with a fine-tooth comb."

His head swiveled toward her, and even in the dim light she
felt the probing weight of his curious, ever-searching eyes.

"Is that the voice of experience?"

She jerked a glance at him and gave a short huff of laughter. "God, no. I fly airplanes for a living, Pearse. You're the one with that kind of experience, not me." He didn't comment, and after a moment she said in an undertone, "I just know he's careful, this Fahad…al-Ramin?"

"Rami," said Cory. "Fahad al-Rami. And he *is* careful. He's had to be, to have managed to keep from getting captured or killed for so many years. He's got to know he's taking a big chance in allowing himself to be interviewed now."

"So are you. Aren't you? Taking a big chance?" It was his turn for that soft snort of laughter. She threw him a look and said dryly, "Bet you never gave that a thought, did you?" She looked away again, quickly, and laughed a little herself. "You probably said, 'To hell with the danger. Tell me when and where, and I'm there.' Like you always do."

"This—" he paused, caught a breath "—it's a news correspondent's dream, Sam." His words were quiet, barely audible, but she could tell by the shape of them that he was looking at her. "It'd be like, ten years ago, going into the mountains of Afghanistan to interview Bin Laden. Who could say no to that?"

She felt a heaviness in her chest, and shook her head, not in disagreement, but in the manner of one shaking off an unwelcome touch. "Okay, if al-Rami's in the same class as Bin Laden? That makes him a terrorist, Pearse. Terrorists kill people. It's what they do."

"Fahad al-Rami calls himself a rebel—which I imagine is one of the things he'd like to clear up in this interview." Cory's voice was sardonic.

Sam replied the same way. "He blows up hotels full of people. That makes him a terrorist in my book."

He didn't deny it. They walked for a while without talking, listening to the scuff of footsteps, the creak of ammunition belts, the rustle of fabric against flesh. The weight in her chest seemed to grow heavier with every step.

Taking a breath that did nothing to make her feel better, Sam muttered, "It's never going to be enough for you, is it?" She'd said it to herself more than Cory, but he answered her anyway.

"It's what I do, Sam."

"Dammit!" And how could she be angry when she'd sworn she didn't care enough to be? "Why do you need this? You've already got your Pulitzer."

His head snapped toward her like a spring letting go, the tension in him so palpable the quietness of his voice seemed a surprise. "Is that what you think this is about? My God, Sam. It's not about prizes—or money, either, for that matter. Or fame or prestige—none of those things matter to me, you should know that. There's a story here that needs to be told, and I'm the one that gets to tell it. To me, that's the only reward that matters."

Sam didn't say anything for a moment. Didn't trust herself to. Thoughts, words, the beginnings of a quarrel simmered in her brain, and the choked-back arguments burned the back of her throat like acid. *You told me to grow up, Pearse. Why? Because I wanted a career...adventure...excitement? What's different about what you do? If growing up means I'm supposed to give up something I've prepared my whole life for...if it means that for me, why not for you?*

The words she couldn't say tasted bitter on her tongue, and her lips felt numb as she murmured instead, "Well, so? Do you think you're ever gonna be ready to come in from the field? To give up the danger?"

There was a long pause, and then his voice came softly. "I thought I *was* ready, once. It didn't work out."

She waited, thinking he meant to say more, to explain. Then, with a little jolt it hit her. *He's talking about his marriage again.*

He'd been ready to come in from the cold, to give up the danger—not for *her,* but for...Kathy, Katie...Carly—whatever the hell her name was. For his *wife.*

It didn't work out.

It all came rushing back—first the shock, icy-cold, numbing. Then the pain. Just the way it had happened then...

She'd finished, finally. Finished her training. She was home after being incommunicado for a whole month of grueling survival training in the Louisiana swamps, exhilarated, keyed-up, dying to talk to somebody, even if she couldn't talk about where she'd been or what she'd gone through. So, naturally, the first thing she'd done was call her best friend...right? Cory had been so much more than that, of course, but first, last and always, he was the closest, dearest friend she had in the world.

The phone at his Washington apartment rings...a recording answers, saying the number is no longer in service. I call Mom and Dad's house in Georgia. Cory and Dad were close, they'll know how to reach him...

Even now, three years later, she felt herself go clammy and sick remembering the terrible little silence on the other end of the line, and the awful fear that had gripped her then.

I think, Oh, God. Something's happened to him. He goes to such awful places, he's almost been killed before....

Then I hear Mom's voice, so sad, so gentle, so...embarrassed. "Oh, Sammi June, honey, I can't believe you don't know...."

Anger. That was the third thing that had come over her that awful day, and it was anger that came back now to save her. Hot, raging anger. It swept through her like a firestorm, carrying all the heaviness and sadness away with it, leaving her feeling barren and brittle inside, but *so* much lighter. As if a good stiff breeze would blow her to dust.

"Too bad," she said to Cory.

And quickening her steps, she left him and moved up to walk beside Tony instead.

"Hey," she said, favoring him with her best smile as she gave him a nudge in the ribs with her elbow. "How ya' doin'? Need any help carryin' those cameras?"

Tony's appreciative grin and undemanding charm didn't do

much to ease the ache inside her, but they did help to pass the time, and more important, hold the memories at bay.

Not long after daybreak they came to a cluster of huts too primitive to be called a village. The morning mists hadn't yet cleared, but the ubiquitous raggedy chickens were already pecking and chuckling in the undergrowth and smoke rose lazily from metal chimneys. The smell of cooking and unfamiliar spices permeated the cool mountain air, and Cory's stomach growled a loud and enthusiastic response.

Again there was no welcoming committee. The three "guests" were herded without ceremony into one of the huts, which, except for a brightly patterned curtain that hung across the width of the hut's single room, partitioning it roughly in half, appeared to be empty of both people and furnishings. Their escort's leader, still carrying his rifle but perhaps feeling more secure now that he was on his home turf, directed Sam to one side of the curtain and Cory and Tony to the other. He did so with somewhat less belligerence than he'd shown them up to now, even giving a little bow as he left them, closing the door behind him.

In the sudden silence, Cory heard Sam expel an exasperated breath.

"You get the idea they might've done this before?" Tony remarked in a sardonic undertone.

"Oh, I think you can bet on it," Sam said cheerfully, pulling aside the curtain to rejoin them. "I imagine they run all their hostages through this way."

"You think maybe they didn't get the message we're invited guests, not hostages?" Tony said.

"They'll be even more cautious with us *because* we were invited," Cory said with a long look at Sam. "They know we'd have had time—"

He broke off as the outer door opened. A woman of indeterminate age entered, carrying a stack of folded clothing. Although her own garments were all-concealing and her head covered with a scarf, the fabrics were brightly colored and looked hand-woven in intricate geometric patterns, and she wore a number of bracelets on both arms. Something about her style of dress reminded Cory of parts of Indonesia and Malaysia he'd visited on previous assignments.

Keeping her eyes averted from the two men, the woman went straight to Sam and spoke to her in a low, halting voice. Sam replied, a few brief syllables of acknowledgment, and the woman handed her the stack of clothing, bowed her head and quickly went out again.

"What'd I tell you?" Sam said as soon as the door had closed behind the woman. Her eyes were bright and sharp as a squirrel's, with an excitement Cory couldn't quite understand. "We're to remove our clothes and put these on instead. Ours will be washed, dried and returned to us—as a courtesy." She gave a smug little chortle. "Courtesy, hah. They want to check them for bugs—and I don't mean the creepy-crawly kind."

Tony muttered one of his favorite profanities. "Do you s'pose they mean everything? Underwear, too?"

"I'd imagine," Cory said, with more equanimity than he felt.

"Well," said Sam, "I don't care what they said, I'm *not* giving 'em my underwear." She shuddered delicately. "That's just…no."

"Sam." Cory gave her an amused look. "You're the one who said they're afraid of us. Don't you think you'd better do as they say? This is no time to be stubborn."

After a long mulish glare, she gave the curtain a yank and subsided behind it, swearing and muttering under her breath. A moment later various articles of brightly colored fabric came sailing over the top of the partition.

"Would you rather I take the single room…let you two love-birds be together?" Tony asked facetiously as he simultaneously snatched several of the pieces of cloth from the air and dodged to avoid being hit by flying flip-flops.

"Very...funny," came from the other side of the curtain.

Cory didn't say anything. Sam's voice had a bumpy quality, and he had a sudden vivid mental picture of her undressing with those quick jerky movements of hers, the way she did when she was in a hurry or out of sorts. The image was clear and bright in his mind...

Long, supple athlete's body, abs arranged in a softer, gentler version of the six-pack, buttocks taut and firm with shallow indentations on the sides, breasts high and round, but with a lot more fullness than anyone would suspect, seeing her fully clothed. Only I know how incredibly pale and fine the skin is there... Not much about Sam can be called soft, but there, and low on her belly and especially between her thighs...

"Hey, man, you want the green or the purple?" Tony was holding up two brightly patterned lengths of coarse fabric, one in each hand.

The images shivered and faded from his mind, and his heart knocked hard against his ribs, as if he'd been caught doing something illicit.

"I'm not fussy." He snagged the garment Tony lobbed at him—the green one—with one hand and showed Tony how to put it on, wrapping it around his waist and rolling the top edge over, like a towel.

"Hey," he said with a shrug when Tony gave him a dubious look. "Whatever works, right?"

"Easy for you to say," Tony muttered, uneasily surveying the portion of one muscular leg that was protruding through the edges of the fabric that barely met around his broad girth. "You've got more overlap than I do."

Ignoring what sounded like muffled laughter from the other side of the curtain, Cory finished dressing in the loose-fitting shirt and flip-flop sandals that had been provided. The whole ensemble was surprisingly comfortable, though he couldn't see himself trekking through snake-infested jungles in the wrap-around skirt and open sandals.

He and Tony had just finished folding their own clothing into more or less neat piles when the curtain twitched back and Sam's face appeared at its edge.

"You guys decent?" Her eyes had that squirrel-brightness again, and her lips seemed to quiver with a grin held in check.

Cory felt a buzz deep in his chest, the urge to grin back at her the way he would have done in the old days. The old days…back when they'd so often found the same things amusing, not always at appropriate times, and would exchange that secret look of barely suppressed laughter.

"What would you have done if we hadn't been?" Tony was making no effort to suppress *his* grin.

"Well, then, I'd've taken a *good* long look," she shot back at him in an exaggerated Georgia accent, thick, sweet and sassy as molasses.

"So, since you seem to be the expert on how these people operate, what are we supposed to do now?" Cory asked, frowning to disguise the pleasure he was getting just from looking at her. The rich, fiery colors she'd chosen—red, orange and yellow— had turned her hair to sunshine and her skin to honey, and she reminded him of some lush exotic flower…the kind that was probably concealing something deadly among its petals.

She shrugged. "I don't know. Wait?" She looked at Cory and Tony, then at the door, then back at Cory again. "Well, the hell with that. I'm starving. Not to mention I could sure use a bathroom. They didn't lock us in here, did they?"

With that, she marched up to the door, took hold of the knob and turned it. Throwing a droll look back, eyebrows raised, mouth forming a little O of mock surprise, she pushed the door open and stepped through it. Cory exchanged a look with Tony, shrugged, and they both followed her onto the porch, which was a ramshackle structure made of small logs lashed together with sisal rope.

Almost immediately, as if she'd been waiting for their signal, the woman who'd brought them the clothing appeared, now bearing a large basket containing fruit, wooden bowls and eating utensils. Right behind her was another woman carrying a large pot from which steam and mouthwatering smells rose into the moist morning air. The two women placed the food on the floor of the porch like an offering to pagan gods, bowed hesitantly, and then, instead of leaving, edged past them and disappeared into the hut. A moment later they emerged with their arms full of shoes and clothing, throwing furtive glances toward Cory and the others like looters fleeing a store during a riot. Then, with eyes averted, they hurried away down a dusty path and disappeared between the clusters of rickety buildings.

"Well," said Cory after a moment of almost comical silence, rubbing his hands together briskly. "I don't know about anybody else, but I'm starving. Anybody for breakfast?"

They ate sitting on the porch, throwing fruit seeds and peelings to the foraging chickens. The pot proved to contain a mixture of rice, hard-scrambled eggs and vegetables, all highly spiced and surprisingly tasty. Together with the fruit, it made for a satisfying—not to mention filling—meal, although some of the fruits were too sour for Cory's taste.

"Filipinos like it that way," Sam told Tony when he shuddered over the tartness. "They eat it with salt—sort of like pickles. See?" She demonstrated, then laughed out loud at the pained expression on Tony's face.

Cory didn't say anything. He was enjoying the sound of Sam's laughter, filling up as he listened with a sweet tumble of joy and sadness that was like hearing an old favorite song, one that brought back painful memories of loss and regret.

At the same time he was wondering, not for the first time, how, as a pilot for a second-rate charter airline service, Sam had gotten to be such an expert on Philippine jungle culture.

They'd barely finished eating when the women reappeared, again right on cue, as if they'd been watching from some secret vantage point. This time they were accompanied by two men with rifles, one of them the leader of the band that had brought them here. While the women silently gathered up the remains of breakfast, the spokesman—using his rifle for emphasis, as usual—instructed Cory, Tony and Sam that they were to go back inside the hut now.

Sam cleared her throat loudly and rose to her feet. "Uh...excuse me, but I'd like to use the ladies' room first?" When the guard continued to look stony and aloof, she added a word in a language Cory didn't understand.

To Cory's relief and amusement, the gunman's face brightened for an instant with understanding—the classic lightbulb over the head—then just as quickly darkened with what could only have been embarrassment. He jerked his head at the women and barked a guttural command, and they immediately jumped up and beckoned to Sam, then led her off toward the cluster of shacks.

Cory watched her go with fear twisting in his gut. Fear that, if he let her out of his sight, he'd never see her alive again. Irrational, he told himself. Crazy.

"Hey, man," Tony said plaintively, "you want to ask him where the men's room is, or shall I?"

Without being asked, the spokesman gestured impatiently toward the jungle with his rifle. Tony and Cory looked at each other and shrugged.

"After you," said Tony, with a sweeping gesture and arched eyebrows.

When all three had assembled once more in front of the hut, the English-speaking gunman again ordered them to go inside.

Cory could feel both his annoyance and that irrational fear growing, rising up in him like fermenting yeast. All the delay was beginning to wear on his nerves. This had been a dangerous enough mission to begin with, and with Sam thrown into the mix... Until now the danger had been trumped by the once-in-a-lifetime opportunity he'd been given to interview the world's most notorious terrorist. He knew it was possibly the most important interview he'd ever done, not just for the knowledge of what made a deadly enemy tick, but for the possibility of securing the release of the Lundquists. The importance had seemed more than worth the danger. He'd been looking forward to this, working toward it for weeks.

Now…dammit, all he could seem to think about was Sam, and the peril he'd put her in. He knew he wouldn't draw an easy breath until she—until all of them were back safe and sound in Zamboanga.

Punching down the fear, fighting to keep the irritation out of his voice, he stepped closer to the gunman and said in a low voice, "Look, I know you're only doing your job, but I've come a very long way to talk to Fahad al-Rami. Can you give me some idea when I'm going to be allowed to do that?"

Something flickered in the hard black eyes. Cory hoped… wanted to believe it might be respect. "Fahad al-Rami is not here. We go to him tonight," the gunman said, and punched the air in front of his chest with his rifle. "Now, you sleep."

"Hey—sounds good to me," Tony said. He was already picking his way across the creaking porch. When Cory and Sam followed him into the hut, they found him making himself comfortable in one corner of the room, his head propped on one of his camera bags. Barely moments later, there arose from that vicinity a soft but distinct snore.

"Holy cow," Sam said admiringly.

Cory gave a huff of laughter.

Sam stood gazing at him, chin up, one leg bent, one hip canted, arms folded, the way she had as a kid every time she'd had to start at a new school. Daring anyone to take her on. Feeling so alone, hating being in a place where she didn't belong, a stranger.

A stranger?

I used to know every inch of this man's body. I still do. I remember the smell, the shape, the taste, the feel of him. I remember it with my flesh and bone and blood and nerves, with every cell in my body.

So, why, right now, when there's barely a foot of space between us, does it seem like we're a million miles apart?

He used to be my best friend. I could have told him anything—and probably did.

Yet, here we stand together in an empty room—well, almost empty—and we have nothing at all to say to each other. Like strangers.

How did we get from there…to this?

Cory cleared his throat and said, "Well."

She glanced over at him and saw that he was looking at her with eyebrows raised in a questioning way, one hand rubbing the back of his neck. She jerked away without meeting his eyes. "Yeah, well."

"So. Here we are."

She looked back at him then, and grinned. "Come on, Mr. Wordman, you can do better than that, I hope. It's gonna be a long day, otherwise."

He laughed, a low chuckle. And she remembered that, too. "It's gonna be a long day anyway. The man's right. If we can manage to get some sleep, we probably should. At least try."

"I don't know about you, but I'm not good at sleeping on bare floors," Sam said with a little shudder as she watched two shiny blue lizards chase each other across the wall.

"You can use me for a pillow, if you want."

She jerked her gaze back to him, but there was no teasing gleam in his eyes, no little sardonic half smile on his lips. Just the look of gentle sympathy that was natural to him.

"Thanks," she said dryly, "but I think I'll just sit and veg for a while. Maybe I'll bore myself to sleep."

"You want the curtained-off part? Give you a little more privacy?"

But privacy, suddenly, was the last thing she wanted, though she hadn't known it until that moment. "No, thanks," she said, keeping her voice carefully neutral. "I think I'll just…take this spot right here…" She squatted down, tucking the wraparound skirt under her thighs as she examined the floor. The wooden planks appeared rough, but reasonably clean. She looked up at Cory as she settled herself with her back against the wall. "Unless you'd rather not have my company."

"Come on, Sam." He eased down beside her, a little awkwardly in the unaccustomed skirt, tucking the overlapping flaps between his legs as he stretched them out straight in front of him. His bare feet in the too-small flip-flops seemed oddly vulnerable. "You know me better than that."

Do I? She thought, but didn't say, because he was looking at her with that deep, penetrating gaze of his, and…maybe it was because of those feet—so endearingly absurd—but already she could feel herself going soft inside…like ice cream in the sun.

"Come on," he coaxed, patting his green-patterned thigh, cajoling with the voice, the husky growl she'd never been good at resisting. "Put your head down here. Try and get some rest."

"You're leg's too bony to make a decent pillow," she muttered. But she was already rearranging herself grudgingly, scooting around, leaning toward him, then sinking down…like something without bones or will…until her head, her ear…then her cheek settled onto the hard ridge of his thigh like a weary bird finding its roost.

Weary… She hadn't known how tired she was. Sleep, like a gate-crasher denied admittance only by the strength of her will, now came barreling through abandoned barricades to overwhelm her. Surrounded by warmth and a familiar feeling of security, she felt Cory's hand come to rest on her hair, touching tentatively, at first, then moving slowly…lightly stroking, fingers weaving through the short, damp strands.

She thought, *Oh, how I've missed this.*

I could have had this. If I hadn't insisted on becoming a pilot…if I hadn't allowed myself to be recruited by the Company…if I hadn't lost my temper that night…if I hadn't walked away.

In her unguarded state that night came back to her so vividly. She remembered the sick cold feeling in her chest and belly, the trembling weakness in her legs as she'd walked away from him down that rainy Georgetown street.

She remembered how she'd held her head high as she walked and stared at the streetlamps through a blur of tears and rain. How she'd listened until it seemed as if her whole head was vibrating. Hoping.

Silly me—I'm hoping he'll call to me, tell me not to go. That he'll tell me he loves me and needs me, that he can't possibly live without me, that he wants me just as I am, that it's okay if I want to be a pilot, or become a spy, or whatever it is I want to do, if only I'll come back.

But of course he doesn't call, and I keep walking down that street in the rain, too proud to admit it isn't what I meant to do. That this isn't what I wanted.

If I'd done it differently…

Moisture pooled in the corners of her eyes, made tiny puddles beneath her lashes. Just moisture—not tears, she told herself. *I'm not crying. Samantha June doesn't cry, not over lost causes.*

But…his touch was so gentle…so soothing. With her eyes closed, lashes floating gently on the cushion of tears, she felt his long, sensitive fingers comb the hair back from her temple…tuck a strand behind her ear. It felt so good. She gave a small, shuddering sigh. Safety and contentment settled over her. Twilight drifted down….

Then, from somewhere far above her she heard his voice, a familiar and comforting murmur, like a lullaby....

"What happened here, Sam? This little scar behind your ear?"

Chapter 6

Awareness and adrenaline stabbed through her with the same brutal stroke, like a lance of double-edged steel. The bubble of safety and comfort and sleep that had briefly cocooned her shattered and vanished as if it had never been. Her body twitched and quivered; her hand jerked protectively to the tender place behind her ear, displacing his. Her mind snapped into focus, sharp and crystal clear. *Too late!*

"I can feel a bump there. It's still tender, isn't it? You flinched when I touched it earlier."

She coughed and mumbled, "I had a few stitches—nothing serious." Vibrating inside, she sat up and moved away from him, swiveling her body around so her back was against the wall and there was a buffer zone of space between her arm and his. She had to force herself to make the movements slowly, making it seem a casual thing rather than the panicked retreat it was.

"Is that why you cut your hair?"

She gave him a look and a short laugh, surprised because,

under the influence of her own guilt, it was the last thing she'd expected him to ask. She looked away again and touched her hair with a self-conscious hand. "Yeah…it looked kind of weird with a chunk cut out of it, so I figured, you know, why not. That was a few months ago—it's grown out quite a bit, actually."

"I like it. Looks good on you."

"Thanks." Even as she accepted the compliment she could feel his eyes on her…hear his mind humming away, thinking up new questions to ask. To distract him, she nodded toward Tony's corner, from which the snoring continued unabated. "How can he sleep like that under these conditions? I wish I had the knack."

"I think it's something you develop in childhood. In his case, it's what comes of being one of eleven kids."

"Wow. Really?" Sam leaned her head back against the wall. "Well, that's something us only children aren't ever gonna know about, isn't it?" Then she checked herself and glanced over at him. "But I forgot—I guess it was different for you, wasn't it? In foster homes." She paused, but as usual he didn't answer. Why had she imagined this might be any different from all the other times she'd tried to ask about his past…his childhood?

She studied his profile…like a menswear ad in a glossy magazine, she thought, with his eyes fixed intently on some far-off place, muscles visible in a jaw too square and uncompromising for the rest of his face. It was an interesting face rather than handsome—she'd always thought so, from the first moment she'd laid eyes on it that long-ago afternoon in the White House rose garden—long and angular, with hollows and creases that made it seem scholarly even without glasses. Without the shield of his glasses, which at the moment were tucked in the pocket of his shirt, his eyes seemed even gentler, somehow, the intensity of their gaze veiled by thick lashes, the fan of creases at their corners more suggestive of humor than that laserlike focus that could be so unnerving.

Maybe it was because of that that she pushed bravely on now, when normally such stubborn and intimidating silence would have caused her to abandon the field like a craven coward.

"What was it like for you? In those foster homes. Were they… good to you?"

Still he didn't reply, and she felt the familiar hollowness inside…the terrible deadness of futility. Then he shifted in a restless way, and when he spoke, in a gravelly voice that didn't sound like him, it wasn't what she'd expected.

"What makes you think I'm an only child?"

For a moment she could only stare at him, unable to make sense of the words, as if he'd spoken in a foreign language. "But you're—I thought—" She stopped, as the meaning of what he'd said rolled over her like the delayed winds from an explosion. Breathless with shock, she said, "Wow. You mean you—I didn't know you had siblings. Is it—are they—I mean, my God…"

"Four," he said, and his voice and eyes seemed almost regretful. But oddly, his body, close to hers but not touching, seemed to hum with tension. "Two of each."

"My God." She said it again, dazed. *Why didn't I know? How could I not have known this? Why didn't he tell me?* After a moment she cleared her throat. "Are they—"

"Younger. All of them. I was the oldest."

It was anger that finally squeezed past the immobilizing shock, both of body and mind. And she was too upset herself, then, to notice the tense he'd used, or heed the quality of his voice—a certain carefulness, as if the slightest puff of breath might scatter memories too fragile to hold up to examination. She plunged on, her outrage building with every word, fighting to keep her voice under control, to keep him from knowing how devastated she was.

"You never told me you have brothers and sisters. I mean— when you said you grew up in foster care, I just assumed…how could you not have told me?"

The better question, Cory thought, wasn't why he'd never told her before, but what had possessed him to tell her *now?*

He hadn't meant to. The words had suddenly appeared, his mind playing a trick like a magician plucking a coin from thin air. And, as it usually was with magicians' tricks, he couldn't for the life of him figure out how it had happened.

Why didn't I tell you?

She'd drawn her legs up and wrapped her arms around them, as a barricade against him, he thought, and her eyes, gazing at him across the tops of her knees, were dark with reproach and betrayal. He stared at her, appalled at the pain he'd caused her, unable to think of an explanation that would be enough for her. She'd always wanted brothers and sisters, he knew that. She'd been born two months early, had spent weeks fighting for her life in a NICU, and for her parents, Tris and Jessie Bauer, one million-dollar-miracle baby had been enough. To think, in all the years they'd known each other, after all they'd been to each other, that he had siblings he'd never spoken of, never shared with her…he couldn't blame her for being angry. One more thing he was never going to be able to make right.

How could he make her understand that some secrets were too shameful to share? That some wounds were endurable only if undisturbed? That sometimes guilt was a hornets' nest to be tiptoed around and left alone?

"So," she said in a blunt voice, with a defiant little toss of her head, "Where are they now? Do you see them often?"

He shook his head. "I haven't seen them in…years," he said, and saw a spark of new outrage flare in her eyes. In Sam's extended family, any kinfolk—brothers, sisters, aunts, uncles and cousins—were a taken-for-granted part of everyday life. Even the ones who lived far away from the old home place in Oglethorp County, Georgia, managed to come home for the major holidays and family events.

"You haven't—" Air gusted from her lungs with the word, *"Why?"*

He looked away. "Because," he said with a soft sigh of resignation, "I don't know where they are."

"What? What do you mean, you don't know?" And even without looking at her he knew she'd be staring at him with lightning bolts in her eyes, bristling with dismay and disbelief.

He put his head back against the wall and closed his eyes. The cat was out of the bag, the initial panic and turmoil were passing, and he felt a strange quietness now…a sense of acceptance and inevitability. Maybe, he thought, the words had come simply because it was time. Because for some reason this moment and this place were the right ones, crazy as it seemed—the middle of a Philippine jungle, with uncertainty and peril all around, and Samantha back in his life again, and maybe, just maybe, another chance for them to get it right this time.

And suddenly he knew for certain he wanted that chance. He always had wanted it. He just wasn't sure he was capable of what it would take to make it happen.

Beginning—that was the hardest part. She was waiting for an answer…an explanation he wasn't sure he was ready to give her. He drew a breath that shuddered with the strain, and when he spoke, the words felt as if they were being stripped from him, like the protective bark from a tree. "We were separated after our parents died. I don't know what happened to the others. I think some of them were adopted."

"God…" It was a whisper. She sounded beyond stunned. Sick. "I don't believe this. They split you up? How could they do that?"

He looked over at her with a faint, wry smile. He took a breath; it was getting easier now. "There were five of us, Sam. There aren't too many foster families willing or equipped to take on five kids. Especially—" He stopped himself on the verge of saying too much, and finished instead, "since I was almost twelve. The others were a lot younger—adoptable. I wasn't. So, they did what they thought was best."

Unappeased, she said huffily, "Well, but—didn't you ever try to find them?"

You were supposed to take care of them, Cory. They were your responsibility. How could you let that happen?

Guilt caught him unawares. It was an old guilt, one he thought he'd outgrown; a child's guilt, irrational, black and terrifying. He fought it off and exhaled in a gust, helplessly, unable to laugh, unwilling to be angry. What, after all, was the point?

"Sure I did. I must have run away at least twenty times. Until they put me in a detention center—for incorrigibles, they called it. I was eighteen when they let me out. By that time, I figured, what was the point? The girls had been just babies—two or three, I think—when I saw them last. The boys weren't much older—"

"No—I mean later. After you…" She was breathing in short shallow sips, as if each one hurt her. "My God, Pearse, you're a reporter. You have resources. Can't you—couldn't you—"

"No." He said it softly and with finality, praying she'd hear the pain in it and just…let it go. Hoping she could read in his eyes the fear that haunted him…fear of the memories he kept shut away in the dank, dark basement of his mind. Wishing he could make her understand that his refusal to share those memories with her had nothing to do with her and everything to do with the fear. Fear…that if he did unlock that door he wouldn't be strong enough to deal with the horrors that lurked behind it.

She did let it go, reluctantly, but he could tell by the stricken look on her face and the reproach in her eyes that she didn't understand, not now, no more than all the times he'd disappointed her before.

It was too hard to look at her, so once again he put his head back and closed his eyes, knowing he was shutting himself off from her. Knowing he was hurting her by doing so. Not knowing how to do otherwise.

After a moment he heard rustlings and scufflings, and felt an emptiness where her warmth had been.

The emptiness and hurt were inside him, too. Probably, he

thought, he should just accept that guilt and turmoil were going to be a part of this trip for the duration. That fact had been inevitable from the moment he'd seen Sam standing there beside that antique plane. They had a way of pushing each other's buttons...of disappointing each other, that no amount of time or distance apart seemed able to remedy.

It's just as well we split up when we did, he told himself. Lord, wouldn't we have made each other miserable?

The day stretched ahead of him, tedious and empty. He wished he dared sleep—knew he *should* sleep—but the memories had been awakened now, and the instant he relaxed his vigil he knew they'd be there, banging on the door.

Banging on the door. Banging and banging...the whimpering of the others, the little ones...

Awake, he could play the mind games that would keep them at bay, but if he fell asleep he knew the dreams would be waiting. Those particular dreams hadn't troubled him since Iraq; why they should have returned now, at this of all times, he couldn't imagine. Was it because of Sam, having her so unexpectedly back in his life? Or something else, some combination of circumstances he hadn't yet untangled?

Either way, he thought, the timing couldn't be much worse.

Sam lay curled on her side with her head pillowed on her arm. Tense and quivering, she nursed her outrage and anger, too stunned to sleep, or even to feel hurt. Thoughts kept exploding through her mind like bazookas, each one more devastating than the last.

Brothers and sisters. He has brothers and sisters! How could he not have told me? Something as basic, as important as that?

Brothers and sisters—they're part of what make you who you are. How can you love someone and not tell them who you are?

Damn him. He's the most generous person I know, except when it comes to sharing what's inside him. When it comes to that, he's the...the stingiest *person I know.*

*It's a good thing we broke up. How could I have loved some-
one like that?*

Oh, God. How can I still love him?

I don't want to love him.

I wish somebody would tell me how to stop.

Eventually, she must have slept. When she woke up, stiff and
aching from lying on the bare floor, the room had become shadowed, and the air had the tired, heavy feel of late afternoon. She
sat up, combed her fingers through her hair and looked around.
Cory was still over near the door where she'd left him, stretched
out flat on his back now, with his arms folded across his eyes.
Tony's corner was empty.

She stood up, raised her arms over her head and did a few
stretches and twists to limber up her back muscles, and then,
barefooted and carrying her flip-flops, slipped quietly out of the
hut.

She found Tony standing on the porch, and as usual, holding
a camera in his hands. He turned when she came through the
door, grinned at her, then lifted the camera and snapped her picture. She held up a hand in protest and stuck her tongue out at
him as she dropped her flip-flops and stepped into them. Then
she plunked herself down on the edge of the porch and sat
hunched and rocking herself, throwing baleful looks at Tony as
he slipped the camera strap over one shoulder and came to sit
beside her.

"Did we sleep well?" he inquired in a mock solicitous tone,
lifting his eyebrows at the cranky glare she gave him.

"Well, I know you did," she retorted, smothering a yawn.
"You were snoring like to wake the dead."

"Sorry about that," Tony said cheerfully. He rubbed the bump
on the bridge of his nose with a forefinger. "I think maybe I have
a deviated septum, or something. Wouldn't be surprised—my
nose's been broken a time or two."

She gulped another yawn and shook herself irritably. *Damn.*

She hated sleeping in the daytime—especially when it was hot and muggy like this. It reminded her of having to take a nap when she was a kid and much too old for naps. Her head felt as though it had been stuffed with wool, and she was thirsty. "I could do with something to drink," she grumbled. "What time is it, do you know? My watch got left behind with my bags."

Tony shook his head and held up his camera. "Mine, too. I figure I'm lucky to have this." He paused, then gave her a sideways look. "Cory still sleeping?"

"I guess so. I really don't know." *And don't give a damn,* her tone plainly said. A surge of disbelief, anger and hurt rose out of the sullen stew of her emotions to swamp her again, briefly, before receding to leave her feeling even more dismal than before.

She jerked a look over at Tony. "How long have you two known each other, anyway?"

He straightened abruptly, as if the question had taken him by surprise. "Me? Oh…'bout four years, I guess, maybe more. I was his—" he coughed, belatedly and almost comically embarrassed "—um…his best man. At his…uh…you know…wedding."

One good thing about this new shocker, Sam supposed, for once the mention of Cory's marriage brought not even a twinge of pain or a sizzle of anger. She brushed it aside with only an impatient gesture. "He ever tell you about his family?"

His exotic golden eyes regarded her thoughtfully from under short straight lashes. "Not much, no." He paused, then added, "I know he doesn't have one."

"But he did," she said in a low voice, hunched and intent. "Right? He had a mother and father, brothers and sisters… Did he ever tell you about them?"

He shifted, fiddling with his camera, lifting it to peer one-eyed through the viewfinder then lowering it again to his lap. He looked over at her, still squinting a little. "I know his parents both died. After that he went into the system. Wasn't kind to him, I know that. He doesn't like to talk about it much."

"No kidding." She paused, then asked, "What happened to his mom and dad? How did they die? Was it some kind of accident?"

He didn't answer at first. He studied his feet, rocking himself a little. Then he took a deep breath. "Look, you wanna know the truth? I've wondered about it myself. Used to, anyway. Don't guess I'd be human if I didn't. Hey, I work in the news media— it's all right there, the information, you know? What I'm saying is, if I wanted to find out, I probably could. I just figure…it's not my place to do that. It's not something I need to know. Guys don't have this need to share their innermost feelings. If he wants to tell me, he will. If he doesn't, fine. He's my friend, he's gonna be my friend no matter what." He paused…shifted his gaze to the cloud-shrouded mountains. "You, though…that's a different thing. I don't know…between a man and a woman, if they plan on being together, seems to me like there shouldn't be any se-crets. So, maybe it's something *you* need to know. Maybe it's something he needs to tell you."

Her throat felt dry, as though it might tear if she swallowed. Instead, she gave a huff of scratchy laughter. "*If* they plan on being together. *That's* not gonna happen."

He turned his head to look at her along one shoulder. "Why do you say that? Anybody can see you two've got feelings for each other." He snorted. "He's sure got feelings for you."

"Oh, yeah," Sam said acidly. "This from the guy who was best man at his, 'uh, wedding.' To somebody else?"

He reared back, holding up a hand. "Whoa, that—okay, that was a bad thing he did, I'll grant you that." He darted a look over one shoulder and lowered his voice to a mutter. "I gotta tell you, though—he'd kill me if he knew I was telling you this—the night before the wedding? I could tell something was wrong. I even asked him if he was getting cold feet—you know, kidding around—and he looked at me like…I don't know, but I've seen that exact same look on the faces of convicted felons right after the judge passes sentence, just before the guard fastens on the handcuffs and leads them away. This...oh-Lord-what-have-I-done look, you know? But he just said, No, everything was fine. Then he went and got blasted. *Drunk,*" he added when Sam stared blankly at him.

"Drunk? *Cory?*" She gave her head a hard little shake of disbelief. "He doesn't get drunk. I've never seen him drink more than a couple of beers before in my life."

Tony nodded. "My point exactly. I'd had my doubts before, but that's when I *knew* it wasn't right. She wasn't the one."

She rubbed at her throat; the ache there was becoming intolerable. "Then why did he do it?" she whispered. "Why did he marry her?"

He gave her a long hard look and finally said, "Can't you figure it out? You're a smart lady—put two and two together." He held up a finger. "He doesn't have a family." A second finger joined the first. "He wants one." Another finger. "Time is slipping by." A fourth finger. "You aren't available, but someone comes along at just the right time, and she is available." The fingers clenched into a fist. "Bingo—end of story."

Sam swallowed hard. Her eyes burned. She whispered, "I don't care. If he'd loved me, he wouldn't have done it. *Couldn't* have done it."

As far as she was concerned that was a fact, irrefutable, inescapable. And intolerable. Which didn't keep her from trying to escape it anyway, as she plunged off the porch and headed blindly for the village.

She had no destination in mind to begin with, just that overwhelming desire to flee from thoughts and emotions she didn't want to face, but after the first heedless steps, she decided she might as well make for the crude latrine the women had led her to earlier. On that trip she'd satisfied herself that their "custodian," the terrorist spokesman, was telling the truth when he claimed al-Rami wasn't in the camp. She was fairly certain the hostages wouldn't be, either—other than the hut the three of them were inhabiting, there simply wasn't a structure that could have held them. Not one with a door, anyway.

Tonight. He said, "We go to al-Rami tonight." That's what I have to concentrate on, she told herself. *The job.* And she was getting close…so very close.

She almost ran headlong into the phalanx of armed men that popped up out of the jumble of vegetation and overgrown huts to block her way, the so-called "spokesman" at their center with his trusty rifle at the ready. Behind them, Sam caught glimpses of several women waiting with heads shyly bowed, arms full of baskets of food and bundles of familiar-looking shoes and clothing.

She tried to explain, in her best Tagalog, that she was only going to the latrine, but the spokesman adamantly refused to let her pass.

"Go back now," he barked in his choppy English, which he seemed incapable of speaking without using his weapon for emphasis. "Eat first. Then put on cloths. We go when is dark."

"Gosh, I was getting to kind of like this outfit," Sam said to the man as she was plodding back to the hut, reverting to English herself. "You don't suppose I could keep it, do you? Like those complimentary hotel bathrobes?"

The gunman, stone-faced, didn't answer. She shrugged and grinned at Tony, who was sitting on the porch where she'd left him, his camera discreetly lowered. She told herself her heart didn't quicken its tempo when she saw Cory there, too, standing with his arms folded on his chest as if waiting for her, like a stern papa confronting a child caught coming in past curfew.

She resisted the temptation to stick her tongue out at him, and instead gave her head a breezy toss and said, "Hey, look who I found." Ignoring Cory, she plopped down on the edge of the porch beside Tony and nudged him with her elbow. "Cheer up, guys, they brought your pants back." And she laughed as he clutched belatedly at the edges of his sarong and tried without success to bring them together over his knees.

Laughing…smiling…making jokes…all to hide the fact that her heart was racing and she was helpless to control it. That her whole body seemed to be singing in response to Cory's nearness, nerve endings lifting to him the way skin and hair react to static electricity, with sparks zapping and crackling at the slightest touch. Sparks…that could cause devastating explosions, if conditions were right.

She laughed and smiled and joked with Tony because she had no wish to deal with the jumble of emotions and memories and hurt feelings and fears that were her thoughts just then. As a pilot she knew better than to try to fly through that kind of turbulence.

That night's trek seemed almost a replay of the first. Cory even wondered at times if they might be traversing some of the same territory they'd covered the night before, their guides using darkness as a substitute for blindfolds as they led them in circles to confuse them. In any case, he was determined not to let his own impatience and inner turmoil distract him from experiencing and mentally recording the adventure, and his eyes and ears—not to mention his imagination—were busy as he scrambled in the wake of his escort, dodging branches and trying not to trip over the tangle underfoot.

In different circumstances, he thought, the jungle by moonlight might have seemed an enchanted place, with silvery shafts stabbing through breaks in the canopy like ghostly fingers reaching for something in the shadows clumped below. It wasn't quiet. Small jungle creatures confused by the half light rustled in the undergrowth and twittered in the branches high above their heads as they kept their nervous vigil against the predators that stalked them by moonlight. It was a hunter's night; every now and then a desperate shriek from an unlucky victim shattered the busy whispering, rustling calm and sent shock waves skating along Cory's nerves.

As the night wore on, though, and they left behind the jungle to follow a zigzag track through cultivated fields, his mind, freed of the necessity for constant vigil, began to wander. Perhaps it was inevitable, given recent events, that it should take him into forbidden places…attics of memory he hadn't allowed himself to visit in years.

A few yards ahead of him, he could see Sam as she walked beside Tony, no doubt trying to comfort him over the loss of his cameras, which were presently in the custody of their armed escort. *Temporary* custody, Sam had assured Tony, most likely to insure he didn't photograph any landmarks that might be used to trace the hideout of the elusive al-Rami. Which meant they were getting close….

Now, Cory could hear Sam's soft laughter, a husky chuckle that seemed to blend with the other night noises, and he felt uncomfortable twinges of…surely not *jealousy*…as he watched the two shapes lean close for a moment, then veer apart. No, not jealousy—he had no right to that—perhaps *envy* was a better way to describe the pang it gave him to see the two of them together like that…his best friend and the woman he loved…or the way they'd been back at the hut, talking together on the porch when they'd thought he was sleeping. Not that he worried about Tony, or was surprised Sam would turn to him the way she had; everybody from old people to little children and puppy dogs tended to trust Tony, in spite of his ominous appearance. But he'd felt those pangs nonetheless, and it was only now, walking alone in the early-morning moonlight, that it occurred to him the pangs might be loneliness.

"He doesn't have a family…. He wants one."

The words he'd overheard on the porch came back to him, along with a stab of resentment. What an oversimplification that was—like something out of a child's storybook. He was an adult, not a child, and he'd made a fulfilling and successful life for himself without benefit of—or hindrance from—family. The thought of using that as an excuse for bad choices embarrassed him.

Besides, he thought, I *had* a family...once. *A happy one.*

As if in defiance, he let them come, then...the sunshine memories.

Dad, coming home from work, and the warm brown smell of oil and dirt and car grease permeating his skin and clothes, and mine, too, when I hug him. It makes me feel safe and good, that smell, and even now, all these years later, the smell of a mechanic's garage gives me a sense of well-being...a sense that all's right with the world.

Mom, bending down to kiss me good-night before she rushes off to school, smelling of hand lotion and the dinner she's left for Dad and me. And that makes me feel safe and good, too, because she's smiling and her eyes are shining, and I know she's happy. Not to be leaving me—even as young as I am I know that. "I'm going to be a teacher," she tells me, and her voice has a breathless excitement that makes me feel it, too. "Maybe I'll be your teacher someday."

Impatient, I ask her, "When will that be?"

"Soon," she tells me. "Very soon—when you're five."

Dad and me, just the two of us now, me in my pajamas cozy in my bed, Dad lying on top of the covers, his head propped on his hand while he tells me a story. Sometimes it's one I already know, like "The Three Little Pigs," and I chime in with him on the parts I know by heart, like when the Big Bad Wolf says, "I'll huff and I'll puff and I'll BLOW your house down!" But sometimes he makes up stories right out of his head, and that's the best thing of all.

They were the last of the good ones, those memories. Very soon after that his dad had gone away to fight a war in a place called Vietnam, and his mom had quit night school and they'd moved to a big city called Chicago, and his mom had gone to work in a store. He'd started school in a strange place, and his mom didn't smile as much, and she never did become a teacher, his or anyone else's.

That was the beginning of the gray times. The black times, the terrible times, the times he wouldn't let himself remember…those had come later.

Dawn came while the moon, now a flat pale ghost, still floated low in the lavender sky, hovering above a bank of clouds that lay on the horizon like cotton batting thrown down to break its fall. The air was cool, and smelled of crushed vegetation and over-ripe fruit. Humidity lay thick on the grass and dripped like rain-drops from the trees. A stillness lay over the jungle and fields and mountains alike, as if the world held its breath in expectation of sunrise.

Before it came, however, the trail they'd been following plunged suddenly into dark green shadows, zigzagging downward into a steep ravine. As they descended into the dense jungle growth Sam could hear the rush of water, muffled by the trees, and from somewhere up ahead, voices calling out challenges. Moments later, she, Cory and Tony were ordered, by the usual method—a thrusting rifle barrel—to halt. A new cadre of armed men, also wearing camouflage, appeared to block the path. Those who had brought them from the village hospital melted away into the jungle, all but the leader—the "spokesman," who instructed them in his usual staccato English to follow the new escort. As they did so, he fell in behind them, stone-faced as always, rifle at the ready, and off they went once more, deeper into the ravine.

A little farther on, around a sharp bend, they halted once more.

"Holy mother," said Tony.

"Yeah," said Cory.

"Oh, cool," said Sam.

Chapter 7

Directly ahead of them, a large, multi-level house had been built close in against the side of the ravine. Supported by stilts and cantilevered decks and constructed mostly of bamboo with a roof of thatch, it appeared almost to be a part of the surrounding vegetation, making it virtually invisible from both above and below.

Tony said in an awed tone, "This reminds me of a tree house I used to have."

Sam threw him an interested look. "Really?"

"No," Tony admitted, grinning back at her, "but I sure do wish, don't you?"

From a balcony jutting off the top level of the house, yet another rifle-bearing guard wearing camouflage waved them on. The path grew steeper and slippery with spray from the numerous small streams cascading down the side of the ravine. Foliage crowded close and obscured the sky overhead, giving the light a greenish quality, as if they were underwater. There was an eerie beauty about the place, a timeless tranquility—like

Eden, Sam thought, and she felt a momentary pang, knowing the catastrophe she was about to bring down upon it. What a shame, she thought, that people have to bring their wars into such a paradise.

Wars. Until now, she hadn't ever thought of what she was doing as fighting a war; she definitely didn't see herself as any kind of soldier. She'd signed on to help track down terrorists, to stop them from killing innocent people. As far as she was concerned, her job was to put an end to the senseless destruction and havoc of war, not cause it.

But…there was nothing to be done about it. She had a job to do, whatever label anyone chose to put on it. And from the looks of this setup, the amount of security in this place, it was going to be going down soon.

The path crossed the tumbling stream on a bamboo footbridge before coming to an end at a series of bamboo steps leading down to the lowest deck. The light here was dim and the air cool, even though beyond the ravine Sam knew the sun would already be climbing, promising another hot and humid day.

They followed their escort across the deck, through an open doorway and into a large, shadowy room. It was even cooler here, the light so weak it was a moment before Sam's eyes adjusted enough to see that the room was already occupied. At the far end of the room, a man was seated cross-legged on cushions covered in brightly colored and intricately patterned fabrics. He was wearing a loose robe made of similar material, which again seemed to her vaguely Indonesian in design. His full beard was liberally streaked with gray, his hair clipped short and nearly covered by a cap of a style that was also more Indonesian than Filipino. His features were neither, however; his face was angular and gaunt, his nose prominent, even hawklike, and the eyes that surveyed them from shadowed sockets were Caucasian.

Her breathing quickened, and so did her heartbeat. Here at last was the infamous Fahad al-Rami.

He lifted a long-fingered, graceful hand and gestured to them as he spoke, in perfect British English. "Ah, my American guests. I am certain you must be hungry after your long journey. Refreshments are being prepared for you, but in the meantime, I hope you will join me in a cup of tea." Framed by the beard, his lips curved in a smile that didn't show his teeth. "A habit I picked up during my years at Oxford. Please—" he nodded at Cory and extended a hand toward a pile of cushions on his right "—Mr. Pearson, do be seated. It is an honor to meet you face-to-face at last. I have found our e-mail correspondence enjoyable."

The eyes shifted and the hand moved languidly through the air—like a frond of seaweed, Sam thought, waving with the ocean current—to indicate Tony. "And this, I presume, is your photographer, Mr. Whitehall. First, allow me to apologize for asking my men to appropriate your equipment. I'm sure you can appreciate the necessity for doing so. Your cameras will, of course, be returned to you, with the understanding that you may take photographs only within these walls.

"But first—we must eat. Please—sit." The hand dipped toward another pile of cushions.

After a quizzical glance over at Cory, who had already seated himself and was presently squirming around trying to figure out what to do with his feet, Tony sank gingerly onto the cushions.

For one horrible moment Sam thought she wouldn't be able to hold back her laughter as she watched the two men in their jungle boots and cargo pants attempting to make themselves comfortable in a setting reminiscent of a Persian bordello. A favorite expression of her Grandma Betty's popped into her mind: *…As out-of-place as a duck on a doily.*

Then al-Rami's dead dark eyes slid toward and then over her, and any notion she might have had to laugh vanished in an instant. Heat rose to her cheeks, and she became aware of the steady thump of her own heartbeat.

But when al-Rami spoke again, it was to Cory, in a voice as

smooth as silk. "As you can see, there will be no need for the services of your…interpreter. In any case, she would no doubt prefer to rest and freshen up in privacy. Quarters have been prepared which I am sure she will find comfortable. My guard will show her to her room. Refreshments will be brought to her there."

A wave of anger washed over Sam, catching her by surprise and testing her self-control even more sorely than the laughter a moment ago. Loathing clogged her throat like sickness. Her vision shimmered. She was barely aware of Cory's face swiveling toward her, his eyes reaching out to her, flashes of warning…beacons of calm. Then, through that mind-fogging rage, she saw his lips quirk sideways in a wry little smile. She could hear his voice, mild and amused, inside her head. *Ouch, Sam—I know you loved that!*

She began to breathe again, but she was still seething. She answered his nod with a sarcastic one of her own as she turned to follow yet another camouflage-wearing, rifle-toting guard from the room. But every fiber of her being, every part of her, from her free-thinking, independent woman's soul to her strong, red-blooded-American woman's body to the bare-knuckled tomboy she still was at heart, raged in mute rebellion over being dismissed from the august male presence like a child. No—even worse, a woman.

As she was leaving the room, she lost the battle with her pride and looked back once more at Cory, reaching for him across the vast emptiness of the room…ashamed to admit even to herself that right now she wanted—needed—the reassuring touch of those wise blue eyes. But he wasn't looking at her, leaning forward to accept a cup from his host as if, she thought, he'd already dismissed her from his mind. A quiver went through her, a manifestation of emotions too intense to contain. She wasn't even sure she could have named them—*resentment…hurt…loneliness*—but she knew for sure there wasn't anything strong or independent or bare-knuckle tomboyish about any of them.

Shake it off, Sammi June.

How many times had her dad said that—before he'd gone away to Iraq and gotten shot down and disappeared from her life for eight years—when she'd been fouled in a soccer game and lay howling and writhing in the grass? And how many times had she pulled herself together and gotten up, sniffling, to wipe away tears and blood and get right back in the game?

You can do it, Sammi June. Go get 'em.

Resolutely, she banished the hurt and the loneliness. But she held on to the anger, tucking it away in the back of her mind like a secret talisman.

She was taken to a room up one flight of bamboo stairs from the large main room. It was sparsely furnished—a pile of those same all-purpose cushions on the floor, a small bamboo table and stool near the only window—but seemed hospitable enough. A basin filled with water sat on the table, and a shelf below held folded cloth towels.

Her escort nodded her into the room, then closed the door and departed—hurriedly, and without a word or a smile, as if anxious to get as far away from her as possible. Alone at last, Sam let her breath out in a gust and went quickly over to the window. It had neither glass nor screen, just a bamboo shutter that could be closed to keep out the rain and indigenous wildlife—the larger varieties, at least. She leaned her head and shoulders out, looked up, then down. It was a long way to the rushing stream below. She was, for all intents and purposes, a prisoner in the room; though she didn't think she'd been locked in, she was quite certain any attempt to leave through the door would be foiled by those ever-vigilant guards.

What had she expected? This was the hideout of the most wanted man in the world; she could hardly have expected to be given free run of the place.

A picture flashed into her mind, of Cory leaning forward to accept a cup of tea from the bloody hand of Fahad al-Rami. A shiver of outrage shook her from head to toe.

*How can he do this? How can he sit there and…and talk with
that man—and drink tea, for God's sake!—as if he were just any
other human being? Knowing what he's done, all the innocents'
deaths he's been responsible for…the suffering he's caused. And
he gets to sit here like a rajah, enjoying this jungle paradise…*

The anger ebbed, and in its place came a cold resolve. *Not
for long!*

Anyway, her fit of pique had been only a momentary thing,
a knee-jerk reaction to the injury to her feminine pride. The
truth was, she knew her "banishment" couldn't be more oppor-
tune. For what she needed to do next, privacy was essential.

Privacy…and a good satellite signal. An awful thought came
to her, and she swiveled her gaze upward again to where only
minute fragments of hazy sky were visible through the dense foliage. *What if the satellite can't pick up my signal?*

It was time for a test. She took in a deep breath through her
nose…whooshed it out…flexed her fingers, then gave her hands
a shake. Loosening herself up, shaking off the tension. Then,
carefully touching back the hair behind her right ear, she lifted
her finger and placed it on the small bump located there, beneath
the healing scar. Head bowed, eyes closed, concentrating on
blocking out the twinges of pain from still-tender tissues, she
pressed the bump in a well-rehearsed code sequence: *Target located.*

She waited, heart thumping. Several minutes later—it only
seemed like hours—the answer came. A single but unmistakable zap: *Message received and copied.*

Quivering and clammy with relief, she tapped out a new message: *Stand by.*

The answer came more quickly this time. Two zaps: *Say
again. Clarify.*

She repeated it: *Stand by.*

And the answer came back—one zap: *Copy.*

It was done. For now, anyway. Wobble-legged, suddenly, she

turned and half sat, half leaned against the windowsill, letting the tension and adrenaline drain from her body and her thumping heart settle back into normal rhythms. Later, when the time was right, she'd send another signal—the signal to move in. But for now, all she could do was wait. Wait until Cory finished his interview. Wait for word on the hostages. Wait until they were all safely away. *Wait.*

Waiting had never been easy for her.

And in the meantime, somewhere out there beyond the ravine, Philippine government forces and their American special ops advisors would be gathering, homing in on her GPS signal. Waiting for the signal to move on Fahad al-Rami's jungle hideaway. *Waiting.* Their objective, of course, would be to capture the elusive terrorist leader alive, but failing that...

A shudder passed through Sam's body. Pushing herself away from the window, she plunged her hands into the basin and washed her face in the pleasantly cool water. After a moment's hesitation and a quick look toward the door, she stripped off her T-shirt, then quickly slipped out of her boots and cargo pants. Dressed only in her underwear, she soaked a towel in the water, wrung it out lightly and sponged herself off as best she could. She dried herself and dressed hurriedly, cringing at the feel of her damp, sweaty clothing on her skin. She'd barely finished and was attempting to finger-comb some order into her hair when there was a discreet knock on the door.

She opened it to find a stone-faced guard with a tray on which were arranged a small pot of tea, a cup, a woven bowl containing fruit, and a covered container she was sure would hold the usual concoction of vegetables and rice. She smiled and thanked the guard in Tagalog, but, naturally, got no response. He merely handed over the tray and retreated, pulling the door shut after him.

"Have a nice day," Sam said dryly. She stood for a moment, holding the tray and chewing her lip, trying to decide whether to displace the basin of water and use the table and stool, or go for the floor and cushions.

"Oh, hell—when in Rome," she muttered with a shrug as she placed the tray on the floor and sank cross-legged onto a tufted purple cushion.

The next few minutes she spent refueling with gusto and efficiency. She hadn't realized how hungry she was—probably, she thought, anger and adrenaline would tend to have a dampening effect on a person's appetite. Gradually, though, as the void inside her filled, a sense of peaceful lassitude settled over her. It was a good feeling; the first part of her job had been done, and for the moment there was nothing more she could do. And she was tired; she'd had only catnaps the past few days, and here, for the first time since Zamboanga, was both privacy and comfort. Her body relaxed…her mind drifted. Once again her guard slipped, and the memories came pouring in.

It's autumn, the days are growing short and in Athens, Georgia, the leaves are already falling. But the sky is wonderfully blue and the air smells crisp and good, and Cory's here! I haven't seen him in a while, he's been out of the country on assignment, but now he's back in Atlanta again, taping something for CNN, and it's the weekend and he's driven over to Athens to see me. We've been to a football game—the Bulldogs won, not that I care, because all that matters is Cory's here, and we hold hands as we stroll through the campus, kicking through the fresh leaves and laughing at nothing, because it's enough just to be together. We spread our jackets on the grass and finish the rest of the tailgate lunch I'd fixed for before the game, throwing bits of bread crusts to the squirrels.

I look at Cory, and he's smiling that gentle smile, and his eyes look back into mine with such understanding, and his face is so beautiful I hurt inside, and I have to fight back tears. I lean over and kiss him, and his lips are warm and the shape of them against mine is the most incredible thing I've ever felt. His lips part under mine, and I laugh, low in my throat, because he tastes like mustard and onions, and so do I, but what do either of us care? I'm trembling when he pulls away with a soft little sigh of regret, and I want him so much...the wanting fills every part of me, and I know I won't be able to hide it from him. I wonder how much longer I'll have to wait for him to get past the notion I'm too young for him, the daughter of his closest friend, and decides it's okay to make love to me. I wonder how it's possible to be so happy...and feel such pain....

She must have slept, because she woke with a start to find herself sprawled in a jumble of cushions with her arms and legs every which way, and the silhouetted figure of a man standing in front of the window. She sat up too quickly, clammy and jangled, and the figure moved away from the light and became Cory.

"Hey. Didn't mean to wake you," he said softly, smiling that gentle smile that was so much like the one in her recent memory—or had it been a dream?—it made her heart flip-flop.

She scowled at him. "What're you doing here, Pearse?" And her voice sounded gruff and cranky, because that was her best defense against the way she felt. *Vulnerable.* There was nothing in the world Sam hated more than feeling vulnerable.

"Are you okay?"

And sympathy didn't help matters, either, especially coming from the person whose whole entire fault it was she felt this way. "I'm fine," she said with an impatient wave of her hand, whisking away the question like an annoying fly. "No big deal. I wasn't crazy about being sent to my room like a—" She broke it off while she pulled her feet under her and prepared to stand up, then amended it. "Being treated that way by that SOB, but hey—I'm over it."

Cory stepped closer and held out his hand to help her up. His eyes were amused. "Come on, Sam, I know you too well. If ever I saw murder in a woman's eyes..." He paused, patiently waiting for her to take his hand, as if it had never occurred to him she wouldn't. "I know that can't have been easy for you," he said, and his mouth tilted wryly. "For what it's worth, though…thank you for not making a scene."

Telling herself it would be pointless—and childish—to ignore his offer of help, she grudgingly put her hand in his. The familiar warmth and strength of it made her breathing catch. "Guess that makes us even," she said lightly as he pulled her easily to her feet.

"Not even close," he said softly, and instead of letting go of her hand, enclosed it in both of his and drew her closer.

She could have pulled away, of course she could have. Should have, no question about it. He would have released her at even the slightest sign of resistance, she knew that. Instead, she let herself be reeled in, all the time telling herself, *This is a mistake…you know it's a mistake…for God's sake, Samantha June, have good sense for a change!*

She did put her free hand flat against his chest, though, maintaining at least that much distance between them, and although she held her head high, she kept her eyes fixed on her captive hand and refused to meet his eyes.

The breeze from his exhaled breath tickled her temple. "I know I hurt you. God, I'm sorry. If I could go back and undo it, I would. But I can't, Sam. I can't."

Bitterly, she thought, *Oh? Which hurt are we talking about this time?*

She shrugged, drawing herself in around the misery inside her, hunkering down behind the questions she wasn't brave enough to ask. "I'm over that, too, okay?"

"I truly did think you were through with me, after that night in Georgetown." His eyes were sad, his smile crooked. "I was trying to move on. I thought…when I met Karen… But it was a mistake to expect someone else…" He paused for a breath, and when he went on his voice had filled with gravel. "We both knew the marriage was a mistake, Karen and I, almost immediately. We agreed the best thing would be to try and undo the damage as quickly as possible."

Oh—his marriage. That's what he's talking about, she thought dismally. And how odd she should feel so deflated, when only a day or two ago the subject had been sore as a toothache for her. She'd have put the day she'd heard the news about Cory's marriage right up there with the day she was told her daddy was dead, shot down in his fighter jet over Iraq, as one of the worst days of her life.

"Of course…" And even through her defenses, though she tried not to, she heard the regret and irony in his voice. "I know some things can't ever be undone."

"Hey," she said distantly as she turned away from him, "it's ancient history. Forget it. I have."

It surprised her to realize it, but it was true. She really was over it—or at least, the importance of it had been greatly diminished—dwarfed, in fact, by yesterday's shocking revelation that the man she'd loved and shared her body, mind and soul with for almost six years had a whole bunch of brothers and sisters he'd never told her about. She'd been trying ever since to get her mind around that, but the questions kept battering away at her like attacking Furies.

What does this say about our relationship? What does it say about you, Pearse?

She was no psychologist, and God knows, no expert on relationships, but she was pretty sure it must mean he didn't trust her enough to share his most basic self with her. Maybe it meant he was afraid or incapable of intimacy—the emotional kind, which even she knew was way more important than the physical, if a relationship was going to have a chance to survive the long haul.

So, what did that mean for her and Cory? His marriage—okay, that had been a mistake—a biggie, all right. A whopper.

But mistakes could be forgiven. But this… If Cory's failure to share something so important with her meant what she feared it did, then there was simply no hope for them. None at all.

It was only then, as the pain of that truth slammed into her, that she understood that until that moment, hope *had* been alive. Somewhere deep inside her, hidden, sure, but *there,* like a buried coal, warm, glowing…*alive.* She hadn't realized it was there until she'd felt it die, but now she grieved for the loss of it as she would for the death of a loved one.

"Sam…"

She felt his hands on her shoulders, the familiar and beloved fingers…so strong and yet so gentle…kneading the rock-hard muscles there in the way only he knew. She endured it for a long, aching moment, holding herself stiffly, jaws rigid, the pain in her throat so terrible she couldn't even swallow, then jerked her shoulders in a futile attempt to shake him off. "That's not gonna solve anything," she said in a slurred voice.

"Maybe not," he murmured, "but it doesn't hurt, does it?"

Doesn't hurt? Oh, God, you have no idea.

And she was being carried on the waves of that pain to a place, a time in her distant past…so long ago—ten years!—but it seemed like yesterday. Or…now, as if it was happening to her all over again, this very minute.

I'm standing in the middle of the tarmac, watching the plane that's bringing my dad home taxi toward me through the heat shimmer. To me, the plane seems to be floating, disconnected from the ground. And all around me are crowds of people, flags waving, a band playing, little children holding up signs that say Welcome Home Lt. Bauer and We Love You, Tristan.

They've put down a red carpet leading out to the plane, and people in dress uniforms plastered with medals, and others in business suits, famous people whose names I can't think of right now, are all out there shaking hands with someone I can't quite see because of all the people. Then—suddenly, Grampa Max is there, too, strong, proud, unshakeable Grampa Max—and he's grabbing hold of this tall, thin man in an aviator's flight suit, wrapping him in his arms and hugging him, and there are tears running down his face.

*Watching, I feel a bubble of laughter welling up inside me, and I know a sob is coming with it, and I press my hands against my mouth and I think—pray—*Oh please, oh please, God, don't let me cry. I don't want all these people to see me cry. Especially my dad. Please…

Then, just when I think for sure I'm not going to be able to keep myself from falling apart, I feel someone's arms around me. It's my mom, and I think how long it's been since I've felt her arms around me—I'm eighteen, after all, and in college; I'm not a little girl anymore. But, oh, how good it feels to have her hold me like this. She says my name…

"Sam…"

Sam. Not *Sammi June.* Because of course it was Cory's arms she felt around her now, not her mother's. The rest, though, was pretty much the same—the awful pressure of tears her pride wouldn't allow her to shed, and thinking how long it had been since she'd felt these arms around her, holding her like this…and how good, how unbearably good they felt. And just as she had on that day of her dad's homecoming, she allowed herself, just this once, to give in and accept the comfort offered.

Just this once, she told herself. *After all, what does it matter now?*

She turned in his embrace and with a sigh, slipped her arms into their special place, low around his waist. She felt the supple strength in his body, a sturdiness unexpected in one so slender…except to her. To her his body was just as she remembered it…so perfect for her, and so *right.* She lifted her face into the hollow of his neck and jaw and inhaled the warm familiar Cory smell, and…*oh, God,* she thought, *how I've missed this.* The sense of homecoming, of belonging, was a sweet and terrible joy.

For another moment or two his hands went on stroking up and down her back, kneading her shoulders in that knowing way he had. Then his breath sighed across her hair, and his arms came around her, wrapped around her like sheltering wings, like fortress walls keeping the world and all its doubts and fears away. He held her close, so close she felt the thumping of his heart against her own chest, but with restraint, too, so that she also felt the minute tremors quivering through his muscles.

"This isn't gonna solve anything," she whispered again.

But this time, instead of answering with words, his hand came to curve around the side of her neck, just below her jaw. Gently, he tilted her head back...raised her face to his...and kissed her.

It had been inevitable, of course, from the moment she'd taken the hand he'd offered. She supposed she'd known that, and had let it happen anyway, for no other reason than that, in the very depths of her being, she'd wanted it, and in her arrogance, believed she could handle whatever might come of it. Now, she knew how foolish she'd been. Because all at once she was eighteen again, crazy in love and filling up with that same terrible wanting she'd remembered—or dreamed—such a short while ago. She'd always been so certain, in her likes and dislikes, her wanting and not wanting. Now she was discovering how wrong she could be, how wrong she had been, because what she'd been so certain she didn't want, ever again, she now knew she'd been wanting with a deep-down yearning all along.

Tears squeezed between her eyelids as he kissed her; she tasted them on her lips, and knew he would, too, but suddenly she didn't mind. The salty-sweet wetness was like rain to her thirsty soul. With a shuddering laugh she opened herself to it, and parts of her that had been parched and barren for years sprang to joyous, pulsing life. She rubbed her hands over the front of his shirt, her skin hungry for the feel of his, and felt his hands grow urgent on her back, gentleness giving way to the restless jerkiness of passion. One quick tug and her shirt was free of her belt, and her skin silvered under his touch. She shuddered again, but with a whimper this time.

"Sam…" He whispered it deep in the kiss, his mouth changing shape against hers, his lips sliding over and between and around hers, slick with that sweet essence that was like a drug she couldn't ever get enough of. And it was both a question and a plea.

Hearing it, she felt something break apart inside her, the way the earth itself rips when the pressure of opposing forces inside it becomes too much to bear. With a wild little cry of anguish she tore her mouth from his and spun away from him, then stood stiffly with her back to him, shivering and hugging herself, trying desperately to hold the shattered pieces of herself together.

It seemed to her the room behind her had gone utterly still—though for all she could have heard above the storm within her, an army might have been marching through it. Her heartbeat was thunder in her ears, her breath like fitful gusts of wind. Tension seemed to crackle all around her as she braced herself, expecting, half dreading, half hoping for, the gentle weight of his hands on her shoulders.

But it didn't come. Instead, when he spoke his voice seemed to drift from far away. "What happened to us, Sam? How did we lose this? How did we let this get away?"

She turned slowly, carefully, keeping her arms wrapped protectively around herself. Cory was leaning, half sitting, on the windowsill, the way she'd been doing herself not so long ago. He wasn't looking at her. His eyes were closed, and he'd taken off his glasses and was scrubbing his face with both hands. For the first time she noticed how exhausted he looked, his eye sockets more shadowed than ever, cheeks gaunt, with sharp grooves etched from his nose to the corners of his mouth. She caught a breath and ruthlessly quelled a fierce and terrible yearning to go to him and smooth those hollows away with her hands.

"'This'…has never been our problem, Pearse," she said bitterly.

He lifted his head. This time the silence was all too real…the tension profound. Breathing and even heartbeats seemed to wait while he looked at her a long suspenseful time. And then he said softly, "No."

Sam let out a slow and weary breath. *So,* she thought. *We've finally done it. Both of us. Admitted we have "a problem." Wow.*

But she felt a small surge of hope, too, because wasn't recognizing the existence of a problem supposed to be the first step in solving it?

Then just as quickly she deflated, because she seriously doubted the "problem" she and Cory had in mind was the same one. He'd be thinking about her job, of course—her career. As far as he was concerned, that had always been the big thing between them, and according to Tony it was what had driven him to marry someone else. Okay, so fine. Just as well, she thought. At least reminding her of that fact had brought her mind back on course.

"What are we going to do about this, Sam?" It was his normal, quiet voice, and he was smiling at her now, his usual gentle smile.

She shrugged and unwrapped her arms from around her body, forcing rigid muscles to relax. She gave an offhand, one-shoulder shrug. "Nothing we can do, is there? Not right now. For *sure* not here. You—" and dear Lord, she'd *almost* said "we" "—have a job to do. Right?" Her lips twisted into something she hoped would resemble a smile. "How's that going, by the way? The interview?"

He let out a gusty breath and pushed himself away from the window. "We start this afternoon—after lunch—or dinner, or whatever. I have some prep work to do first, since all my questions—my research notes—were on my laptop. I've asked for some writing materials—I'm going to have to cobble something up in a hurry. That's where I'm going now, actually." He offered her a rueful smile, though his eyes remained shadowed and troubled. "I just stopped by to see how you were."

"So," said Sam, carefully ignoring the look in his eyes as she settled into the spot against the windowsill he'd just vacated, "I guess this means I'm going to be stuck here in this room for the rest of the day?"

He gave her an uncomfortable, almost embarrassed look, and ran a hand through his hair. "I'll see what I can do about that." A smile flickered briefly as he paused with one hand on the door latch. "Maybe I can tell al-Rami you're my secretary."

"Yeah," Sam said dryly, "that's just what I've always wanted to be. Somebody's secretary. Wahoo."

His smile steadied and grew tender. "*That's* the Sam I know," he said softly.

After he'd gone, she went on sitting at the windowsill for a long time, arms crisscrossing her body, one hand covering her mouth, eyes closed...rocking herself a little...too emotionally exhausted to cry, hurting too much to laugh.

"Mr. al-Rami, I have only a few more questions...." Cory leaned forward into the pool of light.

It was late afternoon, but here, deep in the ravine, twilight had already fallen. Lamps had been lit, lending a degree of warmth and conviviality to the setting that made it hard to remember, sometimes, that the man sitting across from him in the role of gracious host was the same one responsible for the deaths of hundreds, if not thousands, of people, and whose professed objective was the destruction of almost everything Cory loved and believed in.

"Of course," al-Rami said, with a magnanimous wave of a long, graceful hand.

Cory cleared his throat. On his left, he could hear the quiet click and whir of Tony's camera. He had to fight the urge to glance over at Sam, who'd been sitting silently on his right, every now and then taking a sip of tea or reaching to pluck a piece of fruit from the bowl in front of her. She hadn't said a word throughout the meal and the subsequent question-and-answer session, except to murmur an occasional "Thank you" when some new dish was placed in front of her, and al-Rami had treated her with the same courtesy he'd shown to Tony. Cory suspected the earlier display had been only a case of the terrorist leader demonstrating his absolute power and control, over both them and the situation. *This is my game, and you will play by my rules.*

Knowing how important it was at this juncture that he not waver or show weakness, he kept his eyes fixed on Fahad al-Rami's. "Sir, it is known that you are currently holding two hostages. A Canadian couple—" he made a point of glancing down at his notes, although the names were etched in his memory "—Esther and Harold Lundquist." He looked up, once more locking eyes with al-Rami. "Missionaries." He waited.

Al-Rami nodded, his expression unperturbed, even aloof. "That is true, yes. They are in my custody. I can assure you they have not been harmed, and are being well treated."

"Might I be allowed to see for myself that that is the case? A firsthand report from me would go a long way toward changing the perception most people have of you and your organization."

Al-Rami gave a slight shrug, picked up his teacup and sipped delicately before answering. "I wish I could accommodate your request, Mr. Pearson. Unfortunately, the Lundquists are not here at the present time. They are being kept at another location—as I said, safe and unharmed."

"These people are missionaries, Mr. al-Rami. They mean you and your followers no harm. What purpose—"

"On the contrary. They mean us great harm. They have attempted to corrupt the most sacred beliefs of our people." Al-Rami replaced the cup in its saucer with a sharp click.

Cory took a breath and tried a new tack. "Can you tell me when they will be released?"

"They will be released when the time is right, and under circumstances of *our* choosing." Al-Rami's tone was cold.

"Might I suggest," Cory said softly, leaning forward once more, "that *now* might be an advantageous time for you and your cause? Coupled with this interview, such a magnanimous gesture—"

He broke off, his breath catching as a series of sharp, rapid pops came from somewhere outside, not too far distant. Beside him he felt Sam jerk upright and go rigid, as if someone had jabbed her in the back with a poker.

Tony said, "Holy momma, what was *that?*"

Before Cory had a chance to reply, the room filled with men in camouflage. In an instant, it seemed, a phalanx of them had surrounded Fahad al-Rami and were helping him to rise. Others, with less consideration, grabbed Tony and Sam and jerked them to their feet; Cory heard Tony's protests as he tried frantically to snatch up his cameras. Then he, too, was being jerked upright. He just did manage to scoop up the tape recorder and stuff it into the front of his shirt before they were all hustled out onto the deck, down the swaying rattan stairway and into the depths of the ravine.

Chapter 8

All hell was breaking loose behind them. Shouts, small explosions and the crackle of gunfire chased them as they zigzagged through the jungle growth, stumbling and tripping over vines and rotting logs, trying to dodge the stinging slap of ferns and fronds and branches. Then came a flash, and almost immediately after that the *thump* of an explosion—and then quickly two more. From the indescribable but unmistakable sounds of destruction that followed the blasts, Cory felt certain the unique bamboo house in the ravine was no more.

In the confusion he'd lost track of Fahad al-Rami, though he assumed the terrorist leader must be somewhere in the tangle ahead of them, no doubt surrounded and protected by his special cadre of security forces. Only three or four of the guards had been left behind to shepherd the three "guests," and it was obvious the selected ones weren't happy about it. Every time Cory tried to pause to see where Sam and Tony were, he felt the impatient thump of a rifle barrel against his back, and heard the same guttural command repeated harshly over and over. He didn't have to understand Tagalog—or whatever dialect these people were speaking—to recognize *"Go, go, go!"* when he heard it. And go he did, with his head down, heart pumping, adrenaline squirting through his veins and his mind in useless turmoil.

He had no idea how long that headlong flight went on or how much territory they'd covered before he was ordered, with pushes and shoves and barked commands, to halt and crouch down in the dense undergrowth. Moments later, to his intense relief, Sam and Tony came crashing through the brush and dropped—or were pushed—down beside him. Tony's face was glistening with a mixture of sweat and blood from a scratch over one eye. Sam's face was unmarred but stony. The guards, meanwhile, had gone darting and leaping back the way they'd come and were hunkered down in cover a short distance away, rifles at the ready, avidly scanning the jungle for signs of pursuit.

As soon as he had his breath back, Cory rolled over, propped himself on his elbows and wheezed, "Everybody okay?"

He got all the reassurance he needed from Tony when the photographer began swearing as only he knew how. He left him muttering and fretting over his precious cameras and turned to Sam, who was sitting silently with her arms draped over her drawn-up knees, staring into the darkening canopy.

"Sam?"

She flashed him a glance that stung, and in a voice so low he could barely hear it, muttered, "Yeah, I'm fine." She turned her face away from him then, but not before he'd registered, with a small sense of shock, the fact that she was angry.

Angry? Why in the world would she be angry? He sat without moving, the question spinning in his brain. Fear he could have understood—not that he'd have expected it, this was Sam, after all—but...*rage?* It didn't make sense, but there it was: unless he was mistaken, Sam was about as furious as he'd ever seen her. And Sam—the Sam *he* knew—didn't *get* mad. Oh, she had a temper, for sure, but she'd almost never let herself show it. She cared too much about keeping her cool, keeping it together. She'd just about rather die than let anyone see her upset, angry, hurt or scared. He understood that part of her so well, maybe because she'd developed her armor the same way he had, as a fatherless child learning to survive among unsympathetic strangers. It was, he realized, one of the things that had drawn him to her from the beginning, that intuitive recognition of a kindred soul. He'd understood her, then, better than she'd understood herself.

He wondered when all that had changed. Because he sure couldn't say the same thing now.

Night fell with a crash, the way it does in the tropics. The guards returned from their reconnaissance, muttering amongst themselves, and the retreat through the jungle resumed, although in a somewhat more calm and orderly fashion than before.

It was the third night in a row of these moonlit treks, with only catnaps for sleep, but Sam was a long way from feeling tired. She was too angry to be tired.

Idiots!

The word had zapped through her mind when she'd heard the first spatter of gunfire, and it repeated there now like a drummer's cadence keeping time with her plodding, crashing footsteps. *Idiots—they were supposed to wait for my signal! Why didn't they wait?*

She'd given the message. She was certain it had been received and understood. *Stand by.*

Clearly, either the government forces hadn't gotten the second message—the one after *Target located*—or they'd ignored it. Either way, they'd jumped the gun and attacked al-Rami's hideout without waiting for her signal to move in. *What were they thinking? We could all have been killed!*

Even worse, Fahad al-Rami had escaped. The mission had failed. And all this—the risk of seeing Cory again, digging up old memories, stirring up so much pain—was for nothing.

In the singing, sweltering jungle night, she felt angry, and cold…and finally numb.

As nearly as Cory could tell, given the overcast skies, it was getting on towards noon when they came to the village. The smells of freshly turned earth and cooking fires assailed him the moment he emerged from the jungle into the open swath of cultivated fields, scents as rich and brown and mouthwatering as the aroma from a king's banquet table. And carried on the breeze from somewhere out of sight, sharp and heady as wine, came the unmistakable salt tang of the sea.

"Lord, I hope that's food I smell," Tony said plaintively, pausing beside him to dip his head and mop his face on the shoulder of his T-shirt. "I'm so hungry I could eat a bug. Better yet—a whole lotta bugs."

Cory grunted; his own stomach had been complaining loudly and painfully since before daybreak. Small wonder—they'd had nothing to eat or drink since the meal they'd shared with Fahad al-Rami the previous afternoon, other than some fruits they'd found growing wild in the jungle which Sam had assured him were safe to eat. He'd been hungry enough to take her word for that, but once again had been left to wonder where she'd come by such knowledge.

He looked over at her now, walking a little apart from everyone else, her gaze fixed straight ahead, her expression aloof and distant. "Any idea where we are?" he asked her in an undertone, with a wary glance at the nearest guard.

She looked up at the lowering clouds and shrugged. "We're near the ocean. Can't be absolutely sure, we've been doing quite a bit of circling and backtracking, but if I'm right, this would be the south side of the island."

He gave her a long, meaningful look. "That would put us only a few miles from where we left the plane."

"Yep." She aimed an almost undetectable nod toward the right. "Wind's coming from there, so I'm guessing that's where the water is. That puts the plane—" she tilted the nod back toward the left "—over thataway." She flashed him a stiff and humorless grin. "Just in case…"

Once again he didn't question her conclusions, but as he returned her smile he felt the same nagging sense of unease that had troubled him since they'd left the house in the ravine. Truth was, for the first time since he'd known her she was a stranger to him. He couldn't read this new Sam at all, and that bothered him. He'd always been able to tell when something was troubling her, and it had never taken much effort on his part to get her to spill what was on her mind. Which was so typical of Sam— didn't mind telling you about her feelings, even if she did hate showing them. But now he felt certain she was shielding herself, evading, deliberately keeping secrets from him, and it came as something of a surprise to him that he found that so disturbing, and even felt vaguely wounded, as if he'd had a door politely but firmly shut in his face.

The village was as tiny and primitive as the others they'd seen, no more than a cluster of houses tucked away on the far side of the cultivated fields, nestled between the base of a mountain and a wide gully that had been cut by a river on its winding way down—to the right, Sam had been correct on that score—to a small sea cove. There wasn't much water in the river now, this close to the end of the dry season, but when the monsoon rains began, Cory imagined it could become a raging torrent in a matter of minutes.

They crossed the gully on a swaying footbridge, their armed escort sandwiching them, two in front and two behind. As they made their way along a dusty road between haphazard clusters of houses, once again Cory saw few signs of life save for the usual placidly foraging chickens. But here, instead of a feeling of emptiness and abandonment, he had an uneasy sense of eyes watching avidly from shadowed doorways.

After passing through the village, the road narrowed to a footpath that zigzagged up a grassy slope to where a large house with a thatched roof perched, half-supported by pilings, on the side of the mountain. It had a large veranda that looked out over the village and cultivated fields, the fringe of jungle beyond, and probably even, off in the distance, a hazy glimpse of ocean.

A short distance away, to the right of the main house, Cory noted a smaller house sitting by itself in the shade of a large tree. He could just make out the figure of a man leaning against the wall in the shade on the near side of the house, cradling an automatic rifle in his arms.

He moved close to Sam and nudged her with his elbow, then nodded toward the smaller house. Without moving her lips she muttered, "I see it."

As they approached the big house, Fahad al-Rami stepped out from the shadowed doorway and moved to the edge of the veranda. He was dressed in a white robe now, with a colorful open vest over it, sandals on his feet and on his head an Indonesian-style cap similar to the one he'd been wearing before. Above the graying beard his cheekbones looked gaunt, and his eyes were sunk deep in shadowed sockets.

"Now you see what I and my people must endure," he said, his voice cold and austere, looking down upon them as he might an invasion of cockroaches. Al-Rami almost spat words as he continued, "Persecution by government forces, aided by your American army rangers, is constant and unrelenting. Every day my people mourn the slaughter of our innocents—old people, women and children. Where are your highly touted ideals? Your concern for human rights? Your so-called Geneva Convention? Pah—I would be entirely justified in holding you three as my prisoners—hostages, if you wish—to secure freedom for my people and the withdrawal of all invaders from our lands."

He made an angry gesture with his hand as he turned, and said on a regretful exhalation, "But…I have given my word and I will honor it. Again, I offer you the hospitality of my house. Please—come. Rest and refresh yourselves. Food is being prepared for you. Tomorrow my men will return you safely to your plane." With that, he stepped back through the doorway and disappeared inside the house.

"Well," Tony said brightly, looking around at his companions, "*I* feel all warm and fuzzy—how 'bout you guys?"

Cory let out the breath he'd been holding. "We should probably consider ourselves lucky," he said dryly. *Lucky we're here, and not in that other house—the one with the armed guard.*

He was just glad he'd gotten the interview pretty much wrapped. Not that he'd wouldn't have liked to spend more time with his subject, maybe get him to let his guard down and open up a little, maybe get some personal stuff. But it looked as though what he already had on tape and in his notes—and Tony's photos, of course—was going to have to do, and he was grateful enough for that.

Yeah, and all I have to do is get the material—and us—safely out of this place. When I've done that, maybe I'll be able to breathe again.

"Might not be the best time to bring up those other hostages again, either," Sam said in an expressionless undertone as they mounted wooden steps to the veranda.

Cory wanted to glance at her to see if she was needling him, but he didn't, and made do with a noncommittal snort instead. *Yeah, breathe again,* he told himself. *And think about other things.*

Once again Sam was taken to a room segregated from the men—not that she minded; the privacy was welcome, and she'd reconciled herself to these people's attitude toward women. It was just that—and oh, how she hated to admit it—she was beginning to feel annoying twinges of anxiety whenever she had to let Cory out of her sight.

Childish. The hated word whispered derisively in the back corners of her mind. *Maybe he was right about you, Sammi June.*

Except she knew he wasn't. Never had been, really, and especially not now. It wasn't for herself she felt anxious, but for him—for Cory. For Tony, too, of course, but Cory was…well. *Face it, Samantha June, you still love him.* Okay, she did—but even if that wasn't true, she'd have plenty of cause to be worried about two civilians running around in the middle of a firefight, getting caught in the crossfire. Not that both Cory and Tony weren't experienced when it came to being in battle zones; they were war reporters, after all. But they hadn't had the training she'd had. Not by a long shot. *And if anything happens to him out here…how will I live with that?*

Anyway, for better or worse she was alone again, in a room that looked less like something out of the Arabian Nights and more like your basic primitive jungle hooch, with a sleeping mat on the floor and a lashed-bamboo table and chair shoved against the wall under an open and unscreened window. A patterned curtain drawn across one end of the room hid the pre-indoor-plumbing equivalent of a private bathroom: a basin of water sitting on a low bamboo bench, and on the floor, an empty pail. There were towels on the bench, too, and a folded garment that turned out to be a robe, the wraparound kind that closes with a belt tie, made of a heavy white cotton material that reminded her of martial arts uniforms.

She stripped and made use of both the basin and the bucket, then dried herself and put on the robe. It felt stiff and unforgiving against her skin, and chafed her unprotected nipples. When, she wondered, had they become so sensitive? The time of the month, maybe? Hormones, or her mind wandering where it had no business being, poking into long-buried memories and re-awakening old yearnings?

She'd just finished folding her dusty sweat- and grass-stained clothing into an untidy pile and was considering whether to ask someone for enough water to rinse them out with, when there came a discreet knock on the door. She opened it to find a young girl of maybe twelve or thirteen, dressed in a patterned wrap skirt and long-sleeved tunic, with her head covered by a scarf and a single long braid hanging down her back. She was holding a tray on which were several covered dishes and the usual teapot, bowls and eating utensils. With eyes carefully averted, she entered, crossed the room to the table and set the tray down, then turned and, before Sam could even thank her, bent and scooped up the pile of dirty clothes, gave a quick little bow and scurried out, all without saying a word.

"Huh—maid service," Sam said aloud to herself as she went to close the door. Then she had to use all the self-control she had in her to keep from falling on the food tray like a starving wolf.

She felt much better after she'd eaten all she could possibly hold of the customary offering of rice and vegetables and fruit, washed down with several cups of tea. Well enough that her mind could begin functioning again on more than just the most prim-itive level.

She wondered if Cory and Tony had been given trays in their room—rooms?—or whether they'd been invited to dine again with their infamous host, Fahad al-Rami. She wondered if Cory would dare to ask again about the hostages—the Lundquists. She wondered whether it really was the Lundquists in that house the soldier was guarding.

She wondered if it was time to send another target-located sig-nal. And if she did, whether this time the government forces would obey her order to stand by.

Ripples of anger coursed through her when she thought about

what had *almost* happened back at the house in the ravine. *If it hadn't been for Fahad al-Rami's sentries and a well-planned escape route, we might all be dead right now. Those idiots!*

No. She wouldn't send the signal, not yet. Cory and Tony were exhausted—so was she, though she hated to admit it. Tomorrow would be soon enough, after they'd all had a chance to rest. After they'd had a chance to find out whether the hostages were in that smaller house, and whether there was any chance at all Fahad al-Rami might be convinced to turn them over. Tomorrow would be soon enough to risk another government attack and headlong flight for their lives.

Though it was only midafternoon, a full stomach, clean clothes and sleep deprivation were beginning to have a predictable effect on her. The sleeping mat was looking a lot less austere—downright seductive, in fact. And she thought, Well, shoot, why not? Nothing was likely to happen today anyway, and she wasn't going anywhere dressed in a damn bathrobe, so she might as well nap.

She lay down, expecting to fall asleep instantly, thinking as tired as she was, she ought to be able to sleep anywhere, no matter what—even on the floor. But instead she found that, now that she was lying down *trying* to sleep, she no longer felt sleepy at all. Her body felt hot and tense; her skin crawled and prickled, as though all her nerve endings had gone on full battle alert and, like nervous sentries, were overreacting to the slightest sensation. She felt her heart beating in remote parts of her body, and heard her blood whooshing through the arteries in her head. Her mind followed the path of each breath, through her nostrils, down into her lungs and back again; she was aware of every molecule of moisture that welled up through her pores.

The chafe of clothing was intolerable; she longed to throw off the stiff cotton robe and lie naked with only the caress of warm, humid air on her body…but there was no lock on her door and what if someone came in and found her like that? And anyway it wouldn't be enough, because part of her would still be touching the mat. How wonderful it would be, she thought, to be weightless, if only for this moment...to float suspended, rocked by a gentle sea...and the cool kiss of water on her skin. She longed for...yearned for...

She sat up suddenly, then collapsed back onto the mat, arms over her eyes, writhing in chagrin. *Oh, hell,* she thought, *I know what this is. It's* him *I want. The caress I'm longing for...the kiss...it's Cory's.*

It had been so many years since she'd felt like this, but she remembered it now—it all came back to her. The frustration...the yearning...the bewilderment. *I want him so much...I know he wants me, too...why won't he make love to me?* And then the anger, too. *I'm eighteen, damn it—a grown woman. Plenty old enough to know what I want!*

Old enough, yes, but without the experience and confidence to take the initiative, to go after what she wanted. *What if I fail? What if he turns me down?* Her pride wouldn't let her take that chance.

Until the day something awoke inside her—a voice scolding, *Samantha June, your mama didn't raise you to be a coward! If you want the man bad enough, you just might have to sacrifice a little pride.*

She remembered it so well. It had been November, the weekend of her nineteenth birthday, her first birthday since her dad had come back from the dead. Her birthday was on Friday, and that afternoon Cory had driven over from Atlanta to pick her up from school and take her to Grandma's house, where her parents were staying while their new house was being built over near Augusta. There'd been a huge party—naturally all the aunts and uncles and cousins and in-laws had been there, because any excuse for a family get-together, right? It had been great, though, having both her dad and Cory there, one of the happiest days she could remember in a long, long time.

The only cloud in Sammi June's sky that day had been the knowledge that it was Cory's last weekend in Atlanta. On Sunday he was catching a plane to New York, and after that he'd be going off on assignment, back to the Middle East—and hadn't he had enough of that place? She knew it was his job to be where the danger was, but she couldn't shake the feeling that something terrible might happen to him over there, and if it did, she was never going to see him again. Never have a chance to know what it would be like to make love with him.

Or maybe that was just an excuse because she'd been wanting him to make love to her for months, and she was nineteen, now, and tired of waiting.

Whatever the reason, on Saturday afternoon when Cory was dropping her off at her dorm, she asked him to wait for her while she took her birthday loot up to her room, because, she said, she had a surprise for him. And boy, did she. When she came back downstairs she was wearing a little black dress that hit her about eight inches above her knees, and high heels made mostly of see-through plastic, and she'd put her hair up on top of her head. She even had on earrings, which she *never* wore. She'd spent most of the birthday money she hadn't even gotten yet on that outfit, but it had been worth it, because the look on Cory's face when he saw her in it was priceless.

She'd brought her soccer sports bag with her—which didn't exactly go with her outfit, but it was all she had to put her overnight stuff in—and she told Cory, since it was his last night in Georgia for a while, she wanted to take him out and "do Atlanta."

He'd said, "I didn't know there was anything *to* do in Atlanta." And she'd replied, with a sexy and wicked smile, "Have you ever been to Underground Atlanta?"

So they'd joined the Saturday-night crowds strolling the underground mall, and they'd eaten dinner and danced to live music, and Sam was careful not to drink anything except diet soda because she didn't want Cory to think she was doing this just because she was drunk.

By the time they headed back to Cory's apartment—the apartment CNN let him use whenever he was in town—her feet were killing her, and she'd taken off her high heels and was carrying them in her hand. Her heart was thumping and butterflies were fluttering around in her stomach as she rode up in the elevator beside Cory, his arm just brushing hers and her whole body vibrating nervously inside that little black dress.

The elevator doors opened, and she could hear laughter and music, with a thumping bass that crawled through the floors and walls and went in through the soles of her bare feet and joined up with the rhythms of her own pulse beat. Evidently, someone a couple of doors down the hall was having one hell of a party.

Cory had apologized for the noise while he unlocked the door and showed her inside the apartment. Then he'd closed the door, shutting out most of the racket—all but that bass. He turned back to her, and she could see it in his eyes—she just *knew* what he was thinking. And before he could even *suggest* making up that couch for himself to sleep on, she dropped her sexy shoes and her soccer bag on the floor and stepped up to him and laced her fingers behind his neck.

"Actually, the noise is good," she'd murmured, her lips so close to his they tingled. "It makes a good cover."

"Mmm…cover…for what?" His voice had sounded faint and shaken—and she knew that he knew. And she'd felt something inside herself grow strong and sure.

From that well of confidence a laugh bubbled up, one she'd never heard from herself before—husky and deep-throated…a woman's laugh. "What do you think?" she'd said, and then she'd kissed him.

She'd kissed him until she'd felt his muscles begin to quiver and his breathing quicken, and his hands slip around her waist as though they didn't have the will to do otherwise. Then, still kissing him, she took her hands from around his neck and reached behind her and pulled the zipper on the little black dress all the way down. The dress slithered to the floor, and she was wearing only a very tiny pair of black lace panties.

"My God…Sam…" His voice had sounded strangled. "Are you sure—"

She'd silenced him with a finger across his lips. "Shut up, Pearse," she'd said fiercely. "Don't make me have to kill you."

He'd chuckled then, the most beautiful sound she'd ever heard. "Not a chance," he'd growled. And after that there was no more talking.

He kisses me and I know it's going to be all right, I can leave it to him, now, and a good thing, too, because this is about as far as my vast knowledge and experience can take me. I'm shaking, appalled and amazed at this thing I've done, the tremendous risk I've taken. But proud, too, and glad, and so very, very relieved…

He kisses me and his hands are on my body, so passionate and sure, touching me in ways he never has before, but so gently, too, and his tenderness tells me as nothing else could that this is important to him, as important and momentous and miraculous and terrifying as it is to me. And I understand, finally, that the reason he hasn't made love to me before is only because he loves me. I understand that by waiting for me to come to him, without pressure or hesitation, he has given me the most amazing gift, and my heart fills with so much love it overwhelms me and tears rush into my eyes before I can stop them. This is a very special man, I tell myself, awed. An incredible, wonderful, amazing man…and he is mine.

He kisses me, and I him, and my body shudders with joy and awe and wonder and fear, all of those, but at the same time I feel safe and cared for, and suddenly this—everything—every part of him seems so precious to me, I feel a terrible stab of panic at the thought of ever losing it. I rub my face against him and breathe him in, and I love the way he smells...run my hands over his body and tangle my legs with his, and I love the silky slide of his skin on mine...I wrap my arms around him and feel his body's weight and warmth embrace me, and I love the thump of his heart against my breasts, and the quiver of his muscles, and the strong, solid feel of his bones. And I know that I can trust this man absolutely and without reservation, and that I always will.

I hear the belly-deep growl of his voice against my ear: "Sam..." Just that, and it's a poem, a sonnet, a hymn, a prayer and a question.

I answer with only one word: "Yes..."

Cory woke to the crash of thunder. He lay for a moment, jangled and clammy, haunted by dreams already slipping beyond recall, the menacing shouts and thumps and bangs of the dreams so rapidly overtaken and usurped by the cracks and crashes outside his open window he forgot they'd ever been at all. Then, because they were sometimes in his dreams as well, he thought, *Explosions! Mortar rounds! Incoming!* But in the next instant the room lit with flickering blue-white light, and the crack and rolling rumble that followed a moment later sent a new fear racing through him like a cold wind. *Monsoon.*

It had been his greatest fear—hard to remember that, now— that the rains would come before he was able to complete the interview with Fahad al-Rami and get the hostages safely away and off the island. Discovering that Sam—his Samantha—was the person whose responsibility it would be to get them off the island safely had only deepened his sense of dread. Not that he'd ever doubted her ability to do so; it just made the stakes, in case anything did go wrong, that much higher. Now, though, as a wild rushing sound filled the night, he felt a strange, almost fatalistic sense of calm. That was the thing about weather, he thought— there wasn't a thing anyone could do about it. Whatever disasters it brought simply had to be dealt with.

He lay with his eyes closed, listening to it, one forearm across his brow, the thump of his own pulse and the roar of the rain filling his ears, drowning all other sounds, even Tony's snores from the other side of the room. So it was that he never heard the creak of the opening door…the soft brush of bare feet crossing the wood plank floor.

Chapter 9

In the darkness and heat and humidity of the night he hadn't felt her warmth or sensed her presence. The only warning he had came with the rasp of coarse cotton fabric against his side. Something brushed across his face, and instinctively he shot out a hand and his fingers closed around a wrist, one with strong and sturdy bones, but slender nonetheless. A woman's wrist.

He heard the sharp hiss of indrawn breath, then a husky gurgle of laughter and a whispered, "Nothing wrong with your reflexes, Pearse."

"Sam." His heart was knocking so hard against his ribs he wondered it didn't do itself damage, but he sought to keep his voice calm. "Don't tell me you're afraid of a little storm."

Her snort blew a puff of warmth across his cheek. "You know me better'n that—I'm a Georgia girl." He felt her settle herself along his side, and her murmured drawl was smug. "Just thought…be a shame to waste all this noise. Makes a good cover…"

His mind lurched, spilling a memory from his distant past. He groped for it, his heart racing, his skin rippling where she touched him. "Cover?" he said weakly. "For what?"

Her hand skimmed lightly across his chest. "What do you think?" she replied, and her voice was not quite steady.

"My God, Sam…" The powerful sense of déjà vu made him wonder if this was real, or if he could possibly still be asleep… dreaming. "Are you sure?"

He heard a husky sound that might have been laughter. "Shut up, Pearse, don't make me have to kill you," she said fiercely, and the memory tumbled into his mind and unfurled in full light and living color.

No longer in doubt, he growled, "Not a chance," and raised himself to meet her.

The kiss was fierce and wild, the clash of two hungry and frustrated souls—not like his memory of that first sweet, wondering time, when they'd touched each other with such awe, lost in a daze of happiness, like children discovering the gift of their dreams on Christmas morning.

And yet…there was something of the same feeling inside him…a remembered sense of amazement and disbelief, almost, that such a miracle should have been granted to him. Back then, the miracle was that this incredible woman had chosen to give herself to *him,* when he'd never dared to imagine such a possibility for himself—had certainly never looked for it, and had in fact spent his adult life to that point insulating himself against the likelihood that it might happen to him.

But *now*… Now, it seemed lightning had struck him again, because the woman he thought he'd lost forever was back in his life, and inexplicably had once again chosen to give herself to him. For reasons he couldn't begin to fathom, he was being granted a second chance. If only *this* time he could figure out how to get it right.

"You're naked," she whispered, pulling back a little as she

combed her fingers down his chest, grazing his skin with her nails so that he rippled inside where she'd touched him, like water when the wind passes over it.

"And you're not," he whispered back, voice choppy with his fractured breath.

"No problem." He felt a rasp of heavy fabric and a flurry of humid air, and then her warmth and softness covering him from chest to thighs, and his body was remembering her contours, their two bodies melding with the ease and gladness of two old friends meeting again after far too many years.

"Aren't you afraid someone might see you?" he asked with a bump and a smile in his voice as he let his hands follow their well-remembered path over the dip of her waist…the swell of her bottom. Because he already knew the answer, even before he felt her jerk back like an affronted cat. *Afraid? Not my Sam. Fearless Sam!*

"Who's going to see us—Tony?" she scoffed. "You said it— he sleeps through everything. Besides—it's pitch-dark in—" And she gasped as, with magnificent timing, the room lit up with blue-white light and turned her lovely body to silver.

It looked, he thought, as though it should be hard and cold to the touch, like an elegant sculpture in marble or alabaster, but instead she was all firm and giving softness and a fierce, vibrant heat that radiated from somewhere inside her and reached deep into his very core.

In the flickering light her face seemed to come down to his bit by bit, in little jerks and starts that matched the uneven rhythms of his heart, and the rocky rumble of the thunder outside was a growling he felt deep in his chest and belly. Too impatient to wait for her to come to him, he lifted his head and found her mouth, then gasped as passions ignited inside him with a power that threatened to tear him apart. And somewhere in the chaos of his mind a thought flashed clear:

What made me think anyone could take the place of this

woman in my life? This *woman—Samantha—is the only one...
the* only *one...for me.*

He held her as tightly as he dared, quaking with the violence
of his emotions, and felt her legs align and twine themselves with
his, and her body flow up and over his like liquid fire. Then, with
one strong and joyful surge he rolled her under him, and when
he entered her, he felt like a lost traveler coming home.

He heard her sharp cry, quickly stifled, and then her body
shook beneath him and he realized she was laughing, that broken little chuckle of sheer relief and gladness. Tenderly, he lowered his mouth to hers again and tasted the salty-sweetness of
tears.

But when, overwhelmed, he pulled back a little with her name
on his lips, she made a fierce growling sound and surged upward
and claimed his mouth again with what seemed a terrible urgency. And he knew at once, as he'd always known in the old
times, what she wanted to tell him.

*Don't say a word, Pearse. Don't talk, don't think, not about
the past, or what happens tomorrow...just make love to me now.*

So that's what he did. And there was a sweet and desperate
joy to their loving he knew he was going to remember for the
rest of his life.

Sam slipped away from him sometime before dawn, in a silence that told him more than words that she was determined to
make what had just happened between them an anomaly, an isolated incident under special circumstances, like a wartime one-
night stand. There must be no word spoken of this tomorrow, no
acknowledging glances, no remembering blushes, and above
all, no expectations.

Cory let out a careful breath and smiled to himself in the darkness.

Think again, Sam.

He awoke to a gray, dripping morning and a state of mind that
could best be described as chaotic. The rainy season had indeed

begun. Outside the unshuttered window, clouds lay low on the mountaintops and instead of feeling weighed down by humidity, the air was lively with the sounds of water on the move— plops and whispers as it dripped from leaves and the thatched roofs of houses, and the muted and distant roar of runoff racing down the river's course, past the village and down to the sea. And within Cory there was a similar restlessness, an urgent desire to be somewhere else, an itchy sense of things not done, missions not yet accomplished.

For starters, he had yet to learn the whereabouts of the missionary couple held hostage for nearly a year. And he had still to get himself and his crew, along with the material gathered from the interview with Fahad al-Rami—and, he hoped, Harold and Esther Lundquist—back to the plane and safely off the island. And although he couldn't afford to forget, ignore or minimize the danger they were all in, at the same time he couldn't deny the small glowing core of hope and optimism hidden away deep in his heart this morning like a secret treasure, and the name that repeated in his mind like a phrase from a well-loved song.

Samantha...

Of course, he knew last night hadn't really changed anything, and that he and Sam still had big problems to work out, issues to deal with before there could be any real hope for them of a future together. Which was all the more reason why he was eager to put this assignment behind him, so he could concentrate on what he was beginning to realize might just be the most important mission of his life: winning back Sam.

To that end, his first priority this morning would have to be the Lundquists. Like it or not, he was going to have to broach that touchy subject with an already ticked-off terrorist named Fahad al-Rami.

He dragged himself up off of his sleeping mat and stretched away some of the inevitable stiffness—and a contradictory and slightly guilty sense of satisfaction and well-being—then dressed in his own clothes. He'd found them along with Tony's, now clean and smelling strongly of lye and woodsmoke, lying folded and neatly stacked beside two pairs of mud-free boots just outside the door of their room. He fidgeted restlessly while he waited for Tony to get himself up and dressed, and was about to go in search of food and al-Rami—in whatever order he found them—when there was an imperative knock on the door. It was one of the guards, of course, summoning them at the order of their leader.

He and Tony were ushered, in the usual preemptory way, through the quiet house and out onto the veranda, where they found Fahad al-Rami seated at a small rattan table, a basket of fruit and the inevitable teapot arrayed in front of him. Sam joined them there a moment later, also dressed in her own clothes and looking wide awake and fully alert. Her hair was wet and beginning to curl in little dark commas on her forehead and behind her ears, and at the sight of her flushed cheeks and long, moisture-glazed throat, Cory felt juices pool at the back of his mouth, like a hungry man smelling good things to eat.

As he'd known she would, she took great care to avoid meeting his eyes.

Al-Rami waved them to the empty chairs that had been set around the table. When they were seated, he made casual morning small talk while he offered refreshment and served tea all around, inquiring like any good host as to the comfort of their quarters and the quality of their night's sleep.

And even while he cringed inwardly with his delicious and secret guilt—and wondered whether Sam might be doing the same—Cory couldn't help but marvel at the incongruity of the little scene: A man with so much blood on his hands—some would say an evil man, a monster, even—prim as an English spinster, calmly pouring out tea.

After an interval filled with chitchat that, given the circumstances, must to a casual observer have seemed downright absurd, Cory put down his cup, pushed it away and leaned forward, clearing his throat. "Sheik al-Rami," he began, the title of respect coming easily to his lips, though he noted Sam's small start— of objection, he wondered, or surprise? "Forgive me for intro- ducing a serious subject into such a pleasant and congenial morning, but as I mentioned before, I am extremely concerned about the couple you are holding—"

Al-Rami cut him off with an imperious wave of his hand. "You refer, of course, to the so-called missionaries, spreaders of your Western propaganda—the Lundquists. I have given a great deal of thought to your...suggestion." He picked up his teacup, eyes hooded, expression aloof. "I'm afraid what you are asking me to do—" And then he paused with the cup halfway to his lips, as if thinking about what he would say next.

Cory waited for him to go on, as did everyone else at the table. But al-Rami didn't continue, and an instant later, in that listen- ing silence, Cory understood why. The terrorist leader, too, was listening, to a faint and distant sound...coming steadily closer.

Next to him, Sam whispered, "Choppers," on the gust of an exhalation. As she pushed herself away from the table Cory thought he heard her swear violently under her breath, and mut- ter, "Not again, *damn* you..."

On his other side, Tony was hurriedly draping himself with his bags and cameras, all the while blaspheming as only he could. Meanwhile Cory, though aware that al-Rami had placed his cup carefully in its saucer and was rising to his feet, kept his eyes fixed on the village, where people were erupting from the thatched-roofed houses like ants from a disturbed nest. He heard shouts coming from that direction, and the crackle of gunfire. Then...the steady thump of chopper rotors as two helicopter gunships lifted above the distant treetops. Across the cultivated fields, men began to emerge from the cover of the jungle.

Fahad al-Rami's deep-set eyes swept over the three still seated at the table, lashing them with a cold black rage. Cory was sure the hatred in those eyes would haunt his nightmares in the days and weeks to come. Then al-Rami whirled, and in two long strides, crossed the veranda and vanished into the house.

"He's probably got an escape route out the back." Sam's voice was low and urgent, more compelling than a shout. The pops and crackles of gunfire seemed closer already; some of al-Rami's men were working their way up the slope, turning now and then to fire back on the advancing government forces. Small explosions had begun to blossom in the road leading to the village. Near the river a thatched roof erupted in flames.

"Come on, let's go—quick—before we lose him." Sam was already on her feet, lunging for the doorway. Tony was right behind her—though naturally he had to pause first to aim his camera and click away at the chaos breaking out below.

"Wait—" Cory caught Sam's arm, stopping her in midstride. "What if they're in there?" His voice was an urgent rasp as he jerked his head toward the small house perched on its stubby stilts fifty yards away across the hillside. The guard they'd seen yesterday was nowhere in sight. "The Lundquists—we can't just leave them there. They could be hit—killed."

She gave him a long, furious glare, then abruptly nodded. "Okay, dammit—you're right." She pivoted, and instead of ducking into the house, headed for the far end of the veranda.

Once again Cory caught her arm. "Wait—it's too dangerous. You guys stay here. Let me go. If they're in there, I'll—"

"Like *hell* you will," Sam snapped, jerking herself free of his grasp. "What if they need help?" And she was already jumping down off of the veranda, her voice bumpy and breathless as she landed in a crouch on the wet grass. She paused to glare up at him. "What if they can't walk?"

"Fine—we'll all go," Cory grunted as he dropped down beside her, knowing it was no use arguing with her anyway. He looked up at Tony. "Unless you'd rather stay—"

Tony peered down at him as if he'd lost his mind. "Are you

kiddin' me, man? Here—hold this…" He handed down his camera, then lowered himself carefully over the side of the veranda, corralling his assortment of bags with one hand. He landed awkwardly, but was grinning as he reclaimed his camera. "You think I'm gonna miss a possible 'Dr. Livingston, I presume?' moment? What kind of photojournalist you think I am? Come on, man. I'm thinkin' Pulitzer, here."

"Think about staying alive," Sam snapped. "Keep your head down and run like hell—zigzag! Okay, come on—let's go, go *go!*"

And she was off, running like a flushed rabbit, leaping and dodging in an erratic course across the slope toward the little house under the tree. There was nothing for Cory to do but follow her, while trying his best not to think about the thump of explosions and the pop-pop-pop of automatic weapons' fire all around him. Trying not to think about bullets tearing into the soft and lovely body he still carried in his memory the way he'd seen it last: lit by a flash of lightning to the pristine whiteness of marble.

Then they were there, all three of them, breathing hard and taking stock, backs flattened against the same wall where yesterday they'd seen the bored guard lounging in the meager midday shade.

"Everybody okay?" Sam asked. Barely waiting for two confirming grunts, she spun away again, disappearing around the uphill corner of the house. Cory followed, and found her crouched beside a narrow door. She looked up at him and nodded. He reached across her head to pound on the door with his fist, at the same time shouting, "Hello! Is anybody in there?"

He paused to listen, but the explosions and gunfire were almost continuous now, and he couldn't be sure…

"I think I heard voices," Sam said in a low, tense voice. She straightened up and moved aside while Cory tried the door.

He wasn't surprised to find it locked. He knocked again, then said tersely, "We'll have to kick it down."

Sam gave him a sardonic look. "You ever tried doing that? Believe me, it's not as easy as they make it look on TV."

"You got a better idea?"

"No, dammit."

"Okay," said Cory, glancing over at her, "how 'bout we do it together—the two of us? You're the athlete—your legs are probably stronger than mine anyway."

"Okay." She drew herself up tall beside him and threw him a grin, eyes bright with challenge. "On three—my count. One... two...*three!*"

The impact hurt in every bone and joint in his body. It jarred his molars together and made his eyeballs vibrate in their sockets. But when he was able to focus again, he saw the door hanging crooked on its hinges, the screws having come loose from the half-rotten frame. With a great surge of triumph, he shoved the door aside with his shoulder and stepped into the tiny house, his heart pounding now with dread at what he might see.

The single room was dim, but in the rectangle of light streaming past the broken door he could see two people kneeling motionless on a mat made of thatching. They appeared to be middle-aged, a man and a woman, both extremely thin and dressed in almost identical ragged dungarees and T-shirts. The woman's hair was mostly gray—perhaps it had once been blond—and hung past her haggard face in two thin braids. The man looked as if he had once been strong and robust, with a tall frame and sturdy bones. Now his shoulders were stooped, and his gray hair, thinned to almost nothing on top, had been pulled into a scraggly ponytail. His full beard was scraggly, too, and more white than gray. The two knelt facing each other, hands tightly clasped between them, heads bowed...nearly touching...eyes closed, lips moving. Praying.

Something lurched inside Cory's chest. As he moved toward

the couple, still huddled on their mat of rushes, he could hear Tony's camera clicking and whirring behind him, and was aware that Sam had pushed past them both and had gone to peer out the single tiny window that overlooked the valley.

"Mr. and Mrs. Lundquist?" he said huskily, his chest so tight he could hardly speak.

Two pairs of eyes flew open and two faces swiveled toward him…wide eyes in bewildered faces. They stared at him like people who'd been roughly awakened from a sound sleep.

Cory dropped down on one knee beside them, heart pounding. "Are you…Harold and Esther Lundquist?"

"Oh…my goodness," the woman said, and her voice was faint but musical. "You're real. I was sure I must be dreaming…"

"Praise God…" It sighed from the man's lips like a breath of wind.

"Are you okay? Can you walk?" Cory spoke to them rapidly, urgently, touching each one on the arm, half-afraid they might break apart when he did that, they seemed so frail and fragile. "We need to get you out of here. The village is about to be overrun. By government forces, but I'm afraid right now they're in a shoot-first-and-ask-questions-later mode. Do you think you can—"

"Yes, yes—of course." Harold Lundquist lurched to his feet and helped his wife up. He stood staring at Cory, still clutching his wife's hand and swaying slightly, stooped over like an old, old man. "But…" he said in a puzzled voice, "who *are* you?"

"They're Americans, Hal." Esther Lundquist's weathered face was beatific, wreathed in joy.

"Yes, but…surely not…military?" Her husband threw a doubtful glance at Sam, who was still standing vigil at the window in what struck Cory at that moment as a decidedly military manner, even though, oddly, her hair shone like an angel's halo in the light.

"We're journalists," he explained, nodding toward Tony. "Sam over there's our pilot. We came to do an interview with al-Rami. This is the second time he's come under attack since we've been here."

"Yes, that does happen quite a lot," Esther said softly.

"The first time they hustled us away under guard, but I guess this time they must have had other things on their minds. Anyway, we seem to be pretty much on our own. So, if you're—"

"I hate to break up this tea party," Sam broke in, in a hard, brittle voice as she turned away from the window, "but if we're going to get out of here, it'd better be *now*." As if to punctuate that, something—a shell? a grenade?—exploded close by, bringing a rain of debris pattering down from the thatch overhead.

Harold jerked as if the explosion had jump-started his engine. Muttering breathlessly, "Oh—certainly—yes, of course…" he bent and scooped up a small bundle wrapped in what appeared to be large leaves and stuffed it into a metal pot with a wire handle. Tied to the handle was a section of rope, which he looped over his shoulder and around his neck, the same way Tony carried his camera bags. Esther, meanwhile, was doing the same thing, in nearly perfect concert with her husband and with an efficiency that suggested a routine they'd both practiced many times before. In seconds, both Lundquists had slipped into sandals that had been neatly arranged on the floor near the mat of thatching, and were following Sam and Tony outside past the precariously leaning door.

Cory joined them just as Harold reached out with one long spiderlike arm and caught hold of Sam's shoulder. "Perhaps you'd better let us go first," he said in his breathless way.

His wife was nodding eagerly. "Yes—we know where the booby traps are, you see."

"Booby traps!"

"They have all their hideouts ringed with them," Harold explained.

"But," Esther chimed in, the lines on her face deepening with her smile, "we've been in and out so many times, we're quite familiar with the safe route—aren't we, Hal?"

"Well, yes," Hal said, looking thoughtful, "unless they've changed something since the last time."

"Uh…guys?" Sam said, as gunfire crackled and bullets spattered into the banana trees nearby.

"Well, then," said Esther as she took her husband's hand, "we'll just have to let the good Lord guide our footsteps, won't we?" And they beamed at each other as they set off through the chaos of battle, like children on an outing.

"Do you believe these two?" Sam's voice was bumpy as she ran. "What do they think this is, a Sunday-school picnic?"

"They've survived this for nearly a year," Cory reminded her. "Must have *something* going for them."

"You know what they say," Tony said, panting. "Who is it the Lord's supposed to look after? Fools, drunks and little children?"

"Yeah?" Cory managed to gasp. "Which one do you think *they* are?"

"Or…angels. Okay, yeah, maybe it's angels. Drunks, fools and—"

"Will you two shut up?" Sam yelled. "At least 'til we're through bein' shot at?"

Cory could see her point, since bullets were even then zapping into foliage and thumping into tree trunks not all that far away. Not to mention, there were those booby traps. For the next several minutes he concentrated on keeping his head down and following in the exact footsteps of the poor helpless hostages he'd just rescued.

Sam had gone way past angry. What she was feeling now was…well, she didn't know *what* to call it—fatalistic disgust, maybe?

Dammit, she'd done her best. Done everything she was supposed to do. If everybody else involved had done the same, Fahad al-Rami would be dead or in the hands of Philippine forces—maybe on his way to United States custody—by now, his organization in disarray. Cory would be on his way back to Manila with one hell of an interview, Tony with some really great pictures, and the Lundquists... Well, she didn't really want to think about the Lundquists, because if everybody had done what they were supposed to, they'd probably still be in that hut back there, and subject to whatever reprisals the remnants of his organization might choose to take for the loss of Fahad al-Rami.

Still, this morning was the last straw. *Really.* Dammit, she'd thought long and hard before sending that signal, wondering if she dared risk another screwup. Finally, she'd gone with her orders and sent the damn message—the same as last time: *Target located. Stand by.* And not half an hour later...

In fact...now she thought about it, half an hour wasn't really enough time for her message to have made it to Will, then through all the layers of command, down to the special ops forces here on the island. More likely, then, the government troops had tracked them through the jungle from the ravine camp. Or, maybe it was just happenstance—this particular village hideout had been the object of a random raid.

Either way, the damage was done. God only knew where Fahad al-Rami was now; the quarry had flown, slipped through the net yet again. She had another job to concentrate on now. She still had to get four civilians, including the man she loved—*yes, loved, dammit!*—off this wretched island alive and in one piece.

They'd left the noise of battle far behind them when the rain came again. It fell hard and straight, with a rush that drowned all other sounds, and shrouded the jungle and everything in it in a veil of silver.

Ahead, through the curtain of water, Cory could see the Lund-

quists veering suddenly off the rough trail they'd been following to take shelter among the roots of an enormous tree—a ban-
yan, he thought, or a strangler fig. He'd never really been sure
which was which, but it had roots running like pillars from its
huge spreading branches to the jungle floor.

"Come on in, make yourselves comfortable," Esther called as
they caught up with her, peering between the roots like a gracious hostess in a frilly apron inviting visitors onto her front
porch. "It's all right—we should be past the booby traps here."

Cory would have been happier without that equivocal *should,*
but with rain sluicing down the back of his neck and dripping
off the end of his nose, he decided he was willing to take the
chance.

"Find yourselves a dry spot," Esther went cheerfully on. "Just
poke around a bit before you settle in, to chase away any snakes
that might be in residence."

"Great," Tony muttered, wiping water from his face with a
swipe of his hand as he edged nervously between the roots. "Do
you know how much I hate snakes?"

Howard Lundquist was still out in the downpour; having broken off a dishpan-sized leaf from a nearby plant roughly the size
of a minivan, he was laying it out on the ground, turned upside-
down to catch the rain. Esther, meanwhile, had unwrapped her
leaf bundle and was taking out a section of bamboo that Cory
could see had been fashioned into a cup.

"You must be thirsty," she said kindly, offering the cup to
Sam, with a gesture toward the rapidly filling leaf-basin.
"Please—help yourself to a drink of water."

The reporter in Cory was fascinated, thinking of all the questions he wanted to ask, eager to explore more of the contents of
those intriguing bundles, wanting to find out how, exactly, these
two middle-aged people had managed to survive in these conditions for nearly a year *and* keep not only their sanity but their
humanity and good humor as well. He actually envied Tony, who

had already taken a camera from its waterproof bag and was clicking avidly away.

But Cory had other questions more urgently in need of answers. Life-and-death questions. His journalist's curiosity would have to wait.

Though—still thinking like a journalist for the moment— "You still got the tapes?" he asked Tony in an undertone.

"Yep—safe and sound." Tony lowered his camera long enough to pat the camera case hanging at his side. "Got 'em right in here."

His mind relieved on one score, at least, Cory nodded and made his way over rain-slippery roots to where Sam was sitting with her back against a section of smooth tree trunk. She seemed relaxed and at ease, for once, and was holding one of the giant leaves over her head like an umbrella.

"You look like an illustration for a book on elves and fairies," he said. "All you need is a toadstool to sit on."

"Hal gave it to me," she explained with a shrug. "You should get yourself one—it does help a little. Here—have a drink." She smiled as she offered him the bamboo cup. "There's plenty more where that came from."

He took the cup from her and settled onto another jutting root, at an angle to Sam's so that he could see her face. Her eyes. Then he simply sat for a moment, holding the length of bamboo in his hands, stroking its glossy surface with his fingertips…not drinking, although he was thirsty. Strange to be thirsty, he thought, when the world seemed filled with water. It took up all the space around him, occupied all his senses. The rain noise filled his ears; the smell and taste of it was on his tongue and in his nostrils; the wetness clung to his skin like cloth. The curtain of it enveloped him, shrinking around him so that he and Sam seemed in that moment like the only two people alive in a world of water.

The moment stretched. Sam stirred restlessly under his gaze, her smile fading.

"If you're not gonna drink that, give it back." She sounded testy, the way he knew she did when she was feeling ill at ease.

Silently, he drank the tepid water and handed her the cup. He wasn't playing psychological games; he truly did not know where or how to begin. His suspicions quivered and knotted and lashed at his insides, and at the same time he felt weighed down with the knowledge—*the certainty*—he carried, and the dread that it was about to be confirmed.

She settled back against the tree trunk again, wiggling her shoulders as though she had an itchy spot there. "Wonder where al-Rami's gone to earth this time," she said, her relaxed mood gone, her tone sardonic now, and a little breathy, making nervous conversation, he thought. "Wonder why they didn't take us along this time."

"Last thing al-Rami wants is us anywhere near where he is," Cory muttered.

Sam's eyes snapped toward him. "What?"

He shook his head. "Nothing." But that was cowardice. He leveled a look straight at her, took a breath and said, in a voice only a little less quiet than hers, "We'd all better hope they don't come back looking for us."

"Why?" But her body was still, no longer restless, and her eyes were watchful.

"You know why," he said flatly. "Because if they find us they'll kill us. Probably on sight." God, at least he hoped so. The alternative didn't bear thinking about.

Sam's eyes widened with innocence. "Why would they kill us? Al-Rami's been nothing if not cordial and cooperative up to now. I thought you and he had things all worked out."

He had to admire her poise. He went on looking at her for a moment longer, then let out a breath and wiped moisture from his face with his shoulder. He leaned forward, staring at his hands, which were clasped between his knees. He noted the knuckles had gone white, and made an effort to relax them.

"A few years ago," he said, in a conversational tone she would have to strain to hear above the rain, "I did a story on the latest in surveillance technology. Miniature bugs…tracking devices, cameras—things like that. Real fly-on-the-wall, sci-fi stuff, some of it." He'd lifted his eyes and was watching her closely now. Her eyes didn't flicker. He cleared his throat and plowed on. "One of the things they showed me was an implantable satellite tracking device. One that could be surgically imbedded in the body, becoming completely undetectable by any known scanners."

"Oh, heck—" she made a dismissive motion with her hand "—they've had those for years. You can even put 'em in your pets so they won't get lost."

"Yeah," he said, relentlessly holding her eyes, "but these could be used, not just as locators, but to send and receive coded messages." He paused, waiting.

"Cool," was all she said. And she lifted the bamboo cup to her lips, though he could have sworn the thing was empty.

Chapter 10

When she lowered the cup again, he saw her throat ripple with a hard swallow. He had to hand it to her, though; her gaze didn't waver, not even a little.

"That scar behind your ear—" She made a scoffing noise and rocked back as if in protest. He held up a hand to stop the denial he could see poised on her lips. "Don't, Sam. *Don't.*" He waited, expecting her eyes to come back to his, hot with defiance, chin upthrust. But instead she turned her face away.

Anger boiled up inside him. Anger, disappointment—disappointment so acute it felt like physical pain. He didn't know why—it was no more than he'd suspected. No more than he'd *known.*

"My God," he burst out, in a harsh and tearing voice, "what were you thinking? They'd have killed us all, still might, if they catch us. You said it yourself—they were suspicious of us to begin with. Did you think they wouldn't figure it out that it had to be one of us giving away their location? If I figured it out, they sure as hell can. And let me tell you something—al-Rami's no fool; he'd figured it out already. Did you see the look he gave us just before he fled? He'd have killed us then, if he'd had the means at hand, and if he hadn't been more preoccupied with saving his own skin. You can bet we won't be getting a second chance."

"I was doing my job, Pearse." She said it softly, not sullenly…maybe with a touch of pleading.

His anger toward her didn't soften. It filled his throat, choking him. "You used me, Sam."

Her eyes flashed at him, bright and fervent. "It was a chance to get al-Rami. You expected us to pass that up?"

"I gave my word," he said stiffly, bound up by his own anger. "To a *terrorist?*"

"*My* word, Sam. Mine. He trusted *my* word. And I betrayed him. He won't forget that. Or forgive."

"Well, excuse me," she lashed back, "if I don't get too excited about what might upset Mr. *Sheik* al-Rami!"

He looked at her. Just looked. And saw the fire in her eyes slowly fade to anguish. She jerked, and looked away. "It wasn't supposed to be like that," she said tightly. "They were supposed to get in position and wait for my signal before moving in. I would've waited until the time was right. I would've—"

"The *right* time. Exactly when would that've been, Sam? Before or after the interview? Before or after we'd secured the hostages?" *Before or after we made love?*

"After dark, for starters," she snapped back, glaring at him. "A broad daylight attack was just stupid. I would have waited until you'd gotten what you wanted from al-Rami, and I'd definitely have waited until we were safely out of there. My God, Pearse, do you think I don't know what that interview meant to you? Do you think I'd have risked all our lives by calling in an attack on top of us? Who do you think I am?"

"That's just it—I don't know what to think," he said bitterly.

His anger was fading, leaving him feeling cold and tired. Hollow inside. "And I sure as hell don't know who you are. Obviously." He fell silent, too upset to go on, yet unable to bring himself to go and leave her there. She made a sound like air escaping from a tire, and turned her face away.

After a while, gathering his energy and will because he simply had to know, he asked softly, "So, who is it, Sam? Who are you working for—CIA? Homeland Security? Who?"

"You know—" she broke off, cleared her throat "—you know I can't tell you that." Her voice was as soft as his, but muffled and slurred where his was sharp and bitter.

Frustrated, still furious with her, he growled, "At least tell me how long you've been doing this. How long have you been an agent and I didn't know?"

"How long?" Her head swiveled back to him, and she was the old Sam again, the Sam he knew so well, with that lift to her chin and tilt to her head that were both arrogant and defensive at the same time, and an aching vulnerability about her mouth even her defiant eyes couldn't hide. "Those months when we didn't see much of each other? That's where I was—in training. I was recruited in flight school, went into training right after."

"When were you going to tell me about it? Ever?" He tried, but couldn't keep the pain from leaking into his voice. "My God, Sam. I asked you to marry me."

"Yeah, and now you know why I couldn't say yes," she shot back, in a voice as ragged as his.

He stared at her, hot-eyed. After a moment she went on in a whisper he didn't have to strain to hear, and it occurred to him only then that it had stopped raining.

"I'd just finished my training, you know…when I found out you'd gotten married. I'd been in the field for weeks, and that was the last big thing, and then I was done. I came home and the first thing I wanted to do was call you. I couldn't reach you at the number I had, so I called Mom and Dad. And that's when they told me. That you were married."

Cory let a breath out and rubbed a hand across his eyes. When and how, he wondered wearily, had it come back around to *him?* How was it that he now felt guilty again, when it was she who'd kept such a huge, important *catastrophic* secret from him? His Sam, a *secret agent?* He couldn't get his mind around it.

"So, I guess we've both been keeping secrets," Sam said, as if she'd read his thoughts. She paused, and then, in a voice thick with gravel: "The only difference between us is, now you know all mine."

He didn't lift his head or uncover his eyes, but he knew by the scraping sounds and then the sudden emptiness around him that she had gone.

Sam was still shaking—with anger, she told herself—as she dropped ungracefully onto a root beside Esther Lundquist. She held out the bamboo cup—thrust it, her movements as jerky and uncontrolled as a broken windup toy.

"That was great," she said, in a gruff voice that completely belied the words. "Thank you."

Esther threw her a sharp look as she took the piece of bamboo and returned it carefully to the bundle near her feet. Then she reached over and gave Sam's hand a squeeze and said softly, "Dear, you're more than welcome." And her pale blue eyes smiled with gentle sympathy.

Oh, great, thought Sam, cringing inside. *Were we talking that loudly, or is it just my face? Some secret agent I am—couldn't hold my own in a dorm-room poker game.*

Casting about for something innocuous to say, she nodded at the bundle between Esther's feet. "How did you manage to make that—the cup? It's really cool."

The woman's smile broadened, crinkling her eyes. "Yes, it is, isn't it? Hal's made a few things—eating utensils, bowls and so forth. He's quite clever with his hands."

"Yes, but…bamboo this thick is *tough*—like wood. I mean, you must have had to cut it somehow."

Esther hunched her shoulders like a guilty child and touched a forefinger to her lips in a quick silencing gesture. "Shh—don't tell anyone," she said with a crafty glance over her shoulder. Then she plunged a hand into the mysterious bundle and pulled out an oblong object thickly wrapped in leaves. She began to unroll it, and Sam gasped when she saw the dull glint of a knife blade.

"Holy…cow," she said, remembering in the nick of time that she was speaking to a missionary of God. "Where did you get that?"

"I found it," Esther said, with a pleased little laugh. "I imagine one of *them* must have dropped it. You can't imagine how useful it's been. We keep it hidden, of course—I'm sure they wouldn't approve of us having it. Not that we'd *ever* use it as a weapon—heavens no. Hal and I don't believe in violence."

Sam gazed at her for a moment, then shook her head. Her eyes drifted to where Hal and Tony were sitting together some distance away, their heads bowed over one of Tony's cameras. She took a deep breath, wondering when she'd acquired the aching lump in her chest. An alien need, a compulsion to talk to someone, rose up in her and flattened her pride like a steamroller. "You two amaze me," she said softly.

Esther looked up from the task of rewrapping the knife, her eyebrows arched in surprise. "Oh, my, we do? Why?"

"Because…you seem so…*close.*" She gave her shoulders a little shake, not happy with the word but unable to come up with one better. "After all you've been through, in the middle of all of this…you still seem, I don't know…domestic, I guess. Like…you're this happily married couple and this just happens to be your life." Embarrassed, she stabbed at the ground with the heel of her boot and mumbled, "I'm not saying it very well."

Esther's laugh was a little trill of amusement. "I think you've said it beautifully. We *are* a married couple, and this does happen to be our life—for now, at least."

"But it could all end tomorrow." A cold shiver ran through her and she bit down on her lower lip, wishing she hadn't said it, unable to help herself.

Esther glanced up from her task, no longer smiling, though her eyes were serene and unperturbed. "Yes, it could. But that's true no matter where you are, isn't it? Just think of all the people who left home to go to work on that terrible day that changed our world, and never returned. It happens in smaller ways every day, in cities and small towns, all over the world." She shook her head as she went back to her packing. "Hal and I have talked about it, of course we have. We've both agreed that if it ends for one of us—whenever that may be—the other must be strong and carry on—for the sake of our children, if nothing else."

"You have children?" For some reason the notion both surprised and appalled Sam.

"Oh, yes—two lovely boys. Teenagers." Esther's smile was back, brighter than ever. "I'm sure they're home in Ottawa now, quite safe and sound."

"That must be so hard," Sam said inadequately, shaking her head. She couldn't even imagine it.

Esther was still smiling, but with a shine of tears in her eyes—the first Sam had seen. "Oh, yes, of course it is. But Hal and I are both blessed with wonderful families. Our hearts are at ease, knowing our boys are being cared for and loved."

Sam stared at her feet; her throat felt clogged with wistfulness and longing. "It must be wonderful," she said softly, barely aware she was saying it out loud, "to have so much in common. To have no secrets…"

Esther made a scoffing noise and briskly dashed away a tear. "I don't know about secrets—I haven't really thought about that.

But Hal and I have very little in common—well, there's the way we feel about each other, I suppose."

"And religion, surely?"

She made that same disparaging sound, almost a laugh. "Oh, goodness no—you should hear the arguments we have sometimes."

"So…the two of you do…I mean—"

Esther's eyebrows arched with amusement. "Married couples do argue, dear. So do friends, lovers, companions, partners… Hal is truly all those things to me, and I do try not to keep secrets from him, but really, we're nothing at all alike. He's a dour Swede—" she made a face to illustrate "—and I…well, I'm sure you've noticed, I'm something of a flibbertigibbet. I'm nauseatingly upbeat and optimistic. I guess you could say…oh dear, it's such a cliché, but you really could say we complete each other." Her lined cheeks were pink and her eyes bright, making her look slightly embarrassed, and years younger. "He keeps me grounded," she finished softly, "and I suppose I keep him from becoming mired in melancholy."

"Yin and yang," said Sam.

Esther tilted her head, considering that. "Yes—although I prefer the imagery of the oak tree and the cypress."

"The oak tree…" Unfamiliar with the reference, Sam shook her head.

"Kahlil Gibran? The poet? Oh dear—well, I won't try to paraphrase it for you, the language is too lovely to be mangled the way I would surely manage to do. But someday when you can, find yourself a copy of *The Prophet,* dear, and read the chapter on marriage."

"I'm kind of amazed," Sam said.

"Why, dear?"

She felt her cheeks burning, and wondered how she'd managed to talk herself into yet another corner it was going to be impossible to get out of without being rude—religion, along with politics, being one of those subjects Mama had always taught her weren't to be discussed unless you knew for certain the other person held the same beliefs and opinions as you. "Gibran," she said, squirming. "He's Arab, right? Well, isn't he… I mean, he's not—um…"

Esther's smile and voice were uncharacteristically wry. "There are words of wisdom and beauty to be found in every culture, dear. And, if there's one thing I've learned, being out here, it's not to get too tangled up in dogma."

After a long and thoughtful silence, Sam put her hands on the root beside her and prepared to lever herself off it. "Well, I guess we'd better be getting on," she said, "now that the rain's stopped."

But for some reason it was hard to make herself move. She felt heavy, weighed down…tired out by all the emotional turmoil. She let her eyes slide again to Hal and Tony, and her heart gave a painful leap when she saw Cory had joined them. She drew an unsteady breath and slid down from her perch, overcome with sadness and an indefinable fear.

She was turning when Esther caught at her arm, touching it briefly, just long enough to keep her there.

"It is hard work," she said gently. "Loving someone over the long haul." Sam stared at the frail-looking woman, wondering if she had the gift of second sight. And saw a shadow—not sadness…*weariness,* maybe—in her faded blue eyes. "You know, I think even the happiest, most loving couples must wonder now and then if it's all worth the effort."

"But," Sam blurted out, anguish honing her voice, as it so often did, into a sound more like anger, "*you've* done it. You and Hal—obviously, you've made it work. So…so what's the secret? How do you do it? Is it this…Gibran thing—the oak and the cypress? *What?*"

Gentle humor returned to Esther's eyes. "I suppose I do have a secret." Her lips curved with a sly little smile. "A small one—

just one word, actually. I didn't get it from Gibran, though. This came from a book I'm considerably more familiar with."

"Yeah? What is it?" Sam held herself rigid, fighting back tears.

Esther's lined face blossomed. "Forgiveness, dear."

Sam gave a little huff of helpless laughter and turned away, disappointment leaving her with nothing at all to say. Forgiveness? How was that supposed to help her? Forgiveness pretty much had to be a two-way street, didn't it?

Forgive? Okay, I can do that, I think I already have. The question now is, is he ever going to forgive me?

Cory was squatting, balanced on one heel, beside a patch of mossy ground on which Hal Lundquist had drawn a rough map of the island with a sharp stick.

"So," he said, shoving his glasses up the bridge of his nose as he stabbed the similar stick he held in his hand into a spot near the southern tip, "you figure we're about *here*." He moved the stick a couple of inches toward the center of the island and stabbed again. "And the village and airstrip are roughly here." He looked up and pointed the stick at an imaginary point located halfway between Hal and Tony, who was, as usual, photographing the impromptu strategy meeting for posterity. "That is to say, *there*. No more than three or four miles that direction. That's not too bad. We should be able to make it by dark."

"You're forgetting," Hal said as he used his stick to draw a wiggly line between Cory's two points. "The river. We'll have to cross it."

Cory squinted up at him over the tops of his glasses. "There must be ways. Fords…bridges."

Hal scratched his beard and looked doubtful. "Only two that I know of. Of course there's the bridge back at the village…"

"Yeah, well, I don't think we want to go back there. What's the other?"

"Farther upriver there's a gorge—it's not wide, but it is deep. There's a rope bridge across it."

"A rope bridge," Cory said heavily, taking off his glasses and rubbing his eyes, envisioning the sort of swaying contraption popular in action-adventure movies. Behind him he could hear Tony blaspheming under his breath and felt sure he was on the same wavelength.

"It's not fun, but it is doable," Hal said, though his dour expression suggested he hadn't much optimism about their chances of success. "Esther and I used it several times during the last rainy season—during dry weather, of course, you can cross just about anywhere."

"I don't see we have much choice," Cory said, standing up and brushing at his wet and muddy knees. "If you and your wife—"

"There's just one thing…" Hal Lundquist was still scratching his whiskers, and looking more pessimistic than ever.

"Yeah? What's that?" Cory's heartbeat slowed to a leaden thumping. Behind him, he felt Tony freeze in the act of putting his camera back in its case.

"Well, as I said, there are only the two crossings. Al-Rami's men use them, too, and they won't be any more eager to backtrack through the village than we are. Which means—"

"We may run into them at the crossing," Cory said grimly. "Or worse, they could be set up to ambush us when we try to cross. Great."

"I doubt they'd waste their time and ammunition," Sam said as she joined them. "Assuming al-Rami and his men managed to escape the raid on the village, they'll most likely have crossed the river already and are heading for their nearest hideout as we speak."

Silently, Cory watched her hunker down beside the crudely drawn map, and he was trying not to notice the fluid slide of muscles in her back and arms and thighs that not even men's clothing could hide. Or the matter-of-fact way she'd taken charge, with a quiet authority that could only come from absolute confidence in her superior knowledge and expertise.

Of course, she'd been doing that all along, he realized, in slightly more subtle ways. He'd noticed and wondered about it, even felt twinges of uneasiness...entertained vague suspicions. But then, he'd been distracted—to put it mildly—by the flood of conflicting emotions he'd had to deal with since finding her so unexpectedly back in his life, not to mention the reawakened desires rampaging through his system. And even more than that, he thought, he'd been blinded by the image he'd carried in his mind for so long. Sammi June...Sam...his Samantha...who he'd insisted on seeing still as the arrogant but vulnerable college girl he'd fallen in love with that day in the White House rose garden.

Where was that cheeky golden girl now? Had she ever really existed, except in his fantasies? Certainly he could find no trace of her in this tanned and toned creature in camouflage cargo pants and T-shirt, reminding him of nothing so much as the swashbuckling heroine of some action-adventure film he pictured right at home raiding ancient Egyptian tombs or swinging one-handed on a vine while firing an AK-47 and vanquishing villains with the other. He had no doubt crossing a chasm on a swaying rope would be well within her capabilities.

"Besides, they can't even be sure we'd be coming along that way," she went on, squinting up at Hal Lundquist—making a point, Cory noticed, to avoid meeting *his* eyes. "For all they know, we might have been killed in the raid, or managed to meet up with the government forces. Either way, I doubt they'd sit around waiting at some bridge crossing on the off chance we might happen along."

"That's a very good point," Hal said, though he looked no less dubious as he gazed down at the map.

"Well, like I said, I don't think we have much choice," Cory said briskly. "How far is it to the crossing? Can we still make the village and airstrip before nightfall?"

Hall shook his head. "In terms of miles it's not that far, but the terrain and vegetation make for slow going. Then there's the rain, which will make things more difficult. We might make it there by tomorrow morning, if we keep going all night, but I don't think that's such a good idea. The truth is—" he smiled dolefully at his wife as she joined them "—I'm not at all sure we can find the path in the dark. And with all the cloud cover there'll be no moon."

"We'll take it as it comes, then." Cory glanced at Sam, assuming she'd want to weigh in on the subject. But she wasn't looking his way, and what he could see of her expression was aloof and unreadable.

He heard her asking Esther if she could carry her cooking pot and bundle for her, and heard Esther's serene and cheerful, "I'm quite all right, dear, but thank you for asking." And it occurred to him as he looked at the older woman's gaunt face and frail body that both she and her husband, intrepid though they might be, weren't superhuman. They had to be running low on reserves of strength.

"Do you know if there's someplace we can take shelter for the night?" he asked Hal. "Another nice big tree, maybe?"

"Oh, we can do better than that," Esther said, beaming at her husband. "Can't we, Hal? There's the hunter's hut, remember?" She transferred the smile to Cory. "It's on this side of the gorge, very near the crossing. It's quite tiny, but it does have walls— bamboo, of course—and a roof, of sorts."

"It did," Hal corrected her gently, with a dubious wag of his head. "We can't be sure it's still intact."

"Well, then, we'll just have to put our trust in the Lord," Esther said, and Cory saw her throw Sam a broad wink, and Sam smile wryly back at her. "After he sent these lovely people to bring us home I don't think he's going to let us down now, do you? After you, my love—lead on!"

Still wagging his head, Hal shouldered the larger cooking-pot bundle his wife handed him and set off through the dripping undergrowth, following a trail that remained invisible, at least to Cory. Esther fell in behind him, looking much like a terrier dogging the heels of a Great Dane. After a quick, almost involuntary-seeming glance at Cory, Sam followed her.

Tony moved up beside Cory and paused to rearrange the bags and cases that festooned the upper half of his body. "What is this, 'After you, Alfonse'?" he said with a nod toward the others, who were already disappearing in the heavy undergrowth.

Cory gave a dry laugh without much humor in it. "Something like that. Can I give you a hand with some of that stuff?"

"Naw, that's okay, I got it." He took off the bandana that covered his head and mopped at his face and neck.

Cory gave an exaggerated start. "Whoa—I don't think I've ever seen you with hair before." Tony's normally shiny head was now sporting a furring of dark hair. "Looking a bit scruffy, there, buddy."

"Like *you've* got room to talk," Tony scoffed, baring his teeth in a wide grin and pointedly rubbing the sparse black hairs adorning his chin and upper lip. "That's the thing about us Injuns—no whiskers to worry about."

"Injun, *hah,*" Cory said as he ran a hand over the half inch or so of beard on his own face. "What are you, maybe a quarter? You just like an excuse because you can't grow a beard."

"Excuse! What do I need an excuse for? Beards are a pain, man. Couple more days and you're gonna start looking like the reverend, up there. Not me."

"Yeah," Cory said ruefully, "I am starting to feel a little like Robinson Crusoe. Probably don't smell too good, either."

Tony snorted. "Me, either." But his eyes followed Sam as she ducked in and out of the banana trees up ahead. He lowered his voice and remarked, "Seems like some of us are holding up better than others."

Cory grunted a reply, not wanting to notice the way Sam's hair curled dark and damp on the back of her neck, or how her wet T-shirt clung to the smooth, fluid muscles of her back. Not wanting to acknowledge the gnawing ache in his groin whenever he looked at her, or the bigger, less well-defined ache higher up, in the vicinity of his heart.

"Something goin' on between the two of you?" Tony asked in the same muttered undertone.

Cory lifted a shoulder. "Don't know what you mean. I already told you—"

"Hey, I'm not deaf and blind, man."

"Look, I told you, that was in the past." Cory paused, exhaled and muttered, "And I'm beginning to realize she's not the same person I knew then."

Tony threw him a fierce bright glance. "Who the hell is? Look, man, you two have something beautiful going—sparks, some kind of connection. Don't tell me you don't—even an emotional doofus like me can see it. So, maybe you blew it once. You got a second chance now. Don't blow this again, man."

"What are you, Dr. Phil all of a sudden? Since when are you such a big fan of monogamous happy-ever-after relationships? Anyway," Cory said, stiffening himself against hope and a strange wild despair, "that's not my call to make. She's made her choices."

"Oh, right," said Tony, "so it's all *her* fault." Cory threw him a dirty look and got one in return. "When I was a kid? Any time any of us kids got in an argument or a fight—and with eleven of us there were a lot of fights— Mama used to say it takes two to make a quarrel, and she'd take us by the scruff of the neck and she'd march us into a corner and make us sit there together until we'd 'kissed and made up,' was the way she put it." He paused, and Cory felt the stab of his fierce golden eyes, all the sharper, maybe, for being those of his closest friend. When Tony went on, though, it was in a gentler tone. "All I'm sayin', man, is you two need to get in a quiet place and talk this out."

Cory made a scoffing noise, but his heart wasn't in it. He hoped he was still mature enough to acknowledge when someone was right.

After a moment Tony shrugged and said, "Okay, so she did something that knocked you for a loop. Now maybe you know how she feels."

Again Cory snapped him an angry look, but this time the one Tony returned was somber, maybe even a little sad. "Just think about it, man," he said softly, then quickened his step and moved on ahead of him.

Left alone with his thoughts, Cory was in wretched company. *Think about it? What is there to think about? The woman I love, the woman I wanted to marry and have children with, is a field agent—an undercover operative—a spy—for the CIA!* At least he was pretty sure it would be the CIA. Or some agency even more secret he'd never heard of. How was he supposed to deal with that?

"Now you know how she feels…"

Wait a minute, he protested silently, *this is different. It's different. And anyway, I've told her everything. Everything I remember…*

Somewhere in the distance, thunder rumbled, gradually coming closer. Thunder rumbled now, too, inside his head… *Thumping, pounding, banging, angry and insistent, growing louder… coming closer.*

He slammed shut the doors of memory, shuttered the windows and braced himself against them, breathing hard and shaking, his skin grown clammy and cold.

Chapter 11

There was still some daylight left when they came to the hunter's hut, little more than a bamboo cave in a mountain of jungle greenery. While Esther and Sam banged on the bamboo walls with sticks to chase away any rats and mice already in residence, not to mention snakes that might have come to dine on them, Cory and Tony helped Hal cut banana leaves to fortify the roof, using the knife from Esther's bundle. They managed to get settled in before the rain came again.

They ate a supper of some fruit they'd picked on the way, though it didn't do much to satisfy Sam's hunger; she was thoroughly sick of fruit, and starting to hallucinate cheeseburgers.

Then they sat huddled, listening to the rain drumming on the freshly cut leaves above their heads, smelling the cool damp fragrances of earth and growing things, and Sam thought of the first people, crouched in caves and jungle shelters not much different than this one...wondered whether they'd felt this same loneliness and isolation, and whether they, too, had been thankful for the warmth and vibrancy of other human bodies close by in the darkness, their comforting presence felt even without touching.

The rain passed quickly and the moon came out. Sam watched it slip through the cracks in the bamboo walls and paint uneven stripes across the sleeping Lundquists, lying curled together, front to back, like spoons. And she felt the sense of loneliness and isolation inside her deepen into bottomless sadness.

I remember that, she thought. *I remember what it's like to feel so close to someone that he seems like only another part of me, his smell as natural to me as the air I've grown accustomed to breathing every day, and as essential. His warmth like sunshine on my skin. I remember the first time I felt like that…it seems like yesterday…*

I'm in a boat out on the lake at dusk, sitting with my back against Cory's chest, and his arms are around me and his long legs drawn up alongside mine. I feel his chin resting on the top of my head, and sometimes I feel his warm breath as he touches his lips to my hair. Shivers go through me, then, and I turn my head to his shoulder and breathe him in…his smell reminding me of clean sheets right off my grandmama's clothesline, and I recall the way as a little girl I used to like to bury my face in that sweet freshness, and I wish I could do that now, to him. Right now, with Cory, I feel the way I did then, a child in my grand-mama's house…safe, secure, loved. I feel like I'm home.

The evening star is bright in the darkening sky, and far across the water I can see my mom and dad standing on the dock, twined together so they look like one person. I know that my dad has found his way home, too, and a great wave of emotion rushes through me, happiness so intense it makes tears come to my eyes. Everything I've ever wished for is right here, mine, like this wonderful gift I've been given, and everything I want for my life from now on seems within my grasp.

How did I get so far from there? Sam thought as she gazed at the sleeping Lundquists, her eyes dry now, burning with a

sense of loss and loneliness too great for tears. So far from home.
For the first time she truly understood the depths of her father's
despair when he'd feared he might never again find that place
where he belonged.

*Cory was that place for me; I knew it even then. How did I
let that go? Yes, I wanted more...there were so many things I
wanted to do, places to go, possibilities to explore...was that
wrong? I always thought he'd be there for me to come home
to...my place of belonging, where I would always feel safe and
welcome and loved.*

Was I wrong to want so much?

*Would I have given up my dreams of becoming a pilot, and
later this chance to make a difference in the world, if I'd known
what it would cost me?*

*Why must choosing one cost me the other? Why should I have
to sacrifice half of myself?*

It's not fair, dammit, she thought, stirring angrily in the sil-
ver-dappled darkness. She drew up her knees and wrapped her
arms tightly around them, rested her forehead on her knees and
squeezed her eyes shut, hugging herself against a chill too deep
to reach.

"Sam..." It was a stirring in the air, nothing more...a whisper so faint she couldn't be sure she'd heard it.

Her heart never doubted. It leaped within the confined space
of her chest, and a shiver rippled through her. Pride wouldn't let
her reply; she only hugged her knees more tightly, her whole
body going tense in that perverse way it has of armoring itself
against something it wants too much.

She felt a hand on one shoulder...then both...strong hands,
compelling her. She resisted, of course—her stubborn nature de-
manded it—but gradually the patience and quiet determination
of those hands had their way with her, and she gave a small,
testy sigh and allowed herself to be unfolded and pulled into
Cory's arms.

He would have nested her against him, her back to his front, but that wasn't what she wanted—*needed*—then, and she turned in the circle of his arms and wrapped her arms around him, because she needed desperately not just to be held, but to hold on to someone. Holding him so tightly she could feel his heart beating against her own chest, she lifted her face into his neck and pressed her nose and lips against his skin, breathing in the smell of him, pulling it deep inside her, breathing past the smells of sweat and mud and jungle mustiness to the sweet clean goodness that was the most essential part of him.

She felt his hand cuddle her head close into that hollow that seemed specially made for it, his fingers stroking the hair behind her ear. Stroking gently over the spot where the secret she'd hidden from him, the communication chip, lay embedded beneath her skin, and this time she didn't flinch or cringe away, because it didn't matter anymore, because now he knew. He *knew,* everything there was to know, and still he'd chosen to hold her, comfort her like this, as though nothing had ever gone wrong between them. And maybe that meant there was still a chance for them somewhere…sometime, and maybe it meant nothing at all except further proof of his inherent kindness, but still she felt a great brightness come inside her, as if she'd received a gift of grace.

Cory woke to find Esther Lundquist bending over him.

"We must go now," she whispered, touching his shoulder, and her sweet, bright voice sounded breathless with urgency.

"What is it? What's wrong?" Sam was already coming awake, her body taut and rigid in his arms. They both sat up slowly, disengaging tangled arms and legs. A short distance away in the murky green light of dawn, Hal was shaking Tony awake.

"Al-Rami's men are coming. We heard their voices, Hal and I. They must have come from the crossing—maybe looking for us, maybe not, I don't know. But they know this place—they'll surely search here. We'll have to hide in the jungle until they've gone by."

Cory and Sam were already on their feet. Tony was groping for his camera bags. Silently, one by one, they followed Hal and Esther out of the hut and slipped into the cover of the jungle. They moved slowly, trying not to brush against the foliage lest the sound of that give them away, until an urgent hand signal from Hal, passed from one to the other down the line, told them to drop to the jungle floor and freeze.

"Hide your face," Cory heard Sam hiss. "Faces stand out in this stuff."

Not hesitating, no longer needing to wonder where she'd come by such knowledge, he put his head down on his folded arms. Minutes ticked by while he listened to his heartbeat, loud as thunder in his ears. Somewhere in the canopy, awakening birds squawked and chattered, then fell into a listening hush. And now he heard it, too—the crackle and swush of boots trampling through lush vegetation. He found himself counting, counting footsteps, counting heartbeats, wondering if he was counting down the final seconds of his life. And he had to fight the impulse to reach through the undergrowth that separated them and take Sam's hand, because if he was going to die—if they were both going to die, right here and right now—he wanted her to know in this life that he still loved her.

The moment of insanity passed. Like the others, he lay still as death, except for the wild pounding of his heart, listening to the sounds of heavy boots come closer…until they were right on top of him…until it seemed they surely must hear his heart beating. But the footsteps moved on past, and presently Cory heard the muttering of voices, the creak and rustle of bamboo, and knew the stealthy pursuers were searching the hut where they'd all been sleeping only minutes before. Then, after what seemed like hours, those sounds, too, faded. The jungle grew quiet…then noisy, as high in the canopy the watchful birds resumed their delayed ode to the morning.

Hal rose cautiously to his feet and the others followed, Tony fussing over his camera bags and swearing softly to himself, like a broody hen, Cory thought, counting and clucking over her chicks.

"Come quickly," Esther whispered, waving them all past her. "We must get across the gorge. If they come back, we'll be trapped here on this side." She still sounded out of breath, and her face was pale and shiny with sweat.

"Are you all right?" Cory asked in a low voice, touching her arm as he passed her.

"I'll be fine, dear." She threw him her usual smile, but he thought it seemed strained now, rather than sunny. She patted her chest, a delicate, fluttery gesture. "All this excitement…I just need to catch my breath for a moment. But please—do hurry. It will take us some time to get everyone across. You must go. *Go.*" She gave his arm a motherly pat that was more like a shove, and what could he do but obey?

Later, he wondered what might have happened if he'd listened to the uneasy voices whispering in the back of his mind, wondered whether it would have made any difference at all in the eventual outcome. At the time, though, he did what he thought he must do…closed his ears to the whispers and his mind to unease and went plunging ahead after Sam and Hal and Tony, leaving Esther Lundquist behind.

It was only fifty yards or so farther on when the trees suddenly opened up to reveal an expanse of lavender sky and green-flanked mountains, and a pale sun trying its best to rise above the clouds that clung to their crests like some woolly gray fungus. A few yards more beyond the edge of the trees, the earth dropped away into a deep gorge; Cory could hear the roaring of the river tumbling by far below. And now, on the edge of the gorge, he could see what was to carry them across that chasm.

It wasn't exactly what he'd pictured. It wasn't any kind of a bridge at all, swaying or otherwise, but rather a simple pulley system, rather like the ones he'd seen crisscrossing high above narrow streets in teeming slums in European and Asian cities, festooned with drying laundry. A large wood-and-iron pulley was anchored by heavy rope to the head-high stump of a tree, and from it a double strand of the same heavy rope stretched across the gorge to a similar apparatus on the other side. At each end, near the terminal stump, another loop of rope had been threaded through a sturdy length of bamboo and attached to the main rope with a large metal snap hook, to make a swing. In order to make the crossing, all a person had to do was slip the loop over his head and shoulders, sit on the length of bamboo, then pull himself hand-over-hand to the other side—or, if he had companions, hold on for dear life and let them pull him across. When the occupied chair reached its destination, an empty one would be back at the starting point, ready to be filled by the next person in line.

The chasm wasn't wide; with someone to help with the pulling it would only take minutes to cross from one side to the other. But in those few short minutes, the person in the chair would be completely out in the open. Unprotected. Helpless. A sitting duck.

"Oh, my God," said Sam.

Tony's comment was more colorful but no less horrified.

"Ingenious," Cory muttered, but his heart was tangoing around inside his chest and there was a growing queasiness in the pit of his stomach.

Seemingly unperturbed, Hal was already at the terminal, holding the bamboo swing steady. "Hurry, hurry, we must get started," he urged, beckoning them on with a sweeping wave of his long arm. Then, looking past them: "Where's Esther?"

"She told me she needed to catch her breath," Cory said, his belly twingeing with an uneasy guilt. "She said she was coming right behind me."

"I'd better go and see what's keeping her." Hal thrust the

loop of rope and bamboo at Cory, saying as he brushed past him, "Don't wait for us—start sending the others across." And he crashed away into the trees.

Cory looked at Sam. She held up her hands and backed away. "Uh-uh, not me. *You* go first."

Well, it had been worth a try. He couldn't explain the fear that was creeping over him like a deep-down chill, but he knew it went way beyond any rational sense of urgency based on full awareness of danger and pursuit, or the very real need to hurry.

He took a deep breath and said, "Okay, Tony, you take the first shot."

Tony groaned. "Why did I know you were gonna say that?"

"Hey—you've got the equipment, the tapes—let's get that across, make sure it's safe. And, when you get to the other side you can help pull—it'll make it twice as fast. Come on, big guy," he taunted, grinning, when Tony still looked like he might balk, "this can't be any worse than those donkeys in Afghanistan."

"Yeah, but it wasn't nearly as far to fall," Tony grumbled, but he stepped forward reluctantly, shifting cameras and bags out of the way to allow Cory to slip the loop over his head and shoulders.

"All set?" Sam took hold of one side of the loop and Cory the other, and they held it steady while Tony, still blaspheming imaginatively, slipped the length of bamboo under his backside. "Ready...get set—"

"Wait, wait—" Tony dug in his heels while he shifted a camera to the front of his body so he could reach it more easily "—okay, *now* I'm ready."

"Go!" Cory let go of the chair and hauled hard on the rope, and Tony swung out into thin air.

"Is he gonna be okay?" Sam asked nervously as she moved close to Cory's side and took hold of the rope to help him pull.

Even above the roar of the river they could hear a steady stream of profanity drifting back to them from the middle of the gorge.

"He's a photographer," Cory said, panting a little. "He'll be fine once he remembers that camera around his neck. Those donkeys in Afghanistan? Didn't want to get on those, either. Before it was over he was riding no-hands up these little narrow mountain trails, just so he could snap pictures of three-hundred-foot drop-offs. There—see? He's clicking away already."

They devoted their energies then to hauling on the rope, both of them watching Tony slide closer to the opposite bank and the empty loop swing toward them across the last few yards of the chasm.

"You're next, Sam," Cory said quietly between pulls, not looking at her. "No arguments."

She didn't reply. Together they caught the incoming swing and stood holding it between them as they watched Tony get his feet under him on the other side of the gorge, stand and wrestle the loop over his head, then give a triumphant wave.

Cory said, "Sam?"

She threw him a long dark look, one he couldn't read. Then, moving jerkily with the anger that he knew really wasn't anger, she thrust her head and arms through the loop and hitched herself onto the bamboo seat. "Any time, Pearse," she said airily, her chin high, eyes bright with challenge.

He caught his breath…then cupped the back of her head in his palm and leaned down and kissed her. Just once, quickly and hard, but still he felt her lips tremble under his and a shaft of pain went through him, so acute he nearly gasped. "Hold on tight," he mumbled, stepping back. Feeling as though his heart had lodged in his chest, he took hold of the rope and began to pull.

As she slipped out over the edge of the chasm, rotating slowly, almost lazily in midair, the sun rose at last above the mountaintops and, as if by some stroke of magic, a rainbow appeared between them, painted in the mist thrown up by the rampaging river. The incredible beauty of it—and at the same time an overwhelming sadness—caught at his throat. He wanted to call to her, wave…bring her back and touch her…hold her…kiss her one more time.

But she didn't look back.

It wasn't as bad as she'd thought it would be. Kind of cool, in fact—if she didn't allow herself to think about al-Rami's men back there, searching for them somewhere in the jungle, not that far away. And about Cory left behind in that same jungle, a few short yards and half a world away from her, on the other side of the chasm.

She could still feel the imprint of his mouth, a tingle of warmth and moisture that seemed burned into her flesh. She could still see his eyes, in that last moment before she'd turned away from him to lasso herself into this ridiculous swing…those deep, dark blue eyes that could see right through her. She'd be able to see him now, if she let herself, if she rotated that way just a little…but she didn't do it. She couldn't bear to see him getting smaller and smaller, the gulf between them wider and wider…couldn't shake the panicky feeling that he was slipping away from her, that soon he'd be far beyond her reach. So instead she focused on Tony, hauling away on the rope on the far side of the gorge, grinning at her, his teeth white in his mahogany-colored face….

She was halfway across the gorge—she knew that because she'd just drawn even with the returning empty swing—when she heard the shout. From out of the jungle came a wordless bellow of anguish first, and then Hal's voice, raw and broken, calling his wife's name.

Sam got the swing turned around in time to see Cory straighten and let go of the pulley rope, then spin toward the direction of the shouts, lurching off balance like someone who'd taken a bullet. Yelling at Tony over his shoulder to keep on pulling, he plunged into the jungle.

No! She thought she must have screamed it out loud, but it was only inside her head, the word rebounding and resounding there in a nightmare of echoes and alarms. By the time she reached the terminal stump she was muttering and scolding furiously and slapping at Tony's clumsy attempts to help her out of the rope swing, shaking and half-paralyzed with fear. All she could think about was that her worst nightmare was coming true, the gulf of misunderstanding between her and Cory had become tangible and real. Seeing him disappear into that jungle, the thought that she might not ever see him again was unbearable. Unthinkable.

"What the holy hell's going on?" Tony's face hovered over hers, shiny with sweat. He was breathing hard. "I heard shouting. Where are the missionaries? Where'd Cory—"

"I don't know. I think something's happened to Esther. She didn't come, and Hal went to find her." Sam spoke rapidly, her voice low and furious. Her chest felt tight, as though there were chains wrapped around it, so she couldn't get a breath. "I don't know what, but something's wrong. Cory heard Hal shouting and went back to help."

Her voice broke on the last word as she yanked the rope loop out of Tony's hands and threw it back over her head. *Of course he did. Doesn't he always? Just like that day on the lake...he goes diving in after Dad...doesn't stop to think* he *might die, too.*

"What are you doing? Where the hell do you think you're going?" Tony was tugging on the rope and trying to hang on to her at the same time, bracing his feet as if he was engaged in a child's game of tug-of-war.

"I'm going back," Sam said tersely, jerking ineffectively at the rope; she was shaking too hard to have any real strength in her arms and legs. "He's— God knows what's going on back there. Al-Rami's men—they could be—they must have heard— Let me *go,* damn you—I have to help him. I have to—"

And then somehow she was enfolded in Tony's arms, still shaking and muttering furiously against the solid wall of his chest, and his arms were more walls all around her, holding her in, holding her prisoner, yes, but holding her steady, too. Bracing her. Comforting her. Calming her. They were amazingly gentle, too, those massive arms, for someone so tough and brawny-looking.

"I can't let you go back there." Tony's voice was ragged and filled with gravel. "He'd kill me if I did, you know he would. Why do you think he sent us over first? He wanted us safe, that's why. Dammit, Sam…"

Steadier now, she nodded, then lifted her hands, formed them into fists and let them fall with restrained violence against Tony's chest. "Why does he always have to do that?" she said in a low, furious voice. "Why does he think it's all up to him? Who appointed him everybody's keeper? He's always doing that to me—trying to take care of me. Like I'm a little child and he's responsible for me."

Tony eased her away from him, but cautiously, still holding her by the arms. He cleared his throat and looked past her, frowning, yes, but at the same time his pit-bull features had arranged themselves into something softer, something she couldn't read. "Maybe," he mumbled, "he's got good reason for being that way."

A little shiver ran down her spine as she stared at him, and she opened her mouth, questions poised on her tongue. But instead a shout had them both jerking around in time to see three people emerge from the jungle—Cory first, then Hal, carrying Esther in his arms.

"Oh, God…" Sam breathed the prayer as she and Tony sprang forward simultaneously and grabbed hold of the pulley rope.

On the other side of the gorge, Cory had taken Esther from Hal, and the older man was struggling to get himself into the swing. Sam saw him brace his feet, then give a nod, and Cory bend over and place Esther in his arms, as gently and effortlessly as if she'd been a small child, or perhaps a doll.

Cory gave a shout and a wave, and he and Tony and Sam all began hauling with all their strength on the rope. Rotating dizzily, the frail-looking swing with both Lundquists aboard lurched out over the chasm. Sam's attention was focused on that swaying swing and its precious cargo, on pulling as hard as she could on the rope, so she didn't notice at first that Cory's attention was elsewhere, that he kept looking over his shoulder, back toward the jungle. Then she heard crashing sounds and knew her worst fear had only *now* been realized.

Hal's single shout of fear and anguish had brought al-Rami's men back.

Sam's heart leaped into her throat and stayed there. Fear was a living thing, a great black monster, choking her, weighing her down, tying her muscles in knots. It took every ounce of strength she had just to fight against the fear, force her screaming muscles to pull…pull…keep pulling. And still, it seemed, the Lundquists moved toward her with agonizing slowness… advancing across the chasm only inch by inch.

The Lundquists had reached the middle of the gorge. They were passing the returning empty swing. Beside her Sam could hear Tony's grunts of effort and labored breathing and knew he was straining as hard as she was. *Just a little more,* she thought. *Hang on, Cory…just a few more yards…*

The gunshots didn't sound like much—several quick pops, muted by the noise of the rushing river. But across the gorge, Cory seemed to stumble. Then, almost in slow motion, he crumpled to the ground.

No! A shaft of pain…blinding, white-hot agony…ripped through her, as if the bullet had torn through *her* flesh. Then came darkness. Stillness. She didn't hear herself scream, she only felt it, as if someone was ripping her heart out through her throat.

And then…a strange sort of calm settled over her, just as it had that day on the lake so many years ago, the day of the boat accident, when her dad and Cory had both almost drowned. The worst had happened; she was past fear now. She knew what had to be done. Knew she was the only one who could do it.

"Pull, dammit," she said between clenched teeth. *"Pull..."* And funny...she remembered that her arms had felt like this that day, too, as she'd dug them over and over again into the churning water, paddling her knee board toward the place where she'd seen her dad and Cory go down...as if her muscles were on fire...as if she couldn't paddle fast enough...hard enough...as if she couldn't possibly make one more stroke....

The swing bearing Hal and Esther Lundquist was over the lip of the gorge. Sam reached for it to hold it steady while Tony took Esther from Hal's arms and eased her gently down onto the matted and muddy grass.

"Where the hell do you think you're going?" Tony croaked, looking up in time to see Sam lift the swing from around Hal's shoulders and drop it over her own.

"I'm going back for him," she said calmly. "I'm not leaving him behind."

Tony opened his mouth, then closed it again. "Right. I'll go." He lurched to his feet as Hal took his place beside his wife. But Sam was shaking her head.

"Stay here—take care of them." She tipped her head toward the Lundquists—Hal was stroking Esther's sweat-damp forehead as she moaned softly, and Sam had time for one thought: *Thank God, at least she's alive.* "You're stronger than I am—I'll need you to pull us back across."

Tony hesitated only a moment, then nodded. Sam hitched herself onto the bamboo seat. But just as she was about to cast off, she saw something that sent another bolt of adrenaline rocketing through her body.

Across the gorge, Cory was struggling to his feet. Once again struggling to breathe, and with her heart back in her throat, she watched him stagger to the swing, hunched over and dragging one leg. She watched in paralyzing helplessness while he fumbled the loop of rope, clumsily trying to get it over his shoulders, his teeth showing white in a grimace of agony.

Belatedly remembering where she was, Sam yanked the loop of rope and bamboo from around her shoulders just as Tony yelled hoarsely, "He's on! Go!"

Then once again they were hauling on the rope together, pulling hard, and Cory was swinging out over the void, legs dangling, arms hugging the loop of rope in a deathlike embrace. He'd made it almost to the middle of the gorge when three of Fahad al-Rami's men burst out of the jungle. One had his weapon up and was firing wildly, while the other two ran to the pulley terminal, hands reaching, ready to grasp the incoming swing.

Sam swore, one sharp, sibilant oath, full of chagrin and despair.

"What?" Tony yelled.

"The chair! Why didn't I unhook the damn chair! Look at them—they'll be over here after us in a minute—"

"Worry about that when the time comes. Right now Cory's a sitting duck out there!"

"I know—you keep pulling…" Sam stopped hauling on the rope and instead threw all her weight against it from the side…then swung back…then threw herself against it once more.

"What the hell are you doing?" Tony screeched, as out in the middle of the gorge Cory's swing began to bob and sway like a kite in the wind.

"Making him a moving target," Sam yelled back. The pop and crackle of gunfire sounded almost continuously now.

Tony was swearing wildly, rivers of sweat streaming down his face. "Jeez, Sam…what if he can't hold on?"

"He'll hold on," Sam said grimly. "He'd damn well *better* hold on…" *Don't you dare get yourself killed, Pearse. I swear, if you die, I'll never forgive you!*

Or myself, a voice inside her added….

She could see his face now. His beautiful eyes…and he'd lost his glasses somewhere. But his eyes were closed, his teeth still clenched in that grimace of pain, his skin a dreadful chalky gray. Fear spasmed in her belly like nausea, and cold sweat poured from her skin. *What if he's been hit again? How many times has he been hit? What if he's dying at this very moment? Oh, God...Pearse...*

Then he was *there*, and Tony's strong arms were supporting him, and Sam was touching him...finding him warm and alive...tearing the rope from around his body, patting him, touching him, searching for blood...for bullet wounds.

"Think I'm gonna be sick," Cory mumbled. "I think I'm seasick...what the hell were you tryin' to do to me out there?"

"Saving your life, Batman," Sam said, trying to be curt... shaky instead. "Had to go and be a hero—" She managed to free him from the rope swing just as bullets thunked into the turf near her feet. She gave Tony a shove toward the trees. "Go, go, go— get everybody into cover. I've got to try and stop these guys..."

The knife. Please, God, she prayed, let Esther still have that bundle...

Hal had picked his wife up in his arms and was carrying her into the shelter of the trees. Sam caught at his arm. "Her bundle—that pot of hers," she gasped. "Where is it? Do you still have it? The knife—"

"It's here." Hal swung around so she could see Esther's pot dangling from his neck and shoulder along with his own. "Take it—quickly!"

And Sam was already tugging the leaf-wrapped bundle out of the pot...kneeling to open it, spilling its contents helterskelter on the ground. She snatched up the narrow oblong that held the knife and ran to the terminal stump, unwinding leaf wrappings as she went. Her heart felt on fire, her chest ready to burst, as she began to saw furiously at the rope that fastened the pulley to the stump.

As she sawed she was dimly aware that behind her Tony, Cory and the Lundquists had reached the comparative safety of the trees. Blinking away the sweat that was pouring into her eyes, all but blinding her, she risked a glance to check on the terrorist's progress. Then she wished she hadn't.

He'd reached the halfway point; she could see his face now, grinning, his eyes glittering with anticipation. She felt a jolt under her ribs as she realized she recognized him. It was the "spokesman," the leader of the band that had brought them from the village hospital; the one who had looked at Cory with such hatred. She knew they could expect no mercy from him. Fortunately, at the moment he was too busy holding on to the rope to fire the weapon slung across his chest, but Sam knew the moment he stepped onto solid ground they were all dead.

Her muscles burned like fire, but she kept sawing. How much longer could she keep it up, before her arms turned to so much dead wood? *As long as it takes,* she thought grimly, setting her teeth and fighting to block out the pain.

Just when she was beginning to think even her will wouldn't be enough, Tony was suddenly there at her side. "Take over!" she gasped, and almost wept in relief when she felt his hands push hers aside and close around the handle of the knife.

Then she was looking around frantically, looking for something to use for a weapon—a rock, a log—anything. The terrorist was only a couple of yards from the bank, close enough for her to smell his sweat, close enough to see the cruelty in his eyes. Maybe, she thought, before he has a chance to get his feet under him, I can knock him out…push him over the side…

But…just then, there was a triumphant grunt from Tony, and a dry, slithering, scraping sound. And a heavy clank as the pulley hit the ground. A look of blank astonishment came over the terrorist's face…and then he disappeared.

Chapter 12

Sam didn't wait around to see what had happened to al-Rami's man. After a moment of shocked stillness, amid shouts of fury and a renewed clatter of gunfire from the two terrorists left on the opposite bank, she and Tony ran like hell for the trees.

Once the sheltering foliage had closed around them, she dropped back to let Tony take the lead, since only he knew where, in that tangle of jungle, he'd left the others.

"Cory—" she panted as she ran, gasping for breath, her terror returning in a chilling rush "—how is he? Is he okay? He's alive, isn't he?" *Of course he is. I can't think—won't think about the alternative.*

"Was when I left him." Tony's reply was clipped and grim.

Icy fingers squeezed her heart…squeezed the breath from her lungs. "How bad was he hit? How many—"

"Just the one, far as I could see. In his leg. But it was bleeding pretty bad…"

"Oh, God." *Oh God oh God…* She felt the cold and darkness closing in around her.

Then…she saw him, cradled in a nest of mossy roots with his back propped against a tree, and he seemed to be awake and conscious, jerkily tugging at some sort of strap tied around his thigh. His head came up when he heard them coming, like a deer alert to approaching danger. Then his eyes arrowed straight into hers and lit with a fearsome gladness…relief and love so naked and profound it pierced her soul. To her it felt like a shaft of sunlight breaking through thick black clouds. It was light and warmth, and joy and hope, and she wanted to bask in it like a cat in October sun.

So, of course, perversely, she left Tony to see to Cory, and with her heart still thumping painfully and adrenaline ebbing, angled unsteadily to where Hal Lundquist sat with his wife's head in his lap.

"How's she doing?" she asked softly as she dropped to one trembling knee beside them.

Before Hal could reply, Esther's eyes opened and her lips twitched briefly in a pale imitation of her usual cheery smile. "Oh, hello, dear." Her voice was feeble and gasping. "A little better, I think. I must have fainted…bad time for it, I know. Sorry to be such a bother."

Hal's head moved in an almost imperceptible shake. "I think it's her heart," he murmured, and his expression was bleak as he gazed down at his wife's face and gently stroked her hair. Her eyes were closed again, and she looked almost serene now…and alarmingly fragile.

"Her heart?" Sam was shocked; the woman had seemed so robust—so…indomitable. "But why? She's so…" *So not the heart-attack type!* "Has she had problems like this before?"

Again the movement of Hal Lundquist's head was slight, as he continued to gaze down at his wife and caress her forehead. "She wouldn't have told anyone if she had. But I'm not too surprised by this. She has a family history."

"Well, we're going to get her to a hospital," Sam promised grimly as she pushed herself to her feet. "As soon as we can. Do you think you can carry her, or shall we make a litter?"

For the first time Hal's pale blue eyes, fogged now with sadness, lifted to hers. He seemed dazed, almost as if he was surprised by the question. "I'll carry her. No need for a litter—
unless…perhaps for your friend? He seemed to be bleeding
rather badly."

Something hitched painfully under Sam's ribs as she turned
with a murmured, "Right…" and made her way through the foliage to where Tony crouched beside a pale and sweaty-looking
Cory.

"How's he doin'?" she asked as she lowered herself to the
wet, mossy turf, hoping bright and cheery would hide the fear
that was once again robbing her of breath.

"How's he doing? I'll tell you how he's doing—look what he
did!" Tony held up his camera, minus its neck strap. "Damn guy
made a tourniquet outa my camera strap." He was trying his best
to look and sound outraged, but his grin kept leaking through.

"Is it working?" Sam shifted her eyes to Cory, careful to
avoid looking at his blood-soaked pantleg.

His eyes held hers as he replied in a voice that was airless with
pain, "Slowed it down some."

She turned back to Tony. "Got any more of those straps?"

"Right here." He was already reaching for the equipment
bags.

And to Cory again, "I'm gonna need your shirt."

He nodded, gritted his teeth and began to tug at his shirt with
bloody hands. Appalled, she slapped his hands away. "Here, I'll
get it—raise up your arms." And as she pulled the T-shirt out of
his waistband her fingers grazed his belly. His skin felt clammy
and cold. Shaken, she was careful not to touch him again.
Though the desire…the need to touch him was so overwhelming she trembled with it.

Quickly, she folded the damp T-shirt into a thick pad. When
she placed it over the seeping hole in his thigh, he jerked and
breath hissed between his teeth. Sam threw him a mocking look.
"Don't be a baby, Pearse. Can't have you bleeding to death."

"You sure about that?" His voice was breathy with what might have been laughter. "Kinda had me wondering out there, when I was swingin' in the wind. Thought maybe you were tryin' to dump me in the river."

Furious suddenly, and fighting tears, she shot back between clenched teeth, "I told you, I was trying—"

"Sam." He touched her arm, leaving it blood-smeared. "That was a joke. I know what you were trying to do." His eyes seemed bottomless as they clung to hers. A smile flickered briefly, and his voice dropped to a whisper. "Thank you."

She wanted to say "You're welcome," say it flippantly, as if she hadn't a care in the world. But even after clearing her throat the words wouldn't come. And by that time Tony was there with another camera strap—a nice wide one, brightly woven in some sort of Native American pattern—and she made herself busy getting it knotted around Cory's thigh and the pressure pad in just the right place, and she hoped no one would notice that her hands were shaking.

"Okay," she said briskly when she was finished, "that's the best we can do for now. Tony, you want to load up? The quicker we get going, the faster we'll be able to get help. I'm thinking maybe that clinic'll have some supplies we can use to get them both stabilized." She raised her voice and called to Hal, "How far did you say it is to the village? A couple of miles?"

"More like three or four," came the doleful reply.

"Esther said he's a pessimist," Sam muttered under her breath. "Let's hope she's right."

Tony was a short distance away, rearranging his burden of camera and equipment bags, now short two neck straps. Sam was about to stand up, too, ready to help Cory to his feet, when he touched her arm, then beckoned her closer.

"Sam...I want you to know something...in case I don't..." The weakness in his voice terrified her.

"Don't you even *think* about it," she snapped back at him, shaking with fear and impotent fury. "Don't you dare. Just... don't you dare." She shoved herself to her feet, her vision blurred and shimmering, chest heaving. "Trust me—you're gonna have

a whole lot of time to say whatever it is you have to say to me.
Now—if you're *quite* finished feeling sorry for yourself, do you
think you can get your butt up offa there, so we can get going?"

"Yes, ma'am," Cory muttered contritely. But he was quivering inside with a crazy mixture of amusement and admiration,
weakness and fear. He knew he was in a bad way, not just because of the way he felt, which was as lousy as he could ever remember feeling, but because Sam was in a temper. And if Sam
was in a temper, it meant she was either upset or scared—in this
case, he figured probably both. Scared for him, he thought. And
for Esther. Scared she wasn't going to be able to get them help
in time. It was a sobering thought.

But at the same time, as he watched her take charge, shoulder the weight—literally—of the sick and injured, get everyone
moving again, he felt a tremendous surge of admiration. And
pride. And humility. And in a way, shame. He'd always admired
her, of course, both as a woman and as a person, and been proud
of her, too. But he wondered now if there'd been something pa-
tronizing in his enjoyment of her, as if he'd been somehow responsible for her, or as if she were an extension of himself. God
help him, was he only now seeing her as the incredible and
amazing person she was, separate and apart from him? It was a
horrifying, humiliating thought.

And with it came another: *She loves me.*

He felt dazed as her shoulders came under his arm and lifted,
and her strong bones and supple muscles grew taut in support of
his weight…as he felt the heat and energy radiating from her
body, smelled the sweat of exertion and fear, heard the fierce,
determined sound of her breathing. *My God,* he thought, *she
does.* And he realized he hadn't really believed it before, or understood how much. He wondered if he'd ever heard her say it.
Wondered if that was why he'd felt abandoned when she'd gone
off to pursue her career, and why he'd put her to such a terrible
test, forcing her to choose. An impossible choice, he understood
now. What he'd asked her to give up had been nothing less than
what made her who she was. And so much about her he loved.

The thought made him sick and weak with shame. *I don't deserve her,* he thought. *She was right to turn me down. And if I do make it through this, and she decides to give me another chance, I'd damn well better figure out a way to make it right.*

If we get through this…

"Sam," he murmured, turning his face toward her and away from Tony, who was holding him up from the other side. He could feel the wet ends of her hair, like kitten kisses on his face. "That thing behind your ear…"

Her arm tightened around his waist. "Yeah, what about it?"

"Can you use it to call for help? Like…is there a code for Mayday?"

He heard the hiss of a breath and saw her eye crinkle and her cheek change shape with her smile. "An extraction? Yeah, and I mean to do that…just as soon as we get to a clearing big enough for a chopper to set down."

Well, he should have known she'd have thought of it already. That she'd have it covered. Should have known he could leave it to her. This business of trusting her with his life…it seemed it was going to take some getting used to.

He let go, then, let himself slide into a twilight of pain and struggle and jungle growth and dampness that seemed to go on and on…endlessly.

Though he knew when it began to rain again. They didn't stop to look for shelter, but just kept going, following Hal, whose gaunt, heroic figure seemed like a ghostly outrider in that curtain of rain, plodding tirelessly ahead, carrying his wife in his arms and leading the way.

And he knew when at last they left the jungle for the cultivated fields on the outskirts of the village, but he felt no sense of triumph or relief when he was lowered onto the muddy bank of a rice paddy…only terrible cold and weakness, and an exhaustion that seemed unconquerable even by his most powerful effort of will. But, he remembered, they were in the open, now. Sam would call for extraction, using that sci-fi chip in her scalp.

He didn't have to get up, didn't have to move again. He could wait right here for the chopper to come and pick him up....

Except, the next thing he knew Sam and Tony were there again, pulling at him, making him get up, forcing him to walk, making him move on.

"It's the rain," Sam yelled above the roar of the deluge as they struggled on. "I can't get a signal through. Right now, I'm hoping we can at least get some first-aid supplies at that little hospital...clinic, or whatever. We'll ride this out...try for a chopper later. If all else fails, we'll just have to fly out."

Fly out, Sam thought. *Yeah, that's* if *the plane's still intact. And* if *the landing strip isn't knee-deep in mud.* If *we make it that far...*

But she didn't want to think that far ahead—couldn't let herself. One step at a time. First, make it to the hospital in the village. There'd be medical supplies there, and food and water and shelter...maybe even dry clothes, if the bags they'd had to leave behind were still there. Imagining what it would feel like to be dry again nearly made her weep, and her stomach growled at the thought of those nonperishable field rations in her backpack.

It was because of the rain that she had no warning. It had washed away the smoke and the stink of wet ashes and death, so it wasn't until they came out of the trees that lined the road leading through the village that she realized al-Rami's forces had been there before them.

The chaos was appalling. At least half the houses in the village had been damaged or destroyed and the muddy lanes between them were littered with debris and the carcasses of animals. A few people moved slowly through the wreckage, too dazed and numb to pay much attention either to the rain or the five new refugees among them.

Except for a softly uttered profanity from Tony, no one spoke as they made their way through the ruined village. Sam tried to close her mind to the devastation and concentrate only on the task at hand, but it was impossible; she'd never experienced the waste of war firsthand before. She was badly shaken, though she didn't want to be, and already dreading what they would find at the hospital.

"I guess you've seen all this before," she said in a low voice, directing the comment to Tony past Cory's rain-slicked chest but tilting her head to include both men in the pronoun.

"Yeah, we have." Tony didn't look at her as he replied; he was bearing most of Cory's weight now, and his face was set in a bull-dog grimace of effort. "Never get used to it, though."

"Nobody should," Cory muttered. "Get used to it…" His voice trailed weakly off.

Sam and Tony exchanged a brief look. *Please, God,* Sam prayed, *let the hospital still be standing.*

But her prayer wasn't to be answered, not that one, anyway. Where the hospital, the village's pride and joy, had stood, there was only a burned-out ruin, a charred skeleton reeking of soggy ashes.

She'd been looking ahead, her attention riveted on the devastation, her gaze sliding past Hal Lundquist, who was trudging doggedly on some distance ahead of them. But she saw him halt in his tracks, then sink slowly to his knees in the muddy road. His shoulders hunched and his head bowed; he seemed to curl himself over the woman he held close in his arms, and it appeared poignantly as if he was shielding her from the rain. As Sam came nearer she could see his shoulders shaking.

"Can you manage?" she said in an undertone to Tony, and when he nodded, though every nerve in her body screamed in protest at the separation, she peeled her arm from around Cory's waist and eased her shoulders out from under his weight. And as she moved away from him, her side and shoulders where his warmth had been felt chilled and raw, as if her skin had been stripped away.

She bent over Hal and laid her hand awkwardly on his shoulder. "Come on, Hal, don't give up on her now." She'd meant to say it gently, but it came out gruff instead, and she thought, *Damn you, Pearse—you'd have been so much better at this than I am!* Because suddenly, irrationally, she was more than a little angry at him for getting himself shot and letting her down like this.

"It'll be all right," she said to Hal, awkwardly patting his shoulder. "It's gonna be okay." And she wondered who she was trying to convince—him or herself?

Miraculously, though, the lanai adjoining the hospital had survived almost untouched. While Sam supported most of Esther's weight, Hal managed to stagger to his feet, and together they stumbled the last few remaining yards to shelter. They found Cory and Tony there already, Cory stretched out on one of the market tables and Tony standing beside him with his hands braced on the edge, hunched over and breathing hard.

"How's he doing?" Sam asked Tony in a low voice as she helped Hal lay Esther down on another table nearby.

"*He's* doing just fine—awake and lucid and capable of answering for himself," Cory muttered irritably, sounding almost normal, although he slurred his words a little. "Wish you guys'd quit talking over me. How's Esther?"

"Hangin' in there. And don't you dare get testy with me, Pearse." Sam's voice was clipped and breathless. God, it was hard to see him lying there like that...pale and thin, bearded and muddy...shivering like a castaway or the survivor of some wilderness ordeal. Fear blew its icy breath into her lungs and she gasped, momentarily paralyzed by it.

Tony lifted his head, still winded and breathing hard through his nose, and saw Sam's eyes lose their fire and her face go bleak. She's losing it, he thought. *Hang in there, Captain.* "Okay, boys and girls," he said briskly, "if you're all done bickering, what's our next move?"

To his relief, Sam gave herself a little shake and took a breath, and he saw her eyes focus once more. "Okay," she said, "We've got two choices. One, we can wait for the rain to stop and see if I can call in a chopper. Don't ask." She glared at him, holding up a hand to shut him up before he could ask her how she planned on doing that. "Trust me, okay?"

"Okay," he said when he saw Cory nodding his head underneath the arm he'd thrown across his eyes. Tony nodded toward the table where Hal Lundquist sat beside his wife's still form, hunched over, eyes closed, hands clasped…lips moving. Praying, he thought, and from long ago and half-forgotten memory, he felt a sudden impulse to cross himself. Lowering his voice, he said, "I don't know if we've got time to wait."

He saw Sam's eyes drop for an instant to Cory, and the pinched look of fear come back into her eyes—just for a moment, though, like a bird's shadow crossing the sun. "Yeah, I know. The other option is to get to the plane and fly it out—" her eyes flicked to the destruction around her and her face went bleak "—assuming the plane's there and in any shape to fly."

"Right," said Tony on an exhalation. "Maybe one of us should go check it out first. I can—"

"You wouldn't know what to check for. I'll go," Sam said in a hard, no-arguments voice, and he could tell from the way her eyes clung to Cory that she'd about rather chop off her arm than leave him. "You stay here and look after the others. I'll be—"

They both froze as something rustled in the foliage behind the lanai. Both Tony and Sam moved instinctively, almost as one, to shield Cory's body with theirs, and even as he did that Tony was thinking, *Damn, she must love him. I believe she'd die for him in a heartbeat.* He knew without a doubt the reverse was true as well, and he had time for a flash of something that was maybe half envy, half exasperation with the two of them for being so damn stupid, for not knowing what a precious thing it was they had going for them.

While his eyes were darting around the lanai looking for something he might be able to turn into a weapon, a man stepped out of the curtain of rain and under the relative shelter of the thatched roof. Tony relaxed and let out a relieved breath when he recognized the slight and humble figure as the hospital's caretaker, the man who'd met them on their arrival.

Sam went eagerly to greet him, speaking to him in the language they'd used before—Tagalog, if he had to guess. The man rotated his upper body as he replied, and shifted something from his shoulder onto a nearby table.

Damned if it wasn't Cory's laptop.

The man spoke with Sam for several minutes more, gesturing descriptively and pointing, looking excited one minute, weighed down with grief the next. Finally, after a sad little bow to Sam, he nodded toward Tony and the others and slipped back into the rain.

"Hey, Pearse, I brought you a present," Sam said as she rejoined them, taking the laptop from her shoulder and placing it gently on Cory's chest.

He managed a thin and groggy-sounding, "Hey, that's great…" as he clutched it with both hands and struggled to sit up. "Where did you…"

"He said it was the only thing he was able to save when they evacuated the hospital. Personally," she added with a flash of wry grin, "I wish he'd left the laptop and saved the food and clothing. Right now I'd kill for a candy bar and a dry shirt."

"Anyway," she went on, her face grave again, "Tomas said the attack came this morning, just before dawn. Government forces—"

"*Government* forces did this?"

"They were after Fahad al-Rami. Guess they didn't care who they got in the process," she said dryly. "What do you guys call it—collateral damage? Anyway, al-Rami and his bunch arrived last evening and took over the hospital—made everyone else leave. They figured government forces wouldn't attack a hospital. Turns out they were wrong."

"Did they get him?" Cory croaked. "Al-Rami? Is he dead?"

"Tomas doesn't know. He says they all fled when the shelling started, and took their dead and wounded with them. The good news is—" she took a breath, and this time her smile blossomed unrestrained "—he says he thinks the plane's okay. He says al-Rami's forces came in from the other direction and went out the same way, so they didn't get as far as the landing strip. And he hasn't heard any shelling from over that way, either. So—

what about it, guys?" The smile wavered. "You up for one more run?"

"I'm ready," Tony said, and nudged Cory. "How 'bout you, buddy? Think you can hobble that far?"

"Let's get the hell outa Dodge," Cory muttered, straightening up and sliding off the table. He would have kept going right on down to the ground if Tony hadn't caught him.

Like a daddy picking up his child, Sam thought as she rescued the laptop and slung it over her shoulder. She got her arm around Cory's waist to help Tony hold him upright, and her heart lumbered back to its customary location in her chest after another brief sojourn in her throat. And once again it flashed through her mind that Tony Whitehall was really a very sweet and gentle man, and not at all the tough guy he looked like.

She turned to Hal, who was still sitting slumped on the edge of the table, gazing at his wife. She touched him lightly on the shoulder. "Hal? Do you need help? Would you like Tony to carry her now?"

He gave himself a shake, as if rousing from some gentle reverie. "What? Oh—no, no, that's all right. I'll carry her. Don't worry about me." His voice, which had started out breathy and faint, seemed to grow stronger as he went on. "We'll be fine," he concluded firmly. Then he picked up his wife, cradled her tenderly against his chest once more, and without another word walked out of the lanai and into the rain.

"He's got to be going on sheer willpower," Sam said as she and Tony set out after the Lundquists, with Cory, stoic and silent, hobbling loose-jointedly between them.

"Uh-uh," Tony said between panting breaths, "that's *love,* babe. Most powerful force in the world. Willpower can't hold a candle to it."

That would explain why I don't seem to have any power against it, Sam thought bleakly. But why did it have to be so complicated, so hard to identify—at least for absolute certainty? Shouldn't such a powerful force be simple and straightforward, like other forces of nature? Like hurricanes and volcanoes and tidal waves—no mistaking those things for what they were! But love? That was like…like… Frustrated, she gave up trying to think of an analogy that felt right—Cory would probably have had the perfect one, she thought—and it was almost a relief to put the whole thing out of her mind and concentrate on the nearly impossible task ahead of her.

Tomas's guess had been right. The plane was just as they'd left it. Both it and the landing strip appeared to have escaped the devastation that lay barely half a mile away beyond the fringe of palm and bamboo and banana trees.

The big question, Sam knew, was whether the landing strip would be firm enough to hold the weight of the DC-3 during takeoff. The cultivated fields on both sides of the strip were lakes of water, mud-colored sheets that seemed to boil under the bombardment of raindrops. The landing strip was raised above the level of the fields and seemed to be free of standing water, but she had no way of knowing how solid the ground was underneath the grass cover.

There was only one way to find out.

"You-all stay put," Sam yelled in modified Southern, as they huddled in a small grove of banana trees on the edge of the fields. "I'm gonna go check out the runway." Cory caught at her hand, and she flashed a strained and crooked smile, looking past him with unfocused eyes. She couldn't look at his gaunt, pain-ravaged face, or the blood-soaked cargo pants. Didn't dare. "No sense in everybody getting stuck in the mud, if that's the situation."

Hang on, Pearse, she begged him silently as she wrenched her hand from his. *I'm not gonna let you bleed to death, dammit—or lose your leg, either!*

But it was only bravado, and as she splashed out into the flooded fields, some of the moisture she brushed from her face wasn't rain.

She'd only gone a few yards when she heard something that changed all her plans—an all-too-familiar sound—the pop and crackle of gunfire. But where was it coming from? In the rain it was impossible to tell. From the village? Or the jungle on the other side of the fields? Or—dear God, *both,* and they were about to be caught in the crossfire?

She spun around and ran back to the banana grove, waving and yelling as she went. "Come on—now! Everybody. We have to get to the plane. That gunfire might be the government's forces or it might be al-Rami's, but one thing's for sure, we don't want to be caught in between!"

She grabbed Hal's hand and helped him to his feet, waited, shifting impatiently, until he'd picked up Esther and gotten her situated, then tucked her shoulder under Cory's arm and slipped hers around his waist. And once again, she set out across the sea of rain and mud.

How they made it, she never knew. Later, looking back on it, she didn't remember her heart pounding, or her muscles screaming, or her breath tearing through her lungs. She remembered a terrible sense of urgency and purpose. And one clear thought: *Get everybody into the plane.*

She remembered Hal Lundquist's face, set in a zombielike mask, eyes wide and unfocused, and she remembered wondering how on earth he could still be moving, still be putting one foot in front of the other, carrying his sick wife all those miles, through the rain and mud and jungle…

She remembered thinking about what Tony had said: *That's love, babe. Most powerful force in the world.*

Chapter 13

The DC-3 loomed ahead in the rain, its nose in the air and its tail dragging on the grassy landing strip…the great gray Gooneybird, relic from another time, a different war. Sam's spirits lifted with relief and thanksgiving at the sight, almost as if she were already at the controls of the aircraft and soaring toward the sky.

She let go of Cory and scrambled up the short grassy bank ahead of the others, then turned to offer a hand. Hal slipped once, but never lost his dogged grip on Esther, and then Sam was there on one side of him and Tony on the other, holding him up, and together they all made it to the relative shelter of the plane's big wing.

"Get everybody inside," Sam yelled to Tony. "I'm gonna go check out the runway."

She slipped under the wing and ran past the plane's upswept nose…down the grass-covered strip that stretched ahead of her arrow-straight until it disappeared into the curtain of rain. She ran for nearly a hundred yards, and her heart lifted with such relief and hope she felt as if she could have run forever…turned cartwheels…shouted for joy. Under her feet, rather than the squelch of sucking mud or the give of saturated soil, she felt only a beautiful, unyielding…*crunch*.

She turned, finally, and jogged back to the plane, and Tony came hesitantly to meet her, his face tight with suspense. He looked slightly stunned—though pleased—when she threw her arms around him and kissed him resoundingly on his broad wet cheek.

"That's for your grandaddy," she yelled. "Those navy Cee Bees knew their stuff. Must've built this thing out of crushed volcanic rock. It's solid as the runways at JFK!"

"Go Cee Bees!" Tony pumped an arm in the air and grinned. "So, we're good to go?"

"Good to go! I just need to check out the plane. Everybody inside and buckled in?"

"Almost," Tony said dryly, jerking a thumb over his shoulder. "He wouldn't get in until you got back."

She looked past him and her heart lurched when she saw Cory standing beside the plane, leaning heavily on the steps. "Typical…" she muttered, but couldn't deny the sweet warmth—Lord, what could she call it—tenderness?—that flooded her. Though she did try, adding a sardonic, "My God, what's holding him up?"

Tony shrugged and gave her a sly look. "What'd I tell you? It's love—what else?"

Having no answer for that, Sam made a halfhearted scoffing noise. Her heart was beating like a trip-hammer as she left Tony and walked over to Cory, and inexplicably, she felt awkard and shy. Her face ached and the best smile she could come up with was small and crooked as she spread her hands wide and said, "Hey, Pearse, it's okay…the runway's okay. Rock solid. We're getting out of here. We're gonna get everybody home."

He looked at her. Just looked…his eyes sunk so deep in their sockets they seemed almost black…his face chalk-white beneath a dark growth of beard. Then he lifted his hand and curved it around the back of her neck. She felt his arm tremble as he pulled her close, but his lips were warm and firm when he kissed her. Then he folded her one-armed against him…let go of the steps and wrapped both arms around her. And though she could feel him swaying with weakness, she closed her eyes and let herself hold him for a long, sweet moment.

One that lasted not nearly long enough. It was shattered by the thump of a distant explosion, and then, closer by, the all-too-familiar rattle of gunfire.

Tony lurched past her up the steps yelling, "Here they come! Let's get the hell outa here."

New adrenaline spurted into her bloodstream as she hooked an arm around Cory, who was struggling to pull himself up the steps, dragging his injured leg.

"Get him inside and buckled in," she yelled to Tony, and then she was ducking under the end of the wing, trying not to cringe as the sounds of battle rumbled closer, knowing she had only minutes to get the plane off the ground, knowing, too, that if she overlooked something vital in the preflight prep it could mean disaster for everyone on board.

So, she forced herself to shut out the gunfire and concentrate on the checklist in her mind…checked the props, looking for bird nests in the cylinders and hinges…checked the cowls and gear pins. Satisfied, finally, she pulled the chocks from the wheels and sprinted for the door of the plane.

She pulled up the steps and secured the door, then paused to catch her breath. So far so good, but they weren't out of the woods yet. Not by a long shot. A DC-3 aircraft wasn't a car, she couldn't just jump in and start it up and go shooting off into the wild blue yonder. It was going to take a while to run through even the most basic cockpit check, and then the warm-up…the take-off… Thank God, at least she'd had the foresight to turn the plane around before she'd shut it down!

On her way up the aisle she paused to make sure everyone was belted securely, and had to resist the impulse to put her hand on Cory's shoulder…just to touch him one more time.

Then she was slipping into the pilot's seat, running through the preflight check, once again forcing herself not to rush, to concentrate on the task at hand. *Flight instruments checked… gyros…airspeed selector…trims…pitch…throttles…mixture… tail lock…hydraulics…*

Satisfied at last, she cleared the props and put her hand on the engine-selector switch, just as Tony slid into the right-hand seat beside her.

"We 'bout ready to get this thing airborne?" he asked, his voice breathless and light, trying to hide the urgency in it. "Those bullets are getting a little too close for comfort."

"Starting the engines now," Sam replied, tight-lipped, as her fingers manipulated the switches and first one engine, then the other coughed and fired, shaking the plane with their powerful vibrations. Still going through preparations for takeoff, she spared Tony a brief glance. "Buckle up if you're staying, pal."

"Right…" He pulled his harness tight and squirmed himself into the seat, then looked up and through the windshield. "Uh…Captain?"

"Yeah?" Sam said absently, her eyes on the oil pressure gauge. Then, something in Tony's voice got through to her and she looked up, too. Her heart seemed to freeze in her chest.

The rain had stopped, as if someone had turned off a faucet. And she could see, far down the landing strip, a dozen or so men wearing camouflage pants, running, zigzagging toward the plane, firing automatic rifles as they came.

She swore, one sharp, succinct word, as something—a mortar shell or grenade—exploded in the flooded field near the men, sending geysers of muddy water into the air.

"Uh…might want to get this thing in the air while we've still got a runway," Tony muttered, sounding strangled.

"Can't get the rpm's up 'til I've got oil pressure," she said grimly, as her heart pounded and her eyes flicked between the gauges and the advancing gunmen. Al-Rami's men, she assumed, and those incoming shells must be the government's troops. If even one of them hit its target, the runway would be cut in two. She needed a thousand meters of it for takeoff.

"Come on...come on..." With agonizing slowness, the oil and fuel pressure and temperature readings came into line. Sam's eyes burned in their sockets as she watched them. Her neck muscles felt like wire. The plane shook and bucked like a tethered bronc as the rpm's rose....

Then... *"Okay!"* The word gusted from her on an exhalation. "Here we go..."

With her teeth tightly clenched and her right hand light and steady on the controls, she sent the plane forward, straight toward the oncoming gunmen. She didn't even wince when she heard bullets clang into the plane's metal skin, just tightened her jaw, held the plane steady on course and increased speed...and knew a moment's sheer jubilation as the men on the runway in front of her broke and scattered like chickens, some diving head-first into the muddy water alongside the strip.

"Yee-haw!" Tony crowed, but Sam was too busy, now, for celebrations. Her eyes were on the approaching jungle...coming up fast...coming closer...closer. Her hand was on the throttle...increasing speed...faster...faster. And then...at last... Lift off!

She felt her body press into her seat and her heart shoot through the roof of her mouth as the DC-3's nose swept up and over the treetops. It climbed steadily toward the lowering gray clouds, and the growl of the two big engines was the most beautiful sound she'd ever heard. Then they were in the clouds, swathed in filmy gray-white mist...bucking with the turbulence...then above them, where the air was smooth and the sun was shining.

As the warmth and brilliance of it sliced through the wind-shield, nearly blinding her, Sam eased back in her seat and drew a careful breath. She allowed herself, now, to look over at Tony, and saw that he'd put his head back against his seat, too, and that his eyes were closed. His bulldog face looked bunched and tense, as if his skin held in emotions almost too turbulent to contain.

"Hey—you can go tell Cory we made it," she said softly, and a smile burst across her face like a sunrise.

She was drifting with the drone of the DC-3's engines, allowing her mind the luxury of numbness, although her body was still chilled and quivering with adrenaline hangover, when Tony slipped back into the copilot's seat a short time later.

Pulling herself together reluctantly, she shifted and threw him a glance, and though she cleared her throat, her voice was gruff when she asked, "How's everybody doin' back there?"

"Hangin' in," Tony said, remembering without being told to fasten his seat belt. "Esther's asleep. Hal looks like he is, and somebody just forgot to tell him to close his eyes."

"Cory?" The word came with a little hitch in her breathing she couldn't control.

He shrugged and lowered his voice just a bit. "Hard to say. I know he's gotta be hurting. Lost an awful lot of blood. That tourniquet's been on there a long time, too—that can't be good, but he'd probably bleed to death if we loosen it up." He let out a breath. "He says he's doin' okay, but...you can't always tell what's goin' on with him."

"Tell me about it," Sam said softly. She felt weighed down, suddenly: exhausted, worn-out, depressed. Where only a short while ago she'd been soaring on waves of euphoria, now she wallowed in troughs of futility and despair. And there was frustration with herself and anger, too, because depressed and weighed down wasn't who Samantha June Bauer *was*, and for sure not the way she ever wanted to be.

After a long silence, during which her pride wrestled with an unaccustomed and overwhelming need to talk to someone, she drew a deep breath and said, "Tony?" And then, in a voice edgy and tense with all she was feeling, including the anger: "What am I gonna do?"

"You're doin' it, all you can do, anyway. Getting him to a hospital the fastest—"

She shook that off with an impatient gesture. "I mean about *us*. Cory and me."

After a cautious pause and an uneasy glance, Tony shrugged. "You love him. He loves you. I don't see the problem."

"Yeah, but…" She let out a short, sharp breath, fighting to keep her voice steady. "All of this—none of this is real. All our problems—everything that was wrong before—it's all still there. Nothing's changed, not really."

There was another pause while Tony appeared to be thinking it over. Then he said, "Well, I know one thing you can't do."

Sam threw him a hopeful look. "What's that?"

"Live without each other."

Damn. In spite of all her efforts, the tears she'd been fighting so hard welled up anyway. She blinked them furiously away before they could fall. "Yeah, but unfortunately I still have a career and a…a lifestyle I really love, and that isn't what he wants. And he still won't share himself with me emotionally, and that's not the kind of relationship *I* want. *Okay?* So…I'm asking you—his best friend. What do I do?"

He shifted in his seat, clearly uncomfortable with the role of counselor she'd thrust upon him. "Like I said. I think you guys need to talk."

Too upset to let him off the hook, frustrated almost beyond her ability to control it, Sam growled, "Yeah, but he *won't*. Don't you understand? Not about himself, not the things that matter. And I don't know how to make him, Tony."

He was quiet for a long time. Then, looking straight ahead at the hazy horizon, he said slowly, "Yeah, but…I think you're gonna have to."

"What if I can't?" she whispered, wretched and in despair.

"You need to get him to tell you about his parents."

Something in his voice made her look over at him. "He told me they died."

He turned his head, and his exotic whiskey-gold eyes looked straight into hers—briefly, before he turned back to the horizon again. "Get him to tell you *how* they died. *Make* him."

She stared at his profile, and it was like something carved in the side of a mountain. Quivering with frustration and dawning realization, she said slowly, "You know, don't you? You told me you didn't, but that's not true. You did look it up. You *know* what happened. Oh, God. Tony—" she clutched his arm and it came in a rush "—please tell me, please, it's important, I have to know, *please.*"

He shook his head, his jaw implacable, unyielding as stone. "Yeah, you do, but like I told you—it's his story. He's the one who needs to tell it." He unbuckled himself and eased out of the seat, looming over her briefly as he stood, and again, for one moment his eyes arrowed straight into hers. "You have to *make* him tell it, Sam."

The dream came gently, like a parent creeping in to kiss a sleeping child good-night.

It's my mother's face bending over me, laughing and beautiful...her hands are cool as she brushes my cheek...then she hugs me, and her cheek is smooth and soft, and she smells like flowers and sunshine.

I feel my father's shoulder, hard and bony under my head...his breath tickles my forehead and I giggle as his voice growls deep inside his chest: "And I'll huff and I'll puff and I'll BLOW your house down!"

Then, as it always did, in his dream everything turned dark. All around him was darkness, and his mother's face swam toward him and then retreated...drifted around and came back, then floated away again, always out of reach, bobbing like a cork on the ocean.

She's not laughing now, but she's speaking, saying something to me, and her eyes look scared so I know it's something important, something urgent, but I can't hear what it is because of the noise...

There's a loud and terrible noise, a howling sound and a banging, banging, banging...someone's pounding on the door, and I hear a roaring, growling voice saying, "I'll huff and I'll puff and I'll BLOW your house down!" And I don't want to open the door, because I know something terrible is on the other side. It's the Big Bad Wolf, and he's pounding, pounding, pounding on the door and yelling at me to open it, and I know I must not open it, but I do anyway.

And the Big Bad Wolf has my father's face.

Cory fought his way free of the dream, clawing his way toward consciousness by sheer will, and woke chilled, sweating, and desperately nauseated. He felt hands on his shoulders, and clutching at one of them, managed to utter one word: "Sick..."

A basin materialized near his chin, the hands lifted his shoulder and rolled him, and he retched feebly and fruitlessly before subsiding, exhausted, shaking with the most appalling weakness he'd ever known. No wonder he'd dreamed of his childhood, he thought. It was the way he felt—weak as a child...an infant.

"What's wrong? Is he okay?"

The familiar voice, husky and belligerent, jolted him into full awareness. "Sam?" he croaked, struggling to lift his head.

"Don't worry, this is perfectly normal," a heavily accented voice said. He felt the upper half of the bed rise under him and a head crowned with sleek black hair moved out of his line of vision. A blond one came to take its place. Blond hair standing up in tufts as if it had been combed with fingers, surrounding a frowning face with honey-gold skin, a sprinkling of freckles, and fierce dark brown eyes.

In spite of how desperately awful he felt—worse than he could ever remember feeling before in his life—he could feel a smile shivering through his whole body, warming him the way the sun does when it slices through the frost on a cold morning.

"Hey, Sam," he croaked.

Her eyes flickered, but didn't lose their fierceness. "Hey, Pearse."

"My God, you're beautiful," he murmured before he thought, then wanted to laugh out loud when she snorted. It was so typically, beautifully Sam.

"Boy, that's a good one," she said tartly, folding her arms on her chest in a defensive way, as if he'd said something insulting. "I'm so far from beautiful right now, it isn't even funny."

"That's not the way I see it."

She rolled her eyes. "Oh, well, yeah, but you've been under anesthesia. You're probably hallucinating."

"Anesthesia?" His mind clicked into gear, kaleidoscopic memories zapped into focus. Fear stabbed through him and turned his blood to ice. He struggled to sit, to lift his head. *To see.* "Did I—my leg—is it—"

"Still there? Yeah, it's fine. Well, not fine, exactly, the bullet did a whole lot of soft tissue damage—your career as an underwear model is probably history—but at least you get to keep it awhile longer."

He was laughing helplessly, partly with relief, partly delight in her and sheer giddy wonderment that he'd managed to survive the last four years without her.

Then other memories faded in and took on sharpness, and the laughter died. "How's Esther?" he asked half-fearfully.

Sam's smile faltered as she drew a hitching breath. "She's in intensive care. Hangin' in there. As soon as she's strong enough, I guess she'll be flying back to Canada for bypass surgery. Her family wants her closer to home…."

"And Hal?"

She gave another of her dry little snorts. "He won't leave her side. They had to put a bed in the ICU for him." And she was fidgeting, suddenly, as if the subject made her uncomfortable, though he couldn't imagine why.

"Where are we, Zamboanga?" he asked, still groggy.

She shook her head. "I only put down there long enough to pick up a med tech and some supplies. Then it was straight to Davao City. I'd have opted for Manila if I'd thought you two would make it that far."

Cory was silent for a long time, letting the reality of that sink in to his mind and body…taking in the hospital room and the IV tubes pumping various fluids into his arms, no doubt laced with massive doses of antibiotics and painkillers…remembering everything that had happened over the last few incredible days, including things that were already beginning to seem more like a dream to him than reality. Except for the woman standing before him with her arms folded and one hip canted in that familiar, pugnacious way…

He closed his eyes and whispered on an exhalation, "God, Sam…you did it. I don't know how, but you did. You got us all out of there alive. I can't…" And for one of the very few times in his life, words failed him.

When he opened his eyes again, Sam was shaking her head emphatically, making her short hair fan out like ruffled fur. "It was a team effort, Pearse." He opened his mouth to deny it, but she cut him off, sounding half-angry. "Hal and Esther wouldn't be here at all right now if it wasn't for you." Then she caught a gulp of breath and added in a grudging tone, "Well, and Tony, of course."

Tony. For the first time Cory thought about the interview tapes he'd entrusted to his best friend's care…the cameras and rolls of film Tony had shlepped through miles of jungle and monsoon rains, even after he'd sacrificed two of his neck straps to save Cory's life. "Good old Tony…where is he, by the way?" he asked in a careful voice.

For the first time in a while, Sam grinned. "I expect he'll be up here shortly. Last time I saw him he was on a live videophone to CNN in New York. Looks like you'd better get yourself out of that bed in a hurry, Pearse. The whole world's a-waitin' for your side of the story."

He laughed, then let his eyes drift closed again, and for a few moments allowed himself to float on the sweet euphoria of being alive, all too aware the world was out there "a-waitin'" for him, aware of all the things that needed to be done, but content for the moment to let it all drift along without his participation, like flotsam on the same river flow.

Except for one thing. Only one thing in his life was compelling enough, right now, to coax him out of that lovely lethargy. He opened his eyes and let them rest on her with gratitude, like rafters on a turbulent river finding a quiet cove.

She gazed back at him with that poignant mix of toughness and vulnerability that had captivated him the first time he'd laid eyes on her—toughness in the thrust of her chin belied by the soft vulnerability of her mouth…her dark and troubled eyes…

He smiled and said in a raspy murmur, "Do you have to stand clear over there? I can't very well come to you, and I sure would like to kiss you."

She jerked as if he'd startled her, and he saw a shadow cross her face…something that looked like pain. She hesitated, then stepped close to his bed, leaned down, and he heard the small intake of her breath just before she kissed him. It sounded very much like a sob. The kiss was brief and light, and with the taste of her only a tantalizing promise on his lips, before he could bring up his hand to hold her there, she straightened up and looked away, and he saw her throat ripple several times with swallows. An ache formed in his own throat as he realized she was fighting tears.

Tears? But this was Sam, who *never* cried.

"What is it?" His voice was harsh and rasping. "What's wrong?" He groped for her hand. "Come here—sit."

She shook her head rapidly and gave a high little laugh, though when she spoke, her words sounded thick and slurred. "Uh-uh—I'm too dirty. The nurse would probably kick my butt right on outa here if I got mud all over you. Besides—" she caught a quick breath and didn't seem to know what to do with her eyes "—I have to go, anyway."

"Do you have to?" Fighting irrational panic at the thought of her leaving, he took care to make his voice calm…light…gentle. "Where are you off to?"

Fidgeting, she ran a hand through her hair, still not meeting his eyes. "Right now, to find a shower and some clothes. And, if there's a God, a *toothbrush*. Then…" She reached again for a breath. "I guess I'll be flying to Washington."

His heart did a violent skip, but he only lifted his eyebrows. "Flying?"

She gave him a tight little smile. "Commercial flight, Pearse. I have to check in with my…uh, you know. Debriefing, and so on."

He studied her, ruthlessly squelching the part of him that wanted to grab her and hold on to her and wail like an abandoned child. He was well aware that he was treading a narrow and unstable path, and doing it pretty much blindfolded. *You wanted a chance to do it right? Well, here's where it begins. Don't blow this, Pearse.*

The only problem: he had no idea what the right thing was. Should he back off and let her go with his cheerful blessing, show her he was capable of dealing with the demands of her career? Or tell her the truth, hold nothing back?

He still didn't know what he was about to say, not until the words came out of his mouth. "Wow. I hate to let you go." He took a breath, let it out, shook his head, and managed to produce a smile that made his face ache. "I think…we need to talk, Sam. Tony says we do, anyway."

She gave a small laugh like a whimper of pain…looked away, then down at her feet.

"I can't believe all this—meeting again after so long, being together—I can't believe it didn't happen for a reason," he said softly. "We had something…maybe it sounds like a cliché, but we had something special, Sam. We did. We let it get away— my fault, I know—but here we have a chance to fix it." He paused, then took another breath and plunged. "I love you. I never stopped…loving you. If you love me…*if* you do…then I don't see how we can walk away from that without trying to make it work this time. I want to make it work, Sam."

She'd promised herself she wouldn't cry. Had vowed on her CIA oath she wouldn't. She was going to damn Cory Pearson to hell if he made her break that vow. But, oh, how she wanted to cry. Her throat felt as though a giant hand was squeezing it. Her face was a thousand burning knots.

"How can it, Pearse?" she said in a broken voice, barely audible. "How can it possibly work? I love you, but—"

"But—?" he interrupted with a small crooked smile. "That's the first time you've ever told me that, by the way."

"It is not!" she shot back, her pain replaced by anger.

Maddeningly—and true to his nature—he only said gently, "It's true—but never mind. I'll take it. So, why won't it work?"

"For the same reason it didn't work for us before, dammit. I have a career you can't deal with. And if you couldn't handle me being a pilot, what are you going to do with a CIA operative, for God's sake? And—" her voice broke unexpectedly; she drew herself in, fighting desperately to hold fast against the breech "—I love my job, Pearse. Like I started to say, I love you, but I don't want to give it up. Maybe someday. Okay, *someday,* but not yet, not now, when I've just barely started. I want to make a difference; it's important to me. I've worked all my life for this. It's who I *am.* Why should I have to sacrifice that in order to be with you?"

"Everybody makes sacrifices," he said softly.

"You wouldn't give up *your* career. Nobody would ever expect you to."

"Maybe not...but I'd definitely make some adjustments, in a heartbeat." His eyes narrowed as though she'd become a light too bright to look at. "But that's beside the point. What if I told you I'd be willing to accept your career? That I wouldn't ask you to give up a thing?"

She stared at him, devastated, wanting to scream at him, curse him for taking away her anger, the only defense she had. She turned her face away from him and rubbed a hand over her burning eyes. "It wouldn't work," she mumbled. "I know you mean it. You'd try your best, but...I know what you want, Pearse. I know exactly the kind of life, the kind of home and family you want. Because it's what I had, growing up. It was great. No doubt about it. It was...wonderful. And I can't rob you of that. I can't."

"Don't you think you should let me decide what I'm willing to give up?" He punched down on the mattress beside his hips, trying to push himself upright, and she saw anger awaken, now, in his eyes.

She shook her head...closed her eyes...took a breath. "Okay, but...it's not the only thing—"

"For God's sake, Sam," he exploded in a torn voice, "what else is there? If you don't want to be with me, just say so."

She jerked around, trembling violently. "That's just it, dammit—I do want to be *with* you. I want to be with you. I want to share myself with you, and I want you to do the same with me. I don't want this...I can't stand this one-way street. It's too damn lonely, Pearse. It's too damn lonely..." She squeezed her eyes shut, but it didn't stop the tears or the sob that ripped through her throat. "Sometimes I feel like I'm in love with a ghost. A really kind, loving, benevolent ghost. Because...the truth is, I don't have a *clue* who you are. I can't *touch* you." She clutched air with her fingers, then gathered the fistful to her chest. "I can't touch you *here*. I can't get past your barricades. Your secrets..."

"*Secrets?*" She could almost see him cringe away from her

as he said it, and his eyes blazed at her, with anger, yes, but with something else, too. Something that looked very much like fear. "What are you talking about?"

She dashed away tears, grateful at least to have the anger-baton passed back to her. It was much more comfortable than the tears. "Your family, Pearse. Your childhood. Those brothers and sisters you never told me about. Your parents."

And now she could see him withdrawing behind his defenses, like a turtle into its shell. "They died," he said stiffly. "I told you that. It's no secret."

Make him tell you, Sam.

She leaned toward him, shaking inside, knuckles white as she gripped the safety bar on the side of the bed. "Yeah? How did they die, Pearse?"

He made a small violent gesture of denial. "God—I was a kid, I don't remember—"

She held up a not-quite-steady hand. "*Don't*—I mean it. Don't give me that. It was in the papers. It's in the record. Tony looked it up. If he knows, you sure as hell do."

He glared at her, and he'd never looked at her that way before…with his face a mask of anger and fear. In a voice so icy it made her shudder, he said, "If Tony knows, then why don't you ask him?"

She almost gave it up, then. She'd never felt such anger before, not from her Cory, gentle, empathetic Cory, not directed at her. It devastated her; she wanted to turn and flee, run away from it as fast as she could. But somehow she stayed. She stayed because somehow she knew that for a man like Cory, such anger could only mean wounds too deep and raw to deal with any other way. Wounds beyond the scope of her experience, or her power to heal.

You have to make him tell you.

Yes, and she'd started this. She'd gone this far, opened the door, grabbed the tiger's tail. She couldn't let go now.

Pulling back a little and drawing in a calming breath, she said, "I did ask him, actually. He wouldn't tell me. He said it has to come from you—whatever *it* is—this terrible, deep dark secret. He said *you* need to tell me."

Cory jerked and made a scoffing noise. "Since when did Tony become a shrink?"

"You know what?" said Sam, ignoring the sarcasm. "I think he's right. I think you need to tell me. Because if you can't, if you can't bring yourself to share even that much of your past with me, then I don't see how there's anything more for us to talk about."

She saw the anger drain from his face, leaving only fear. Fear that bleached his skin to a muddy gray, and misted his forehead with sweat. Fear that lurked behind his eyes like the monster in a child's closet. "You're not being fair, Sam," he said, in a gritty voice, barely above a whisper.

It seemed a very long time that she went on gazing at him, while her heart thundered and her body trembled, while voices of protest and rejection and denial screamed and echoed inside her head. She closed her ears to them all and said softly, "Goodbye, Pearse." Then turned and walked away on legs of glass.

Chapter 14

He was losing her.

What she was asking of him was too much. He couldn't do it. If he talked about it, he'd have to remember. And if he did, the memories would overtake him like an oncoming freight train. They would surely crush him. He couldn't do it. Couldn't.

If he didn't, he was going to lose her.

The pounding is only in your head, Pearse. You know that. It's a nightmare. Nightmares can't kill you.

Except…he knew they could. Nightmares could kill, and they could destroy.

And by God, he wasn't going to let it happen to him.

Sweating, teeth clenched, Cory lifted a shaking hand and drove his fingers into his hair, pressed them against his skull as if doing so could keep it from cracking under the pressure of the din inside. A din so loud he couldn't hear his own voice call out her name.

But he did call, and she heard. He saw her pause. The noise

in his head subsided to a muted thumping, and this time he heard himself hoarsely croak, "Sam—wait."

She turned halfway, one hand still on the doorknob. Waiting.

"My father killed my mother," he heard himself say in a voice carefully stripped of all emotion. "He shot her. Then he turned the gun on himself."

At the first words her head jerked the rest of the way around, and she stared at him, her eyes nearly black in a face bleached white with shock.

He went on in the same relentless, expressionless voice. "That's what happened. That's what I was told." And then, gently, cruelly, "Are you happy now?"

"My God..." And he could hear the soft, sticky sound of her swallow.

He couldn't take pleasure in how shaken she was. "I'm sorry," he mumbled, contrite and emotionally drained, and put an arm across his eyes. "You wanted to know."

He felt her come closer, creeping uncertainly toward him as if he were a wounded animal, or some unknown and possibly unstable substance. Both of which he supposed he was, at the moment.

She cleared her throat. "Where were you when it happened? Were you there? Did you see it?"

"I don't remember." He moved his arm and looked at her, eyes aching with exhaustion, and the unaccustomed strain of functioning without glasses. "Really, Sam. I don't remember. The newspaper accounts said the children—the little ones and I—were in the house at the time. But I have no memory of it. Sorry."

"Do they know why it happened?" She was frowning intently at him and trying to sound totally unemotional, the way she did when she was trying to hide how emotionally touched... shaken...hurt she really was.

Encased in his own shell of numbness, and thoroughly regretting, now, that he'd done this to her, he shrugged and said gently, "Classic posttraumatic stress, probably. He'd been in Vietnam. I'm guessing he had a violent flashback, attacked my mother, someone called the police and when they arrived, he shot her, then himself."

Sam's eyes narrowed. "But...he didn't hurt you or the other children?"

"No." The pounding had started up again. He wanted to put his hands over his ears to block it out, but he knew it wouldn't help. Nothing did. He rubbed his eyes instead. "Evidently not."

"You were there...and you were how old? Ten? Twelve?"

"Eleven," he said woodenly. He could feel the fear creeping up on him, like icy fog.

Her voice was disbelieving. "Pearse...Cory. Surely, you must remember *something*."

He felt the bed dip with her weight, and then a soothing coolness with a little bit of sandpaper roughness to it touched his face, stroked his hair back from his forehead. He'd never known Sam's hands could be so gentle.

Emotion, a devastating mix of love and despair, shivered through him. He caught her wrist and heard her gasp as he said in a voice tight with pain, "Maybe I don't want to remember. Did you ever think of that?"

She sat for a long time without speaking, just looking at him with her wounded eyes, and that dauntless and defensive lift to her chin. Then her gaze shifted past him to the IV bag hanging above his bed, and he saw her throat working.

"You know," she said in a flat voice with a huskiness in it she didn't bother to clear, "during my training for...this job, they covered PTSD pretty well...the causes and effects, symptoms, prevention...treatment. All of it. I guess they do that, now. Anyway, one of the things they told us is that PTSD can take lots of different forms. Violent flashbacks like your father had, or nightmares and depression, flirting with suicide—the things my dad had to deal with after Iraq—those aren't the only symptoms.

When you can't—or won't—let yourself remember, when you shut yourself off from people emotionally...that's PTSD, too. And you're not going to get over it, Cory. Not unless you talk about it."

Her eyes came back to his, and he was shocked to see them brimming with tears. One sat shimmering suspensefully on her lower lash, then tumbled over. Devastated, he lifted his hand and brushed it with his thumb...cradled her head with his palm, fingers sliding through her hair to touch the tender spot behind her ear. The moisture from the tear felt warm and soft, and he watched in awe as his thumb smoothed it like oil across her cheek.

Maybe, he thought. *Maybe...*

He held his breath...the door in his mind he'd kept barricaded for most of his life creaked open...just a hair. And he heard the noises...the pounding. *Boom...boom...boom...* A voice...thundering. *"Open up this door, Cory! I'm gonna break it down!"* Terrible sounds...cracking, splintering, screaming...the little ones crying. *"Mama!"*

Terror overwhelmed him. The door slammed shut.

"Don't ask me to do this," he whispered brokenly. "I can't. Not now."

For a long minute more she looked into his eyes. Then she jerked her gaze away and swiped recklessly at her tears. She caught his hand in both of hers to pull it away from her face as she rose. "I have to go," she said, breathless and rushed.

And then, impulsively, she bent down and kissed him, one quick hard brush of her lips, and to him that was worse than nothing at all. Pain knifed through him. It felt as though his heart was being ripped out of his chest.

She crossed the room in her long, tomboy's stride, then paused at the door and said without turning, "I'll be going home to Georgia to see Mama and Daddy after I'm done in Washington. When you're ready to talk, that's where I'll be."

She opened the door, and was gone.

* * *

Sam sat in one of the old creaky white-painted rocking chairs on Grandma Betty's wide front porch. Her eyes were closed and the sleeping baby on her chest made a small puddle of warmth as she rocked them both gently in the hazy heat of a Georgia July morning. The humid air was heavy on her shoulders, and scented with the roses that sprawled across the porch roof and the lighter, softer fragrance of the baby's down-covered scalp just below her chin. Birds and insects sang them a lazy lullaby, and Sam's mind drifted on meandering rivers of memory.

The scent of roses, and Cory's finger stroking a velvety petal in the garden at the White House...and I tell him I'm worried about my dad, because he won't talk about what happened to him in Iraq. "You talk about it," I tell him, and he replies, "I'd much rather write about it. Writing is what helps me. Everybody's different. Your dad has to find what works for him..."

Then...I talk about Vietnam, about how some who went there never did find their way home...and he looks at me with his gentle eyes and smiles his gentle smile, so full of compassion and understanding, and because I'm young and selfish and wrapped up in my own trials at the moment, I don't see the pain that's in them, too.

He sees inside my soul, and all I see is myself reflected back in his eyes. I don't see him at all.

Oh, God, Pearse...I'm so sorry.

Tears made warm puddles under her lashes, and for once she let them stay. The grief and regret lay lightly on her, now, a poignant ache that, like the sleeping infant, the humid air, the scent of roses, seemed only a natural part of this particular morning. Tomorrow, she would leave all this again. The day after the July fourth holiday, she'd be back in Washington, and after that, off to only God knew where. It had been over a month since she'd left Cory in that Mindanao hospital...nearly three weeks that

she'd been here in Grandma Betty's house, waiting for him.
Three weeks and he hadn't come.

When you're ready to talk, Pearse...

She had to accept that maybe he never would be.

The crunch of tires on gravel wasn't loud, but it destroyed the
mood of the morning nonetheless, the way even a twig dropped
onto the smooth surface of a pond shivers the mirror image.

Sam hastily dashed the tears from her eyes and brought the
rocker upright, careful not to disturb the sleeping baby as she
looked across to where an unfamiliar car was just pulling to a
stop under the huge oak trees on the edge of the yard. She
stopped breathing and her heart thumped beneath the baby's
warmth as she waited for the driver to emerge.

The car door opened, and there was a long suspenseful pause
before someone appeared, unfolding awkwardly to stand with a
hand braced on the roof of the car while he tugged at something
still inside. Then the tall figure was moving toward her across
the lawn, limping, leaning heavily on a cane.

She watched him come, rippling inside, and waited until he'd
reached the steps before she said, "Hey, Pearse." And dipped her
head to hide her trembling smile against the baby's downy head.

He paused with one foot on the step, one hand on the newel
post, and his smile grew wry. "I must say, in my wildest dreams,
this isn't how I expected to find you."

"What? Oh." Of course everything she was feeling must
surely show, and he would know it already, but to protect herself a little while longer, she kept her eyes on the baby's open
mouth and fat velvety cheeks, impossibly delicate lashes. "I'm
babysitting. This is Lizzy-Beth—well, actually, it's Elizabeth
Ashley Starr—she's my cousin J.J.'s—Jimmy Joe and Mirabella's first grandbaby. Isn't she sweet?"

"How old is she?"

Her breath caught as she heard the top step creak, and then
his uneven footsteps cross the wooden porch floor. She lifted her

head and shook back her hair, and began to rock gently as she watched him. "Five weeks yesterday. She was born while I— while we were in the Philippines." *There. No sense in avoiding it, pretending it all hadn't happened.*

A few feet away from her he stopped and leaned his backside and the cane against the porch railing. His face seemed even more angular than she remembered...the interesting lines and hollows hinting at even deeper secrets. And he was wearing new glasses, she noticed. Very stylish, with narrow, trendy lenses. She decided they looked good on him. Behind them his eyes rested on her with compassion, as all-seeing as ever, but with something different, now, too. Something she'd never seen before. Something she couldn't quite name.

After a moment he shook his head, and once again she saw his smile slip. "Don't take this the wrong way—I have to say it, Sam. She looks good on you."

She snorted. "Hey—I never said I didn't want one of these, eventually. Just not right *now,* okay? Actually, you might not believe this, but I used to be crazy about little babies when I was a kid. I don't know, maybe it was because I always wanted brothers and sisters..."

"Sam—"

Ignoring the interruption, she dipped her lips once again to the baby's head, ignoring, too, the tear-glaze that had come to fog up her vision. She drew a quivering breath. "God...I'd forgotten how good they smell... I remember the first time Jimmy Joe brought Mirabella here. And her baby, Amy Jo—he'd delivered her himself, you know, in the sleeper of his truck, on Christmas Eve. He fell in love with her then, but Mirabella was too stubborn to believe it. So one day, Jimmy Joe just went and got her. He drove up to the house with her and the baby in his big blue truck. Mama and J.J. and I all ran out to see what the fuss was, and there was Amy Jo sitting in the middle of the front walk in her car seat. We all just fell in love with her, right then and there. J.J. and I fought, I remember, over who'd get to hold her first." She twitched her gaze up to Cory, and her smile felt brittle and false. "Amy Jo's in college, now. Scary…"

"What is?" His voice was gentle.

"How fast the time goes." She lifted her head and suddenly tears were streaming down her face and for once she didn't care. "You think I don't know how much you want this—all of this? The thing is, you know, I want it, too. I do. Eventually. But I'm only twenty-eight. Can't I have a couple more years?"

"I think I'd give you the moon, if you asked me," he said softly. "If it meant we'd be together." But he wasn't looking at her. His head was turned away from her and his haunted eyes were fixed on one swaying tendril of the climbing rose, thick with red-pink blossoms.

Sam closed her eyes. She could feel her heart tearing in two. "Oh, God, Pearse…"

He jerked as if he'd struck her, and she could see he'd misunderstood her tears. "Sam—what we talked about in Mindanao…"

"Wait—" she rushed to interrupt him, to get it said. "That's what I wanted to tell you. I was unfair. I did ask too much. I had no right. If you're not ready—"

He was shaking his head. "No—you didn't ask too much. It was time. Past time." He dragged a hand over his face, then said grimly, "I don't know if I'm ready or not, but I've been trying to remember what happened. Letting myself, I guess would be a better way to put it."

She waited, heart thumping, slowly wiping away her tears. She knew, now, what it was she'd seen in his eyes. The horrors of his memories, lurking like monsters in the dark.

"I don't think I can do it by myself, Sam. And…if I'm going to talk to anybody, I…the truth is, the only person I trust to see me through this is you."

She could only stare at him…and go on holding the baby,

rocking gently, heart pounding… She felt both humble and proud at the same time, overwhelmed and exhilarated, as if she was standing on the edge of a volcano, something awesome and beautiful beyond imagining, but terrifying, too.

Cory shifted with the new restlessness that seemed to have become a part of him now. Hell, she's in shock, he thought as he watched her face drain of color. *I shouldn't have dropped it on her like this.* "Is there someplace we can go? Where is everybody?"

"Um…" She cleared her throat and said unsteadily, "They've all gone to the lake house for the holiday—fireworks are legal in South Carolina. I volunteered to babysit."

"You didn't want to go?"

She shook her head and a smile flickered briefly. "That place has too many memories."

He snorted. "You can say that again. I almost drowned there."

"And," she said softly, "you kissed me for the first time there."

He gazed at her until his eyes burned, and the silence filled up with the rocking chair's slow creaking…bees humming in the rose bush…a cardinal calling…a squirrel scolding…

"I know she's beautiful and sweet and all that," he finally said, nodding at the baby in Sam's arms and trying his best to smile, "but is there someplace you can put her down for a bit? I'd really like to kiss you now. That peck you planted on me in Davao City—"

"Hold that thought." She stopped rocking suddenly and rose, supporting the baby's head as naturally as if she'd spent a lifetime doing that rather than flying World War Two airplanes and hunting down terrorists and rescuing journalists and hostages from Philippine jungles. Looking at once distracted and purposeful, she swept past him and into the house.

By the time he'd collected his wits and his cane and followed her, she was already halfway up the stairs. He paused at the bottom to wait for her, thinking she meant to come back down so they could talk, but she threw him a look over one shoulder and said, "Coming?" in a breathless and impatient way, like a child with a secret to share.

So he made his way up the stairs as rapidly as his healing thigh muscle would allow, feeling thoroughly bemused, and his heart pounding with more than just physical exertion.

He found her in a spare bedroom, bending over a portable crib. She straightened and turned when she heard him, then crossed to him in a flurry of motion, her arms already lifting around his neck, and her body came against him in a rush that knocked the breath from his lungs and every lucid thought from his mind.

The cane toppled onto the braided rug and lay there, unneeded and forgotten. His arms tightened around her as she kissed him, but only for a moment; there was too much urgency, too much hunger in him. His hands wandered, shaking, over her back and shoulders, her nape and the silky dampness of her hair…followed the taut ribbons of muscle along her spine to the firm and modest swell of her behind…relearning the shape and feel and texture of her. He felt dazed all over again at the miracle of her, astonished and humble and exalted at the same time.

Oh, but the kiss…he didn't think she'd ever kissed him quite that way before. With exuberance and fierceness and fire and passion, yes—that was only Sam, the only way she could be. But not with this wildness. And something else, something deeper… something he didn't dare hope for or give a name to. Something that felt…irreversible.

She kissed him hard and deep, holding nothing back, and he tasted blood and hoped it wasn't hers. By the time she came up for air his lips were swollen and hot already, pulses thumped in his belly and loins, and his breaths were ragged gasps. With his focus narrowing, his goal and purpose suddenly urgent and clear and the word *bed* uppermost in his mind, he dragged his mouth from hers and croaked, "Don't you want to—"

Misunderstanding his intent, she growled, "Shut up, Pearse," and reclaimed his mouth like a hungry lioness. Her hands tugged at his shirt, his belt buckle.

Caught off guard and off balance, he staggered back against the door frame. She gasped and clutched at him, then burst into helpless laughter, which she instantly tried to smother against his shoulder. "Oh, God, Pearse, I'm sorry." She cleared her throat, lifted her head, shook back her hair and gazed at him, eyes glowing with a fierce, wild light. "I didn't even ask. How is your leg?"

"Healing," he told her absently, as his hands worked their way along her shoulders to the sides of her neck. Cradling her head between them like a precious treasure, stroking her cheeks with his thumbs, he tilted her head back, lowered his mouth to her throat. She smelled poignantly of baby powder. When she moaned softly he moved his mouth to hers and kissed her, slowly and with infinite tenderness, in direct and deliberate contrast with the way they'd kissed before. And when at last he lifted his head and gazed down at her, her eyes were still closed.

"I wanna see it," she mumbled drunkenly.

"What, my leg? Sam…it isn't pretty."

"Like I care." She swayed forward, and her mouth was hot and humid on his throat…her tongue measured his hammering pulse.

He closed his eyes and said weakly, "Right here? Right now?"

"Nuh-uh…" Working her way up to his mouth in determined nibbles, she backed him across the hall and through another doorway. "This is better. It's my room…"

She drew back from him, then, and placed her palms on his chest. She lifted her eyes to his and there was no trace of laughter or wildness in them. Instead they looked bruised and wounded. "Please, Pearse," she whispered. "Let me see."

Slowly, he began to unbutton his shirt. Slowly, he pulled it free, and his hands moved on to his belt buckle…then the zipper of his slacks.

She didn't help him, didn't hurry him, simply clung to his

eyes as if they were the only thing in the universe, and he felt suddenly that this was the most intimate thing they'd ever done together, even more intimate than all the times they'd made love. It frightened him a little…more than a little…because he knew this wasn't about sex, it was much more important than sex, more binding than sex…more permanent.

Her hands slipped lightly down his hips and thighs, following his slacks as they slid to the floor, and she sank onto the edge of the bed without a sound…heavily, as though her legs wouldn't hold her any longer.

He held himself relaxed, trusting her completely, and she looked a long, silent time, her hands almost absently stroking the outsides of his legs. Then she leaned forward and carefully touched her lips to the ragged half-healed scar on the inner part of his thigh. His breath hissed between his teeth, but he didn't move, and let his hands lie easily on her shoulders as she moved her mouth over him, lightly as breath, and the ends of her hair grazed his fevered skin, soft and cool as tears.

Then suddenly he couldn't be still any longer. His hands slid upward along her neck…gathered her hair in greedy handfuls as he tipped her head back and bent down to kiss her. But instead of claiming her mouth as he'd meant to do, he paused and looked down into her fierce bright eyes, and his heart seemed to stop and the earth beneath him quake at what he saw there.

"Sam," he whispered. "My Samantha…"

A radiant smile broke over her face, at the same moment tears seemed to burst from her eyes. Tears and laughter…like rain and sunshine. He'd never seen anything so beautiful.

He kissed her then, reverently…adoringly, bearing her slowly backward onto the tulip quilt that haphazardly covered the bed, and when he would have followed her down, she put her hands on his chest and held him away, still laughing through tears while she squirmed and tugged at her clothes. Then he was helping her skin off her shorts and T-shirt, and shoes and various articles of clothing were sailing into unknown corners of the room, until at last he brought his body and hers together with a profound and grateful sense of homecoming.

He held her close…so close he felt the shape of her ribs and the heart beating madly beneath them. Her woman's scent and quivering warmth overwhelmed him, and yet he felt famished, as though he'd never be able to get enough of it. He felt her strong, capable hands on his back, and the tiny flaws and imperfections her occupation had given them, and it seemed the most erotic, the most exquisite pleasure he'd ever known.

He wanted to stroke her…explore every inch of her body with his hands…worship her with his mouth…feast on her with his eyes. But she was already moving beneath him, shifting in the small adjusting ways that would bring her body into perfect and intimate alignment with his, and who was he to resist? There would be time enough…a lifetime, he hoped…for the feasting.

And so her body welcomed his, and their coming together was different than at any time before…quieter, perhaps, but at the same time infinitely more intense. Though his jaws ached and his body shivered with the pressure of building emotions and passion thundered in his blood, he felt no sense of masculine triumph, no sense of coming into, of entering her body, nor even of a mutual giving and taking. Instead it seemed to him a gentle merging of mind and body, complete and irreversible…like two quiet rivers coming together, then flowing on as one….

And flow on they did, faster and faster, navigating giddily over rocks and rills, clinging together through wild rapids and crying out in terror and exhilaration as they tumbled over thundering falls…to drift at last into quiet pools, all their turbulence, for the moment, spent.

Afterward, it was Sam who spoke first. "Okay, Pearse," she

said in a gruff and crusty voice that was classically, typically
Sam, as if trying to deny the emotional white water they'd just
come safely through. "What the heck was that?"

He smiled down at her, framing her face with his hand, wiping the sheen of sweat and tears from her flushed cheeks. "Don't
you know?" he asked, amused and tender.

She gazed at him in silence for a moment, her eyes growing
bright again, like stars. "Yeah," she finally whispered, "I think I
do. This is us from now on, isn't it, Pearse?"

"You bet it is," he said softly, lying back and drawing her
against him, dazed, still, at this happiness that had somehow
found him when he'd never expected it to happen at all.

She popped up again almost at once, restless as a child fighting nap time, to place a hand on his chest and gaze down at him,
her face earnest and grave. "I meant what I said, though. You
don't have to talk about your past if you don't want to. It was a
dumb thing to do, giving you an ultimatum like that. I'm really
sorry—"

"Shh…" He laid a finger gently across her lips. "It was an ultimatum I needed to hear, I think. It made me realize—something
did, anyway—that I've spent my whole life being afraid of something that can't possibly harm me. *Memories,* Sam. Just memories. How can those change who I am, or where my life is now?
The answer is, they can't. I've survived a lot, and by some miracle I have you…"

She kissed him, then asked carefully, "Have you remembered, then? What happened when your parents died?"

He shook his head and closed his eyes. "I've tried, Sam. I truly
have. All I get are bits and pieces."

"What kind of pieces? Maybe if you told me about them, it
would help you remember."

He opened his eyes and gazed up at her, memorizing the
shape of her forehead as he lifted his hand and idly stroked back
her hair. "Sounds, mostly," he said, smiling a little. "Just sounds.

No matter how hard I try, I can't seem to get any pictures. I don't know why, but there just aren't any."

"Maybe that's why," she said, blinking at him in a solemn way that made him think of owls. "Maybe you can't remember pictures because there aren't any."

He stared at her, a faint little buzz of wonderment beginning deep in his chest. "What do you mean?"

She shrugged, as if it were the simplest thing in the world. "What time of day did it happen? Probably night, right? Maybe you were hiding. Maybe it was dark where you were. So, the only thing you would remember is sounds."

"My God." He rubbed a hand over his eyes and began to laugh, weakly and helplessly. "My God, Sam...trust you to cut through all the crap and solve the mystery of my life in one fell swoop."

She snuggled down beside him with a pleased, almost smug little smile. "So—what noises do you remember? Tell me."

Any urge to laugh vanished. He swallowed and closed his eyes. "Pounding," he said thickly. "That's always the first thing. Someone—my father—banging on the door. Banging...pounding...with his fists, feet, I don't know. Trying to break it down."

"And...where are you?"

"I'm in a bedroom, I think. I don't remember which one. I have the little ones with me. It's my job to look after them when my father is having one of his...spells. I have to keep them out of his way. Keep them safe. I've taken them into the bedroom and I've locked the door, except...I don't trust the lock, so I've wedged a chair under the handle, like my mom showed me. Only...now I'm afraid...terrified even that won't be enough. I can hear the wood splintering...breaking. I know it will only take a few more blows and he'll be through. My mother is screaming...crying. I hold on to the little ones...I have my arms around them, and they're all trembling. The twins, the little girls are sobbing and crying, 'Mama, Mama...' but the boys just cry quietly.

"I hear sirens…more sirens, getting louder and louder until it seems they're coming right into the room, and there's lots of people shouting…and all of a sudden the pounding stops. There's a moment…several minutes…when all I hear is the little ones whimpering…and then, there's a loud *bang*—so loud we—the children and I—all jump. We hold each other even tighter, and there's another bang, and we flinch again, and then there's just confusion…voices shouting…footsteps running… glass breaking…the little ones crying…and I think I might be crying too…"

"Oh, God…Cory—it's all right…it's all right…I love you… I've got you…"

He discovered he *was* crying, but he knew that was all right. He was all right. Sam was holding him tightly, cradling his head against her, and her hands were gentle as they wiped the tears from his face.

Lizzy-Beth's crying woke them. Cory groaned in protest when Sam slipped away from his side. She threw him a dark look as she tugged on her underpants. "Better get used to it. That's what you're asking for, you know."

"I can't wait," he murmured. She felt his eyes following her as she moved around the room mostly naked, gathering up her scattered clothes.

"Yeah? That's definitely one of those 'be careful what you wish for' things, Pearse." But she was smiling as she left him and went to pick up the howling baby, liking the look of him all relaxed and tousled and sleepy in her bed. Liking the way she felt, too—feminine and powerful, gentle and strong, proud to have been gifted with the wisdom of women, passed down from the caves and campfires through uncounted ages.

Later, after Lizzy-Beth had been fed and changed, they put her in the infant carrier—which Cory insisted on strapping on himself—and went for a walk down the lane that arrowed past the house, through the hay fields and down to the woods and the creek beyond.

"My father wasn't a monster," he said quietly as they strolled slowly, the uneven crunch of their footsteps and the scrape of Cory's cane the only other sounds. "I have good memories of him, from before he went to Vietnam. He was a kind and gentle man, he liked to read books, and he told the best stories, stories he'd make up himself. But…" He hitched in a breath and looked away, across the fields. "He went to Vietnam, and he died over there. As surely as if they'd sent him home in a body bag. The person that came home to my mother and me was someone else…a stranger.

"I've often thought that's why I became interested in covering wars…because I wanted to find out what happened to my dad, wanted to understand what it was that destroyed him." He gave a short, humorless laugh. "My only question now is, why wars don't destroy more of the people who fight in them. Funny thing is, you know—they screen people before they let them become policemen…firemen, but they take ordinary people out of their everyday lives—family men, loving husbands, fathers—put them through a little bit of training, then send them out to kill. Some people can handle it, I guess. Others—like my father—can't. He had too much empathy, I think."

"Like you," Sam said softly.

It was a hot and muggy Fourth of July evening, but she was remembering a day of soft May sunshine, and Cory's very first visit here, and walking with him down this very lane, side by side but not quite touching…knowing she was probably about to fall in love.

It was harder to recall the girl she'd been back then. The woman she was now couldn't help but feel a tiny bit ashamed of her arrogance and carelessness, the giddy and selfish way she'd plunged into Cory's life, too full of herself to really see him, too naive to recognize the shadows behind his quiet, compassionate eyes.

Still…she could forgive herself for being young, she supposed, and there had been a kind of innocence about that time: the newness of the feelings, delicious excitement, the roller-coaster ride between euphoria and despair, the awe and the fear. And she knew it didn't begin to compare with what she felt now for the man walking beside her…the love she felt for him, and the awesome challenge and responsibility of having his heart and soul entrusted to her keeping. Forever after. It was humbling… thrilling. And terrifying, too.

But Sammi June Bauer's mama hadn't raised her to be a coward.

"Pearse," she said without looking at him, watching her feet as they strolled along. "That question you asked me four years ago…is it still on the table?"

She felt his fingers tighten around hers, though he didn't reply right away, and in his silence she could feel him weighing her words, making sure he understood. Then he said softly, "You know it is."

"Well then," she said, "the answer is yes."

He stopped walking and turned toward her, taking both of her hands in his. His shadowed eyes gazed at her solemnly over the baby's bright, uncurious eyes and bobbing head, as he uttered one word: "When?"

Her breathing hitched, and she tried to smile. "As soon as possible, I think."

He leaned carefully past the baby and kissed her. "I want that, too," he said in a husky, breaking voice. "But there's something I have to do first."

She closed her eyes, leaned her forehead against his shoulder and said with a tremulous sigh, "I know."

"I'm going to find them, Sam. My brothers and sisters. I have to find them."

She felt warm moisture seep between her lashes. "Of course you do." She lifted her head and took his face between her hands and smiled fiercely at him through her tears. "But not first—after. Marry me, and we'll find them together."

Wordless for once, he hooked his arm around her shoulders and buried his face in her hair.

Slipping her arm around his waist, she turned her face against his neck, breathing in his scent, his warmth, his goodness. "We'll find them, Pearse," she whispered. "I promise you we will."

Epilogue

He married Samantha in the garden of her grandmother's house on a hot July day, with grass underfoot and the scent of roses in the air. There were children running unauthorized between the folding chairs borrowed from the Baptist church down the road, and birds singing and babies crying and old ladies rocking and fanning on the front porch.

In spite of the short notice, everyone was there, all the aunts and uncles and cousins—Jimmy Joe and Mirabella, Al and Tracy, Troy and Charly, C.J. and Caitlyn, Joy and Scott, Roy and Celia—and their kith, kin and kids. It made quite a crowd, this new family of his. A lot to take in all at once.

Sam's cousin Amy Jo was her maid of honor, and her dad, Tristan, walked her down the aisle, then came to stand with him as his best man. She wore a dress her mom, Jessie, had made for her in a hurry—a simple white sheath that showed her long, slender legs, and her Grandma

Betty's wedding veil. Her bridal bouquet was roses, picked from the bush that rambled over the front-porch roof.

Standing there under the big oak trees, he watched her come through the front door of the old family home and start down the porch steps. And then, at the bottom, just before she slipped her hand through Tristan's arm, she paused...lifted her head and stuck out her chin and looked straight at him. And he saw her again, as he had on that first day in the White House rose garden...vulnerable and scared...fierce and proud and brave.

She came toward him, and he felt...

Cory sat for a long time, staring at the blinking cursor. Then he shook his head, moved it to the Save icon and with a sigh, hit the mouse button.

There were no words on earth powerful enough, it seemed, to describe the joy of loving Samantha.

She came to the door of the bedroom, and he felt her there, even before she spoke.

"Pearse? You 'bout ready? Everybody's waitin' for us, fixin' to pelt us with rice and old shoes."

He smiled at her over his shoulder. "Just about. Let me shut this down."

She came toward him with her tomboy's stride, wearing her honeymoon outfit, a short skirt and sleeveless top in the sunshine colors he loved. "What's that you're workin' on, on this, your weddin' day? Don't tell me you're on a deadline."

He shook his head. "Just something I've been working on for a while. A book, actually."

"Really? Cool." She wrapped her slim, strong arms around his neck and leaned over his shoulder, trying to peek. "Can I read it? Is it finished?"

"Oh, no," he said, laughing huskily as he closed the laptop and pulled his brand-new wife into his lap. "Just barely begun."

* * * * *

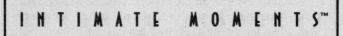